DATE DUE

5-1-09		

Demco

ERASED

OTHER GENERAL JACK MYSTERIES BY JO BAILEY

Recycled
Bagged

ERASED

A GENERAL JACK HOSPITAL MYSTERY

JO BAILEY

THOMAS DUNNE
ST. MARTIN'S PRESS
NEW YORK

ERASED. Copyright © 1996 by Jo Bailey. All rights reserved. Printed in the United States of America. No part of this book may be used or reproduced in any manner whatsoever without written permission except in the case of brief quotations embodied in critical articles or reviews. For information, address St. Martin's Press, 175 Fifth Avenue, New York, N.Y. 10010.

Design by Ellen R. Sasahara

Library of Congress Cataloging-in-Publication Data

Bailey, Jo.
    Erased / Jo Bailey.
       p.   cm.
    "A Thomas Dunne book."
    ISBN 0-312-14330-3
    1. Police, Private—United States—Fiction.   2. Policewomen—United States—Fiction.   3. Hospitals—United States—Fiction.
I. Title.
PS3552.A3722E73   1996
813'.54—dc20   96-4793
                                                                              CIP

First edition: May 1996

10 9 8 7 6 5 4 3 2 1

For all the Smuckabooleans in this world
and the next.

PART I

1

For Jan Gallagher, the hardest part of her job in Security was the isolation. Circumstances had reduced her to running conversations with pencils, erasers, and coffee mugs. When one of the hospital's social workers stopped by to ask for a minute of her time, Jan didn't know what to say.

"Were you talking to me?"

The social worker poked her head into Jan's cubicle to look from one blue partition to the other and arch a puzzled eyebrow. Roughly the size of a Jacuzzi bath, Jan's office was filled with a surplus metal desk instead of water. A studio portrait of Jan's four daughters stood on one corner of the desk; a quote-of-the-day calendar got the other. A God-grant-me-the-serenity poster, plastic vines, and home-sweet-loan cross-stitch took care of the walls. Unless Thumbelina was picnicking under the desk, Jan appeared to be alone.

"I hope so," said the social worker.

"I think a minute could be arranged," Jan said. Reaching into a drawer, she pulled out a tissue and dusted off the chair wedged beside her desk.

"Somewhere private?"

"Believe me," Jan said, "there's nowhere more private."

"Somewhere very private," the social worker said, dropping her voice to a whisper.

"Would outside do?"

The social worker nodded eagerly.

At five-two, Jan came up three or four inches short of the social worker. She was dressed in a security supervisor's uniform of black trousers and white top. Its paramilitary insignia and silver badge created a flash of gender confusion whenever Jan found herself facing a woman in a skirt and nylons, as was the social worker. She overcompensated with small talk so small it was tiny. At age thirty-nine, she still had a few lingering freckles, a slim figure that remained energetic, and hair that was still mostly black, despite her being a single mother of four. She liked to think she had a forthright tongue, when it was given an opportunity for meaningful exercise. In fact, honesty was something she prided herself on.

The social worker's name was Felicia Smith, and Jan knew her through the woman's live-in boyfriend, Lyle Brown, who also worked in Security. She and Felicia regularly exchanged pleasantries at the department's mandatory Christmas bash, where the two of them annually grew tired of the dispute over who was the best practicing middle linebacker in the universe. In the hospital halls they exchanged hellos. Until now that had been the extent of their friendship.

From Jan's cubicle, they adjourned to the courtyard outside Administration, with Felicia putting as many evergreen shrubs as possible between themselves and any windows. The courtyard was a relatively new addition to Jackson General, whose campus, as hospital brochures called the odd assortment of buildings, was a quaint history of the city's pork barrel. Felicia picked the farthest corner, where only the midday sun could see them. They were on the leeward side of the General's oldest building, seven stories' worth of slouching brick, and the early May sun heated up the surroundings enough for them to be comfortable without a coat. Felicia twice peeked around the last evergreen before joining Jan on a cement bench.

"Someone following us?"

"Don't say that," Felicia scolded. "Lyle would skin me alive if he knew I was out here."

"Sounds serious."

"Serious monkey business," Felicia said with a frown. "They're planning to play a big joke on you, though it doesn't sound so funny to me."

"Who's planning?"

"The graveyard shift."

"I see," Jan said, without having to ask why she'd been singled out. Slightly over two years before, she'd sued the county for discrimination in its promotion practices. And won. Following that victory she'd briefly held the position of night supervisor, which turned out to be more grudge match than job. Not for long, though. Soon she was promoted into oblivion, which at Jackson County Medical Center had the title of Head of Special Projects for Security. The only special projects that came her way were lighter than air. After the promotion, isolation settled in thick as river-bottom fog.

"I thought you might," said Felicia, checking behind them again. "You're going to be asked to fill in for old Gavin Larsen while he's on vacation."

"That's news to me."

"You'll be finding out. And everybody's planning on calling in sick."

"What's so funny about that?"

"We're talking about men," Felicia reminded her. "All I know is that the boys were playing poker at our place and feeling awfully good about putting one over on you."

"Anything else?"

Felicia shook her head and said in a troubled voice, "What are you going to do?"

"Something brilliant," Jan said with a hollow grin. "But don't worry, I won't let on that I heard anything."

"That wasn't troubling me," Felicia said, but she sounded relieved when she added, "I don't think Lyle's going along with it, but I can't promise you anything."

"You've done enough," Jan said.

"I just hate to see them get away with something like this."

"They won't," Jan promised, sounding more certain than she felt.

A COUPLE OF days later she was called into her supervisor's office, a rare occasion, and told she would be replacing the late-night supervisor while he was on vacation, starting in two days and lasting two weeks. She dryly thanked her boss for all the forewarning but didn't turn the assignment down.

When the fated day arrived, she called in sick herself. But not before paying her doctor a visit late in the afternoon, complaining of nausea and vomiting after eating lunch out. That night the entire graveyard shift phoned in with everything from bad backs to rotten teeth, forcing most of Security's evening shift to pull a double. Although everyone got called on the carpet for the stunt, Jan alone had documented her illness, a fact that increased her reputation for sharpness. The remainder of her replacement duty went down with remarkable smoothness.

AFTERWARDS, SHE REPAID Felicia's kindness by inviting her to supper on a night when Lyle felt well enough to work. To her mild surprise, Felicia accepted. Their evening out was a success and for the remainder of May and the entire month of June, they occasionally repeated the performance, picking a bistro or rib joint far enough removed from the hospital to insure that Felicia wouldn't be made as Jan's source.

They talked about many things, both work related and personal, and by the time July was upon them, they'd discovered they both had divorced parents, were divorced themselves, shared a rich sense of irony when it came to men, although not rich enough to do without them, and that they never felt as though they were living up to their potential. Cancer ran in Felicia's family, and she was the sole survivor, which made Lyle her only family, even though they hadn't tied any knots. Jan's whole family was alive but never got together anymore, which struck Jan as a different form of cancer, a thought she didn't mention. The comparison seemed to belittle Felicia's losses.

The one other thing neither of them mentioned was that Jan was white and Felicia black, although strictly speaking, Jan was more strawberry white, thanks to noontime sunning, and Felicia closer to royal brown. Since skin color wasn't supposed to matter in America, they worked overtime living up to society's expectations—a tried-and-true recipe for tragedy.

2

The Jeep Wrangler nearly tipped as it took the corner into the emergency drive at Jackson General. For a fluttery heartbeat the topless vehicle teetered, causing three of the four young men hanging on to lean into the turn. Rider number four lay unconscious in the back with no idea he'd almost been flipped out on his head.

"Little turn," Cut T, the driver, called out.

"Crazy fool!"

The opinion of his front-seat passenger.

"Who askin'?" Cut T said, righting the wheels, shooting the gap between a parked ambulance and an arriving Yellow Cab, and all the while chanting over his broad shoulder to the wounded friend in back, "Hang mean, Rainy. Hang tough, motherfuck. Hang in there, badass. Hang on . . ."

Pure superfly except for the moist sheen of sweat riding his rich black skin and making his hands so slippery on the steering wheel that he gripped it hard enough to cramp his forearms.

It was then shortly after eleven P.M. on a Fourth of July, over two hundred years past the signing of the Declaration of Independence. It felt as though the oven had been on high for most of those two centuries, cooking the juices out of the city's sewer system. You could feel the smells and smell the heat.

Moments before the Wrangler's arrival, patriotic fireworks had commenced two miles to the northeast, over the lake. The business district's well-lit skyline blocked the hospital's view of the orange and silvery star bursts, but the muted concussions of the exploding rockets carried down the city streets, echoing off brick and fake brick alike, amplified by strings of lit Blackcats, jalopy backfires, and the barking of Saturday night specials, all of which coincided so neatly with Cut T's hasty approach that it seemed as though the city he tore out of was under attack. That was hardly news, not at Jackson General, otherwise known as General Jack in the trenches. Its staff had been tending to the city's casualties for so many years that in the wrong light, such as sunrise or sunset, patients had been heard to comment that the hospital's brittle bricks appeared to be bleeding.

Up front on the Jeep's passenger seat hunched a chocolate-colored young man called Last—short for Last Word—who was struggling to be the first to ditch his firepower as they swerved toward the ER entrance. He succeeded in stuffing the magnum into the bouncing glove compartment as Cut T stomped down on the brakes. In back, a gangly kid named Sweet Sixteen, his shoe size, held the unconscious Rainy as a lifeguard would a drowning victim. With his other arm hooked around the roll bar, Sweet Six, as his name was usually shortened, had to wait until the Jeep quit hopping before fumbling his nickel-handled automatic under a seat. As the motor died, Cut T whipped a Beretta out from his belt, stashed it under the dash, and cracked his door to sprint for help.

"Tell 'em we gots every fuckin' kind of 'surance," Last shouted.

"Twice," Cut T answered without a look back.

Just as he disappeared into the greenish-yellow lights of the hospital entrance, two cop cars flashed onto the scene, blocking either end of the ER's drive, a synchronized light-and-sound show.

At the same instant, Last cried out, "Rainy's piece!"

Sweet Six clawed at Rainy's gun, which the wounded young man clung to as if he might have to shoot his way into heaven. As soon as the gun was pried loose, Last blurted, "Lose it."

Sweet Six obliged, flinging Rainy's Uzi over his shoulder, a dumb-ass move that turned out to be their first stroke of good luck for the night. The gun landed on top of an ambulance pulling away. Then they got the most-wanted treatment: spotlights, loudspeakers, riot guns. Real gangster status. Meanwhile, Rainy's heater rode off into the night unmolested.

THE LEBARON TRAILING the cop cars and Jeep had to punch it up to fifty on some narrow one-way streets to keep pace with the procession. Inside the speeding car, two brothers, known to friends and foes alike as Little Whip and Brew, had their buttons stuck on fast-forward. Short and muscular, they had complexions black as coffee beans; their small, intelligent eyes darted everywhere. Other than the fact that they rarely got along, the only thing that identified them as brothers was the Colt pistols in their stubby hands. Police officers in the city's gang detail referred to the pair as the Colt brothers, .38 and .45.

As the LeBaron shot past the hospital, Brew told Little Whip to lower his window. The smoky glass might have saved their asses more than once during daylight, when they found themselves wrong-siding Ninety-eighth Street, the border between the Golds and Sevens, more fully known as the Golden Horde of Plenty and the Seven Crime Lords, two of the city's deeper gangs, but at night the tinted glass threw everything into shadows. Leaning forward, Brew squinted at the emergency entrance and made a soft clucking sound.

"Now how we gettin' at him in there?" Little Whip complained.

"They be ways."

"Dumb ways." Eyeing the cop cars in the drive, Little Whip added without conviction, "Maybe that one Seven who already dead."

"Not that one. He think he some kind of superstar. Want to go out big-time. And now that he shot up Little Donny, we goin' to see to it. Trust me on that."

"Shit. S'pose you wants me to drive through them doors so's we can jump out all trigger happy."

"A mind's a terrible thing to waste," Brew observed. When he didn't get a reaction, he added, "I'm talkin' 'bout yours."

"You talkin'," Little Whip grimly agreed. "What now?"

"I say," Brew drawled, tapping the side of his head to show he had something brilliant cooking, "that we need a little up-close work. Why don't you drive us back to Shotgun Mountain, Rasmus, and don't go collectin' no admirin' traffic po-lice-men along the way, huh? Nice and easy does us. We know where ol' Rainy goin' make his last stand. The rest is linin' up a good shot for some deservin' Gold."

"Shit."

"That right, and enough to go around too."

FIFTEEN MINUTES LATER the other half of the shoot-out, Little Donny, arrived at the General in a Jackson County ambulance, his condition nowhere near as mint as Rainy's. Two nine-millimeter portals made his chest look like a first-class cabin with a view of a wine-dark sea. Although the paramedics rushed him into the stabilization room where a full medical team waited, it was mostly a formality, done partly because it was expected, partly to show support for a badly overweight plainclothes cop who'd been on the scene when the cross fire broke out. He'd been thumping up and down on the loser's bubbling chest so long and hard that he looked like a wet T-shirt contestant. Within minutes the second patient was declared dead on arrival, DOA in rubber-stamp talk.

In the meantime the gooseneck of patients waiting to get placed in the ER continued to grow. Whenever someone in a life-or-death condition arrived, the new patient's care sapped the ER's resources, slowing down everyone else's treatment. Near the triage desk just inside the entrance, conversations grew ugly.

"There goes another one in front of us."

"Looks of it, they be patchin' on him for hours."

"Maybe he won't make it."

"He don't look that lucky."

The wait to get a foot stitched up, a fishing lure cut out of an earlobe, or a medication renewed—those waits and many others stretched into hours. The fact that the emergency room and its entrance had recently received a facelift so that it looked like a shining, state-of-the-art medical facility complete with an overabundance of computers and electrical instruments only made matters worse, for the surroundings led people to expect something other than the same old slow boat to the cemetery. Patients were lined up clear around the corner from the remodeled triage desk, "like fuckin' bumps on a fuckin' log," as one self-proclaimed chump put it. Yet despite all the gleam and dream, it still smelled like a hospital. Sounded like one too, people moaning, emesis basins being filled, patients complaining.

There were other tensions involved as well. Even a blind woman wouldn't have taken long to guess that a majority of those seated beside her weren't white. Nobody was talking like an investment banker.

"You can be sure there ain't no whiteys waitin' for hours like this."

"Hey," a lady of the night in high heels and leather minidress said, "what about me?"

"You? Pffft. You don't count."

"I'm Irish."

"You got a car?"

"No."

"A house?"

"No."

"A job?"

"Hey . . ."

"Insurance?"

"No."

"Then it don't matter how white you thinks you is, you black. Just don't know it."

"Why ain't she red?" a Native American down the line objected. "Black ain't the only color waiting 'round here."

"You want her?" the first man asked. "She yours."

That drew a mean chuckle out of everyone but the lady of the night, a small flock of Southeast Asians who were talking in a language that sounded like birdsong, and, of course, anyone who hurt too much to laugh.

About all the staff could do to cool everyone down was turn the thermostat settings lower and lower. Not that it helped. Asthmatic vents kept churning out lukewarm air. After the surface remodeling, there hadn't been enough left in the budget to rehab the air-conditioners.

ANOTHER HOUR AND a half passed before a shapely black woman steamed past the triage desk as if intending to ram her double-wide baby stroller through the closed emergency room doors. The salt-and-pepper pair of security guards stationed in front of those doors traded ugly glances with each other and held their ground. Lyle Brown, the black half of the security team, stood a whisker under six feet, had muscles well defined as body armor, and eyes so deep and still that people were always looking away for fear of falling in. Frank Huey, the paler half of the pair, went six-two, had a whiskey drinker's soft but mean muscles, and eyes friendly as two cracked steelies.

"One of yours," Frank Huey remarked, nodding at the woman bearing down on them.

"What gave her away?" Lyle asked, unamused by the crack.

"The rhyming."

"Right," Lyle said, knowing that in Frank Huey's world all black people spoke in rhyme. "So I'll handle her."

It looked as though he would need both hands to do that. The woman before them was more than a sight, she was almost an apparition. Her eyeballs had voltage, her spiked hair had had some current run through it too, and her clothes, what there was of them—blue jeans cut high as panties and a sleeveless T-shirt fashionably torn off below her breasts—definitely created an electromagnetic field. The two infants hanging on to the stroller plowing in front of her crimped their lips together as if about to cry.

"My man's in there," she called out.

"Sorry," Lyle answered in an even voice. "This area's closed to visitors."

"I ain't no visitor. I's family." Although coming to a full stop, she kept rolling the stroller back and forth, as if revving its motor.

"It's for everyone's safety, ma'am."

Which was true. Whenever the victim of a violent crime—a

shooting, knifing, or general whomping—landed on the ER's doorstep, Security went to a low-level alert. In the past there had been some diligent shooters, stabbers, and whompers who had shown up full of hate for an unfinished job.

"He been shot," she said, outraged. "You can't be keeping me out of there."

"What's your man's name?" Lyle said, making a point of not checking in with his partner. It didn't take eye contact to know Frank Huey's response to any leniency.

"Rainy. Rainy Penshorn. And don' you be tryin' to tell me that man not in there."

"What's he look like?" Lyle asked, hoping that she didn't describe the short and chubby dead kid.

"Like some nigger with a hole in him."

"Lady, I'm trying to help you."

"Then open them doors," she said, raising her voice for the sympathy vote from the people watching from the far side of the triage desk.

"You have some identification?" Lyle said, matching her volume rather than backing down. A certain amount of all security or police work came down to showmanship.

Muttering, she unslung a small patent-leather purse and made a good show of digging though it, but finally she quit searching to look up, her brown eyes going flat clear to the edge of the world while her voice went all tiny and meek. "Couldn't you just tell me how he doin'?"

That didn't wash. The change in tactics only succeeded in arousing Lyle's suspicions.

"As soon as we know who you are, ma'am."

"Now who the hell would I be?" she said, ditching the tiny and meek.

"That I wouldn't have any—"

"Where a phone?" she demanded.

Lyle pointed down a hallway that led away from the emergency room. Pivoting her stroller on its rear wheels, she stalked off, vowing over her shoulder, "I be dealin' with you suckers later."

"Hurry back," Frank Huey added, unable to resist a contribution.

Lyle, however, was more interested in the extrawide berth the woman gave a scrawny black teenager who'd been hanging out near the triage desk for the last fifteen minutes, as if waiting for someone. At least that's what Lyle had assumed until now, but when he crossed over to tap the kid on the shoulder, the boy froze up solid as January ice.

"Stay cool," said Lyle.

"Definitely," the kid answered, at the same time leaning toward the exit.

"You know that woman?"

"All depend," the kid said, pulling a tough face even though he couldn't have been more than eleven or twelve, with doe eyes and long lashes. "Who she sayin' she is?"

"Rainy Penshorn's woman."

"No way," the kid scoffed. "She ain't got nothin' to do with Rainy."

"So you know Rainy, huh?"

But Frank Huey chose that moment to appear at Lyle's shoulder and say, "This little clucker know something?"

One look at Huey dummied the kid up big-time. Lyle tried to guide his partner away by the elbow, but Huey ripped his arm free and shot him the kind of glance that starts crosses burning on front lawns, among other places. Nearby patients held their collective breath, but Lyle disappointed everyone—Huey most of all—by remaining calm. Raising his two-way to his mouth, he requested backup, which arrived almost immediately, taking up the vacant space in front of the ER's doors.

"Let's find that woman," Lyle said.

"We just going to listen for the rhyming?" Huey asked.

"Right," Lyle said, already leading the way.

The voices of the waiting patients died away as the two guards strode by, only to pick up again once they were past. On a stretch of empty hallway, Huey swore out of the side of his mouth, "Keep your black hands off me, Brown."

Lyle didn't have a chance to say that he put his black hands wherever they needed to be put. Just then they rounded a corner to face, dead ahead, the woman with the double-wide baby

14

stroller. She was arguing over a pay phone, her tone sharp and mean as anything she'd put on Lyle, but that all ceased as soon as she spotted the guards. For a couple of seconds a stillness, maybe even an utter stillness, captured the twenty yards separating them. Frank Huey took it upon himself to end the trance.

"Hey you!"

She broke for a fire exit before they could start running. Even more amazing, she left her babies behind. A fire alarm went off, as did the infants. Frank Huey—the faster of the guards, or perhaps the more motivated, since Lyle was beginning to doubt that he really wanted to know what this was all about—reached the fire exit first, laying his shoulder into it and bursting outside. Lyle joined him in time to watch the woman dive into an orange Toronado that squealed off down Wabash Street.

"Bitch," Huey swore, kicking the pavement.

"Right again," Lyle said, heading back inside to the dangling telephone and two bawling kids.

Whoever was on the other end of the phone clicked off as soon as Lyle asked in a streetwise voice, "What's happening?"

By the time Huey stomped in, Lyle had picked up one of the babies to comfort her. Before Huey could spew out anything hateful, Lyle thrust the first child at him and scooped up the second. That's when they saw the shiny barrel of a Smith & Wesson peeking out from the baby covers and knew they'd stumbled across something more than Rainy Penshorn's woman.

As soon as the two hospital guards quit hassling him, the scrawny kid who'd been hanging out by the triage desk slipped out the ER's entrance with the lightness of Tinkerbell. He sprinted to an idling Cherokee, where in between gulps of air he reported all that he'd seen.

"You sure it's that crazy Gold bitch?" the man in the backseat asked him.

"Seen her up close."

"And she had the Swann twins?"

"Pushin' 'em like they her own."

"Then they after Rainy bad. We better get us some muscle or he meat." Picking up a cellular phone, the man in the backseat started tapping out numbers and delivering a single message over and over, "Get your black ass down here."

It took about a half hour for Lyle Brown and Frank Huey to finish threatening each other, to report to their supervisor, and to hand off two squalling infants to a pediatric nurse in the ER. Lyle's explanations to the nurse were cut short by a radio alert for all guards to report, code 1, to triage. Frank Huey thundered to the rescue first, nightstick bouncing on his hip, key ring jangling like sleigh bells at his side. On the last stretch of corridor, Lyle could hear angry shouts but couldn't see beyond a knot of waiting patients blocking the way. Those at the rear of the crowd stood on tiptoe and moved their heads side to side as if trying to glimpse a tennis match, except it felt way too mean for white shorts and handshakes at the net.

When Frank Huey plunged through the onlookers, the crowd pushed back until they spotted his uniform. The ringside glee on people's faces was quickly replaced by hostility. Once Lyle got through the crowd, he found out why.

Fifteen to twenty young black men milled about in front of the triage desk, talking hot, talking angry, talking tall, talking fire . . . talking, talking, talking. All wrapped in loose T-shirts, jeans, and high-tech running shoes, they also wore green hats or bandannas or jackets, the green of a pool table which to the practiced eye announced they were Sevens. The only barrier between them and the emergency room was four unarmed security guards whose puffed-out chests didn't have any expansion left in them. The evening security supervisor, Victor Wheaton, was struggling to reason with whoever was in charge of the small mob, but no one acted as though in charge and every time he asked a question, a different one or two or three of the young men answered him.

"What do you want?" Victor Wheaton called out, his face a shade pasty.

"What do we want?"

"*What* do we want?"

"Wants to know what we want."

"We wants our man out of there."

"Ain't safe for him in there."

"That what we want."

"Who's after him?" Victor Wheaton asked, trying for calm.

"You some kind of fool?"

"Golds after him."

"Want to plant him deep."

"That why we here. To protect our man."

"Well," Victor Wheaton said, "you can't stay. There are sick people here."

"Shit," several said at once.

"You want to clear us out? Give up Rainy."

"We can't do that," Victor Wheaton said.

"You been workin' on him two hours."

"How much time you need?"

"More than you've got," Frank Huey contributed from the sidelines, drawing everyone's wrath to himself.

"I can tell you that he's doing fine," Victor Wheaton promised, at the same time drawing a line across his throat for Huey to shut up. Gradually the Sevens turned back toward Wheaton, although a few continued to point themselves at Huey.

"We s'pose to take your word?"

"We wants to hear Rainy say it."

"That's it."

"That's right."

"Uh-huh."

"I'm afraid we can't allow that," Victor Wheaton said, his voice going wavery. "He's under arrest."

"Arrest!"

"For what?"

"For gettin' shot? That some kind of crime now?"

"He's perfectly safe," Victor Wheaton said, but it was doubtful whether anyone heard him.

That was when Frank Huey took it upon himself to cross to the line of guards blocking off the ER entrance. When one of the young men leaned in his face to say, "Shoo!" Huey sucker-punched the kid on the chin, sending him reeling into two others. Then, before any Sevens could regroup and charge back, squad cars began arriving outside and the curtain went up on the city's first race riot since the sixties.

From then on it was pure barroom-brawl choreography: bodies hurtling like freight cars through space; the crisp sound of shattering glass; big guys bear-hugging one another and pip-squeaks doing their Bruce Lee imitations. Red flashing lights reflected off broken glass and tile to make the floor whirl like a disco's. The dancers were cheek to cheek, fist to cheek, and everyone wanted to lead. One cleared a space by swinging a framed picture that he'd lifted off the wall; another played tag around a gurney; a third tried to strangle an orderly with a stethoscope. But none of it was entertaining, the way it was on a movie screen. All of it was hateful and deadly serious, strictly combat.

Most of the intruders stampeded back out the entrance; assorted others spurted down the hall leading away from the ER and banged into waiting patients, which started additional scuffles. Crutches swished, chairs flew. Lyle wrestled one fleeing Seven to the floor, but the boy reminded him too much of a neighbor's son for his heart to be in holding him. When the kid broke loose, Lyle didn't pursue but joined the guards struggling to push the last of the intruders, by then mixed in with quarreling drunks and counterpunching orderlies, outside so they could lock the doors.

Somewhere in there several carloads of youths with gold bandannas or jackets or sneakers arrived, cutting off the first gang's retreat. That was when two of the Sevens jerked Frank Huey outside for a shield, applying a knife to his throat to steer him.

For an instant the glass door closed in front of Lyle, shutting out the sirens and gunshots and rallying shouts of one gang or the other. He tried to watch them carry Frank Huey off, even for an instant silently cheered them on, but then he checked around and saw that he was the only security guard aware of what was happening. Everyone else was busy slapping on handcuffs or attending to the injured, which meant that Frank Huey's life was in his hands. It wasn't an agreeable sensation, but after only a moment of hesitation he acted, springing outside to save him. At least that was the plan.

In the great outdoors bricks had wings. More squad cars and sirens were being sucked into the riot's vortex. The barking of dogs filled the low registers, gunshots the high.

Lyle managed to yank off the Seven holding the knife to Huey's throat before tear gas hit the street. The second Seven swung on him at about the same time that Lyle's eyes started to burn. Ducking the punch, he staggered backwards, instinctively rubbing at his eye sockets. For a minute he caught flashes of crouched figures and faces masked by gold or green bandannas. That was the last he saw before a brick collided with the back of his skull. Crumpling, he came to while being dragged by his armpits to safety. He struggled, not about to let Frank Huey save his ass, but his legs buckled, leaving him no choice. With his closed eyes still stinging, he realized too late that it wasn't Frank Huey who had ahold of him and that they weren't dragging him back to the hospital but toward an idling car. His rescuers pitched him inside the car's trunk the way the post office flings mailbags. Then darkness, followed by a single thought trapped in his spinning head. *They grabbed the wrong asshole.*

3

When Jan Gallagher's phone woke her at four in the morning, the voice on the other end was a man's.

"Gallagher, this is Larsen, at the hospital. We're activating the call-in list and for some reason you're on it. How long to get down here?"

"What's going on?"

"Riot," Larsen said, wordy as ever.

"Give me thirty," Jan answered, making sure she hung up before he did.

Her first thought was to wake her mother, Claire, who shared the master bedroom with her. Her second thought was that she couldn't wake Claire because her mother had remarried and moved out. She had a panicky moment until rationalizing that she ought to be able to depend on her oldest daughter, Leah, age seventeen teetering on eighteen, to provide somewhat adult direction for the three younger girls until Claire could be called in.

But when she tiptoed into Leah and Amy's room, the red night-light made Leah look as though she were laid out on a funeral barge. She was dressed in black silken pj's, and her hands were folded flat across her chest. She wore earphones. The foot poking out from beneath the iridescent green bedcovers had cat eyes tattooed on either side of the ankle.

"What is it, Mother?"

The question came from Amy in the other bed. Jan should have known better than to think the phone hadn't woken everyone.

Jan's second ex, who had fathered the three youngest girls, was a city cop, and his whereabouts and health put everyone on edge when the phone rang in the middle of the night.

"Work," Leah answered for her mother without cracking an eyelid.

"That's right," Jan said. "I'm going in to the hospital. Leah, you're in charge until Claire gets here."

"I will crack the whip," Leah promised in her best fiendish voice.

"Making breakfast should be enough, thank you."

"They *will* eat their fruit."

"That's doubtful. Do you work today?"

"It's my constitutional right," Leah spitefully said, displaying her justly famous attitude.

"I'll make sure Grandma gets here before you have to leave. Now go back to sleep."

After a pit stop in the bathroom, Jan landed in her security uniform and almost made it out the front door without tripping over the assorted softball mitts, misplaced dresses, and Barbie dolls along the way. She couldn't evade Tess's science project, though, a gerbil named Valvoline who nearly lost his tail.

The first thing she heard outside her suburban ranch house was a siren. On the way to the hospital, she counted three helicopters passing overhead. Twice she had to pull over for fire engines. Whatever was happening at the General, she didn't intend to report directly to Gavin Larsen. What she needed was someone who could string several words together without breaking into a cold sweat. But upon reaching General Jack, she was the speechless one. Through a lingering haze she saw a wheelchair pitched through the frosted glass of the emergency room's entrance sign. The chair hung half in, half out, looking as though a patient had been dumped inside the sign. Jan laughed in disbelief, then sobered considerably when she saw, then smelled, the smoldering husk of a flipped car. Camera crews were circling, and a plywood patch job had been done on the sliding glass doors leading into the ER.

No gawkers, though. The police had cordoned off the streets fronting the hospital. Jan had to detour four blocks to reach the hospital parking ramp and on the way counted a half-dozen over-

21

turned litter bins, several shot-out streetlights, a bus shelter listing to one side, a score of shattered windshields, and a coin-operated newspaper dispenser impaled on a fire hydrant. Newsprint blew across the landscape and the stink of burning rubber tinged the air. With no intention of parking in a remote corner of the ramp at this time of night, she grabbed a slot reserved for a hospital director, slipped out the Twentieth Street exit, and dashed across a deserted avenue to an employee entrance. Leo Kennedy, Security's resident red-haired walrus and yakmaster, as in yakity-yak-yak-yak, unlocked the glass door for her. Before she'd stepped through he was rambling on, wound up even tighter than usual, as he hurried to close the door behind her.

"They didn't call you all the way down here for this little bitty thing, did they, Gallagher?"

"Larsen said there was a riot."

"Might call it that," said Leo, backing away from the locked door as if standing too close to the glass might prove unhealthy. "He tell you about Lyle Brown?"

"What do you think?" Jan said, stiffening as she thought not of Lyle but of his girlfriend, Felicia.

"Sevens snatched him."

"Not funny, Leo." She managed to keep her voice level, eyebrows too.

Leo got right down to telling her how unfunny it was, throwing in the rest of the night's festivities as he went, from the arrival of the gunshot victims, to a pistol-packin' mama, to the riot and Frank Huey's failed attempt to rescue Lyle Brown from the Sevens who'd grabbed him.

"Huey tried to save Lyle?"

"So he says," Leo answered, smiling in disbelief himself. "Didn't see it myself."

"Why'd they want Lyle?"

"Frank says he didn't have time to ask."

"And nobody knows where they've taken him?"

"Not yet we don't," Leo said, making a gesture toward the street. "It's a big goddamn city out there."

"So tell me," Jan said, her eyelids feeling heavy for the first time since rolling out of bed, "what do they want me to do?"

"Something important, I'll bet."

"Save your money, Leo. Has anybody told Felicia?"

"Not likely," Leo said, sobering plenty.

"Well, I'd say we just solved one mystery."

"Care to name it?"

"Why they had to have me down here."

WITH THE ENTIRE hospital in lockup, nobody on the first floor could move from one area to another without clearing control points. To reach the ER, Jan had to pass through three locked fire doors that were normally blocked open. Every checkpoint was secured by a guard who had war stories to tell, each of which involved a hero they were far too modest to name outright.

When she reached the ER the slumped or scowling patients were two to three deep and there was gurney gridlock in the halls. Thanks to tear gas, every third or fourth face had a damp cloth draped across the eyes. A strained, buzzing hush had befallen the land. Staff conferred in hoarse whispers; nurses rushed about with tunnel vision, hoping to complete at least one task before being given three more; patients called, cursed, or grabbed for anyone wearing white or a scrub suit. The noisiest of the wounded was an overfed city cop bellyaching about his lack of VIP treatment. His manners didn't enhance the amount of goodwill present amongst his handcuffed neighbors or the medical staff.

Jan spotted Gavin Larsen's balding head bent over a bellowing patient whose wrists and ankles were being tied down, four-pointed—as the staff called it. A nurse waited in the wings with a needle. During a lull in the proceedings Jan asked where Larsen wanted her to help.

"Hodges's office," he said with a grunt.

The patient started bucking before Jan could ask why the royal summons. On the way out of the ER she pinched herself but—regretfully—didn't awaken. Meetings with her boss, Eldon Hodges, the head of Security, often left her feeling that way.

* * *

So she trooped back through all the checkpoints with a couple of new ones thrown in because she had no intention of venturing outside. To avoid the streets, she went underground in a tunnel, coming up in the remodeled administrative wing where every light was shamelessly blazing and the air-conditioning worked exceedingly well, causing Jan to shiver. When she reached Hodges's office, she found his secretary, Miss Pepperidge, diligently licking envelopes despite the hour. Jan couldn't help but wonder if Hodges's secretary was higher up the call-in list than Jan herself.

"Hodges wanted to see me?" Jan asked as she approached.

"He's in conference."

"At five in the morning?"

"Some days we start early." That was a royal "we." The bad chemistry between Jan and the secretary was as old as their first handshake. Jan had mistakenly addressed her as Ms. instead of Miss.

"Would you mind telling him I'm waiting in my office?" Jan asked, stepping into her nearby cubicle.

She'd barely sat down before the door to Eldon Hodges's office opened and two men hurried out. Not an unusual reaction to the contents of that office, but it meant that he actually had been having a meeting and wasn't just making her wait. She sneaked a glimpse but saw nothing beyond broad shoulders and tight-fitting plaid suit coats. Cops, she decided. Detectives. Who else would bother with ill-fitting suits and clashing ties at that time of the night?

Hodges's door closed, allowing Jan to wait in the manner to which she was accustomed—for no good reason. But then something unexpected happened on her phone console. The light for Hodges's extension flashed on. Unless he was listening to the dial tone, not an impossibility, he was talking to someone, perhaps about something related to work. It was one revelation after another, but before Jan could get her bearings and wonder who might be pinned beneath Hodges's doublespeak, the console light flicked off, his door reopened, and he called out for Jan to join

24

him. He didn't ask Miss Pepperidge to summon her, just called right out himself.

"Gallagher."

Jan waited a moment but no gong sounded. As she paraded into Security's inner sanctum, she did her best to avoid peeking at Miss Pepperidge but in the end couldn't resist. Rather than showing shock, the secretary was smiling almost serenely. Something bad was spreading its wings.

"Close the door," Hodges instructed. "Have a seat."

Jan did so.

The only light turned on in the office was the famous green-glass desk lamp that had been around the world with Hodges during his years in the merchant marine, years that earned him the tag Little Admiral. At present the Admiralty had clasped its pudgy hands together atop the desk. His clean-shaven, splotchy face remained in the shadows.

"You've heard about Lyle Brown?" he asked.

Here it comes, she thought but said, "I have."

"The police are doing everything they can to find him," Hodges said, glaring down at his fleshy hands. "And we're going to do whatever it takes to help them."

"I'm sure Lyle will be relieved to hear that."

"Have you heard about the woman with the baby stroller?" Hodges said, refusing to rise to the bait.

"And the gun she left behind."

"That's right. She left something else too."

He paused. Jan did too, not about to ask.

"Two babies," Hodges said, managing to make it sound like an indictment of all womankind.

"And?"

"The police want some help looking into those babies. They're trying to find their mother to see if she knows anything about all this. I thought of you."

"The babies?" Jan said, frowning.

"Let's not make a federal issue of it, Gallagher. We thought a woman's touch might be needed there. Your personnel folder says you qualify."

"All right," Jan said at last. "To help Lyle."

"Good," Hodges said. "This looks bad enough that he might need it."

That sounded sincere, if begrudgingly so. Abruptly, as if to purge his mind of any sincerity, Hodges assured her that the police officer in charge of finding Lyle, a Lieutenant Harry Crenshaw, from the Gang Squad, was eminently capable. Having said that, he dismissed her. Jan remained seated.

"What about Felicia?"

The Little Admiral's jawline hardened further.

"Has anyone told her about Lyle?" she asked.

"We're talking about his girlfriend?"

"They've been living together for three years. I'd say she's got a right to know."

"That's up to the police."

"I don't think—"

"You're not to do anything," Hodges said, cutting her off, "that interferes with the police's investigation, and right now they're trying to involve as few people as possible. Am I understood?"

"We're talking about his family."

"If we allow the police to do their job, there's every chance Brown can tell his girlfriend all about it himself. Now, go find out what you can about these babies, give your report to Lieutenant Crenshaw, and try not to involve the county in any lawsuits."

Hodges had been the manager named in Jan's discrimination case. When he slid her a slip of paper with Lieutenant Crenshaw's name and number, their fingers didn't touch.

4

By five in the morning the Pediatrics nurse Jan talked to was frazzled as the old woman who lived in a shoe. The lobby in Peds ER was beat as the inside of that shoe—strewn toys, fermenting diapers, *Beauty and the Beast* flickering on a TV mounted out of the reach of smudged little hands. The townspeople were after the beast. The nurse rocked a croupy infant in her stout arms as she updated Jan on the abandoned twins. Young as they were, there was no way the babies would be identified unless someone showed up to claim them. They'd already passed a physical examination, been found basically healthy, if hungry, and been passed on to the Barnabas Shelter to await disposition by the courts.

Jan supposed step two was finding out Frank Huey's backwards slant on the night. It was that or try tracking down all the patients who had been waiting at the triage desk on the slim chance they'd seen something. Even a visit with Frank Huey was more appealing than the legwork that would entail. Since he'd been ordered over to the Fifth Precinct to peruse mug shots of women who might have been pushing the baby stroller, she headed there herself.

On her way over, every second or third car had swirling red lights on its roof and was traveling fast. Located a mile and a half from the hospital, the Fifth Precinct building was two stories high and had three colors of dark brick and one shade of grime. Its air-conditioning had taken the holiday weekend off. The desk sergeant was gulping ice tea and positioning a toy electric fan toward his shiny Roman nose when Jan arrived. He waved her upstairs to where they'd stowed Frank Huey. It got hotter each step of the way up. On the second level, large floor fans rippled the edges of papers thumbtacked to bulletin boards and weighted down on desks with everything from bowling trophies to a Batman doll. The smell of fresh paint was overpowering, but what had been touched up remained a mystery. Every dingy wall within sight had its original orange paint job, a fading Day-Glo tint that had probably broken down many a hardened criminal in its day.

Upstairs she had a creepy sense of déjà vu. An on-again, off-again romance with Detective White, one of the Fifth's finest, could be thanked for that. There was the head-sized hole in the plasterboard that he'd romanticized. Glancing up, she saw the single brown shoe atop a light fixture, right where he'd said it was stationed. He'd been gone on a personal leave for three weeks now, and she wasn't sure if she missed him or not. The only clue she had about why he'd taken the leave was a cryptic postcard he'd sent that read *Bears 3, Honeybees 0*. Detective White had his quirks. The fact that he wasn't presently on hand was a relief, for he had a way of confusing matters with emotions, his and hers.

She found Frank Huey at the back of the room, eavesdropping on a knot of shirtsleeved, sweaty detectives standing in front of a wall map of the city. They were either jabbing fingers at the map or talking animatedly into phones whose extension cords stretched from the nearest desks. The whir of the floor fans drowned out their voices. Frank Huey watched them with all the intensity of a wanna-be and pulled such a long face upon Jan's arrival that she felt like a kid sister. When he spoke, it was low and out of the side of his narrow mouth so that no one would notice them talking.

"Find anything?" Jan asked. The precinct's photo books were spread out on the table before him.

"Of course," he said, as if that was a given whenever he was involved. "They already pulled her in."

Jan waited for more, got a sneer instead.

"And?"

"She's not talking," Frank Huey said, making it sound as if that much should have been obvious.

"Were you expecting her to?"

"There's ways." The corners of his lips turned up.

"What can you tell me about those babies?" Jan asked, unwilling to inquire about his ways.

"I left them in Pediatrics."

"So you did. Tell me about this guy whose arrival started it all."

"Check the operating room."

"Any ideas on what happened to Lyle?"

"Ask his people."

Having talked himself out, Huey did his best tough-guy amble over to the water cooler. Jan might have tripped him if one of the cops hadn't broken away from the others and approached her.

"You Jan Gallagher?"

He had a strong chin, clear eyes, and a nearly unnoticeable speech impediment that caused him to hesitate before saying her name. Extending a hand, he introduced himself as Lieutenant Harry Crenshaw, Gang Squad. Harry to friends. He had a surprisingly limp handshake considering that everything else about him, from the scrupulous part in his short brown hair to the buffed black shoes, said he still believed that clean should squeak. He even had the decency to skip any mention of Jan's dalliance with Detective White, which was no doubt common knowledge in those parts. Cops talked. She knew that much after being married to one. For the courtesy she agreed to call him Harry.

"Any word on Lyle?"

"Nobody's talking," he said, leading the way to his desk, the neat one without any bowling trophies or Batman dolls. Frank Huey remained over by the water cooler looking like no one ever asked him to dance.

"You up to speed?" Lieutenant Crenshaw asked.

"I know there was some excitement."

"Started over a drive-by. We got that much down cold. Two undercover cops saw it all." The lieutenant wagged his head at the wonder of that. "A Jeep Wrangler cruised by a Gold's stash house that Narcotics had under surveillance and started spraying. One dead. The younger brother of one of the Golds' head honchos. That's going to make this ugly. Golds fired back and winged the gunman, a Seven by the name of Rainy Penshorn. You've got him over at your place for now, minor stuff, a nasty head bump and a clean wing shot. He'll be fine. We've also got the three who drove him in—illegal possession of firearms, for now—but we probably won't have them for long, and they know it. The rest of what we've got, you probably heard from your boss."

Rather than point out the error of his ways, Jan said, "Do we know why they grabbed Lyle?"

"Not a clue. And as far as I can tell, we've only got one good shot at getting something soon."

"The woman Frank Huey ID'd?"

"Tina Cassidy?" he said, puzzled.

"Huey didn't give me any names," Jan said. "But he said he picked out the woman who left her babies at the hospital."

"Weren't her babies," the lieutenant said. "But you're talking about Tina. Doesn't matter, though. Aside from the fact that she'd never tell us a thing, she's a Gold and the only witness we have—" he nodded reluctantly toward Frank Huey "—says the guys who grabbed your man were wearing Sevens green. No, I'm thinking about someone else. The babies' real mother."

"You found her already?"

"She found us would be more accurate." Resting his elbows on the desk, he leaned forward to gaze into the shiny desktop. He didn't appear to be seeing anything hopeful. "Let me level with you, Jan. With what's brewing out on the streets, Lyle Brown's abduction isn't getting a high priority. Everyone's too busy thinking about how smoky Los Angeles got after the King trial. The chief of police is worrying about whatever the mayor's worrying about, and the mayor's worrying about whether the governor will call the National Guard in time, although not so soon that he seems like a wimp, and the governor's worrying about . . ."

Here the lieutenant faltered, unsure what occupied the governor's mind and not about to falsely fill in the blank, which was generally acknowledged to be an exceptionally big blank.

"Anyway," the lieutenant continued, "I'd say that it's a safe bet that for the next forty-eight hours every able-bodied cop will be out on the streets with orders to be seen but not heard. So far it's a series of small incidents but it's spreading."

"It sounds like you're leading up to something."

"Working on it," the lieutenant said with regret. "What would you say if I told you that you're sitting next to the investigative team looking into Lyle Brown's whereabouts? And it's not all I have to do, either."

Jan grimaced and asked, "Does Felicia know all this?"

"Who would she be?"

"Felicia Smith. Lyle Brown's girlfriend or significant other or whatever you want to call her. They've been living together over three years."

"Why didn't your boss mention her?"

Jan shrugged artfully.

"Well," the lieutenant said, writing Felicia's name down on a pad, "I hope to meet with her and the victim's brother as soon as possible. But don't ask me when that might be."

"Lyle has a brother?" Jan asked, taking a turn at being surprised.

"According to his personnel folder, he does." The lieutenant's voice lowered to a whisper, causing Frank Huey to squirm. "Now, the reason we've got the real mother is this: Shortly after midnight a young woman named Raeshawn Swann came screaming into the Second Precinct claiming her twins had been kidnapped. Three men busted her door down and took 'em. First look said domestic. Second look says maybe not."

Jan frowned and listened.

"We probably wouldn't have made the connection to the kids dumped at your place if all the excitement hadn't left us short on manpower. When those two infants left with you had to be transported over to the Barnabas Shelter, we had to pull patrolmen from the Second to do it, and they remembered hearing about the kidnapping earlier on their shift. The rest was just good teamwork. But here's the rub. We go out to pick up this Raeshawn Swann and now she won't tell us anything. Not a peep. All she wants is her kids back. That's it."

"Do you want me to talk to her?"

"It'd be a help. Lord knows she's tired of seeing me."

"What are you hoping to find out?"

"Anything beyond my being a blankety-blank would be appreciated," he said with a tired grin. "Number one is the point you raised earlier. Why did they grab Lyle Brown? If we can nail that down, all this might start to make some sense."

"So I talk to her," Jan said. "What tack should I take?"

"Direct as possible. The Second Precinct's in the heart of Sevens country, and this Raeshawn's connected. After the doings tonight, there's not a Seven telling me anything but go spit."

"But with this Raeshawn you've got some leverage?"

"We should have but it's not working yet. All we want, Jan, is to get your man back. We'll make any kind of deal they want. Access to the media, a mayor's task force, they can name it. As long as it's within the law, we'll bargain with them, but we've got to get that word out."

"And you'll let this woman have her kids back?"

"Doesn't matter what I say," he said. "If they're her kids, she's going to get them back."

"But you might help her get them back sooner?"

"That's the way it works," he said with a nod.

Jan glanced toward the detectives grouped around the city map. They were arguing and pointing in several different directions at once, which didn't leave her feeling exactly out of her league, particularly not with Frank Huey trying out for the team.

"I'm game," Jan said.

"Good," the lieutenant said, standing. "We keep it straightforward. I'll tell her you're from the hospital where the babies were found and that you want to help her if only she'll help you."

"In other words, lay it on."

"That's about it."

THEY HAD THE mother in a gray interviewing room, bare gray table, two gray chairs, one light bulb protected by a wire grill, and one gray moth batting about the light. As seen through the door's one-way glass, the young woman pacing in that room had to be a teenager, and a teenager with a strange tic. She kept glancing behind her as if someone was trying to sneak up on her. So slight was her build, so smooth-complected the rosy brown of her high cheeks, that disregarding the difference in skin color, she could have been one of Jan's middle daughters, even down to the oversized white T-shirt hanging well below her waist. Her shirt said Pepsi; Jan's daughters favored Coke. The little lady certainly didn't look sturdy enough to have carried twins. At present she had her arms crossed as if fighting off a chill even though the room lacked a fan to circulate the stifling air.

Lieutenant Crenshaw entered first, introduced Jan as an officer from the hospital where Raeshawn Swann's twins had been taken, and then retired to a chair in a corner where he became grayer than anything else in the room. As soon as the lieutenant stepped aside, Raeshawn ceased pacing and glared at Jan hard enough to strip-mine some earth. Jan crossed to the table and seated herself, but the girl remained standing. Even with the lieutenant just behind her, Jan felt vulnerable and stood back up herself.

"Your children are fine," Jan said, thinking she sounded cold and distant.

"You can't make me give up my babies," Raeshawn cried out.

"What makes you say that?" Jan asked, almost taking a step backward.

"Don't give me that shit, lady. You do whatever necessary to make me talk."

"Why don't we slow down?" Jan said, unconsciously running her hand across the back of the chair in front of her. "Can I get you anything?"

"My babies."

"Some water?"

"My babies," she said, but this time more softly, shoulders slumping, chin dropping.

Jan's instinct was to put an arm around her but when she moved, the girl's head bobbed up, eyes still cooking.

"You belong to the Sevens?" Jan asked.

She made a disparaging, spitting sound and said, "Where I lives, the only ones what don't can't count."

"The Sevens have grabbed a friend of mine and I'm trying to help get him back."

"What about my babies?"

"I can help you get them back," Jan said after only the slightest of hesitations.

"Ain't fair," the girl weakly protested. "I only wants my little ones."

"Can you at least tell me what happened tonight?"

"Ain't nothing new," she said, dropping heavily into a chair, then twisting unexpectedly about to check behind her. "Week ago Sevens went shootin' 'cause of the dirt them Golds done."

"What dirt?"

"Blinded a Seven. So a week back some Sevens tried to even up but blammed some little baby. Tonight them Golds gone creepy and had my childs grabbed."

"Can you give me a name?" Jan said. "Someone to talk to? A man's life's at stake here."

"You think I's crazy?" she said, her mouth open to cry but no sobs coming out.

"You could save my friend's life."

"Save some white ass?"

"Who said he was white?"

That's when it all caught up with Raeshawn Swann, whatever had been chasing her, and the tears flowed. The sobs choked her, and all she could manage to say was, "I wants my little girls." Jan knew then she wouldn't find out anything more, even though she kept at it for another half hour, more than long enough to make her feel cheaper than she ever had before.

5

As far as Po' Rind was concerned, respect didn't grow on your average pear tree. You wanted some, you had to go out and steal it, the old-fashioned way, which was what occupied Po's thoughts through all the night of July fourth and well on into July fifth. It had, in fact, been bothering him for the past three weeks, dating back to the night a pair of ug-faced Golds had planted a tire iron upside his head and stolen what respect he had built up in his neighborhood, along with a lunch bag of genuine drugs, which he was muling for his elders.

Of course he was set up, but that didn't matter. It didn't matter either that they jumped him when he wasn't looking, and it didn't matter that he got a good fleshy bite out of one of their thighs. None of that mattered. What mattered was that afterward no homeboy short of crazy wanted to be seen walking the walk or talking the talk with him. And tiny little g-sters, sprouts half his age, or nearly so, were getting jobs ahead of him.

All he wanted was to bring himself some justice, and on the night of the fourth, soon as he heard about Rainy Penshorn's misfortunes, he saw the silver lining. Thanks to his little mama, who'd recently dropped a litter down at the General, he knew all about how to find a patient in that so-called hospital. While trying to reach the place where babies arrived, he'd gotten lost so many times that he knew all the ins and outs, a fact that he intended to cash in on. Rescuing Rainy single-handedly ought to buy him some stock back home.

The only trouble was, he might need some muscle to pull it off, and when he tried to arrange some help through Maxi, the original gangster who ran their little corner of Seven's heaven, he couldn't get within shouting distance of the man. Too much bureaucracy. Ever since the Sevens had made up their minds to get organized and take over the entire city from the other sorry-ass street companies, it'd been nothing but one layer of punk after another between Po' and anybody driving around behind smoky glass with a cellular phone. And every one of those punks between Po' and anyone who counted carried a hoop, and a Bic lighter to light it, and considering the things they asked you to jump through, could just as easily have been working down at the county welfare department taking general assistance applications.

" 'Portant that I see the Maxi man."

"For what kind of bizness?"

"Kind of bizness? You talkin' like you don' know me."

"Oh, we know you, Po'. You the man lost a sizable chunk . . ."

"Like I's some nigga just wander in off the street."

"Cool those jets, Po'."

"Ain't nothin' gonna cool 'til you tells the Maxi man I got IMPORTANT bizness. Too IMPORTANT to be sharing with any midget I meets along the—"

"I got specific orders on you, Po'."

"That more like it."

"I got orders say you don' get close enough to Maxi to waste a second of his time, not 'less you has one thing."

"What kind of one thing?"

"A one thing what got put in your hands 'bout three weeks ago and disappeared out of your hands three weeks ago, and—lips sayin'—maybe disappeared up your nose. You just lucky yo' cuz happen to be Maxi's go-down woman, or you might be considerable uglier than you already is. Are we reachin' any understandin' here?"

End of interview.

But hardly the end of Po's aspirations. He knew his plan could return his rep, and he wasn't sharing even a whiff of it with anyone but Maxi, or higher. But seeing as how Maxi had left specific instructions concerning Po', and seeing as how Po' liked the way his mouth lined up over his chin and how his eyes felt so at home on either side of his nose and how he'd recently gotten the gold in his mouth all paid for—considering all that, maybe he ought to make positively sure that he could find Rainy's room number before bothering the Maxi man with a request for some traveling muscle.

But the first thing he ran up against down at General Jack was a black hospital cop who acted like he never looked in the mirror.

"Sorry," that hospital cop said, "but we don't have a Rainy Penshorn in house."

"You sure 'bout that?"

"Absolutely."

"No way he not here," Po' said. "He got brought down here the other night, shot up considerable, and bleeding all over your shiny floors."

"You related to him?"

"Related? The man's my brother."

"I see. Let me check again. How do you spell the name?"

"Don' jerk me, man. It spell just the way it sound."

But nothing, even though he knew, and the guard knew, and anybody who watched channels 2, 5, 6, 9, or 13 had a pretty good idea, where Rainy was. Po' couldn't even get inside the hospital.

So he backed off and tried again, but got nothing when he called Emergency Admissions from a corner phone booth. Nothing when he called the hospital operator either. That left him but one option, and it wasn't a pretty one, but this was for fame and glory and he didn't plan on scrimping. He would have to call his sister Willie.

6

Lieutenant Crenshaw acted as though Jan's interview with Raeshawn Swann had been a blazing success, but he had to interrupt further positive reinforcements to field a call. A thirsty mob had looted a liquor store overnight. They were now lounging about in a cemetery across the way, lobbing empties across the street. Jan found her own way downstairs.

By seven that morning the sky was an overcooked blue except on the edges, where it was a hung-over brown. With the coming of light, the city turned quiet, too quiet, like a cat watching a mouse hole. Traffic on the main thoroughfares was sparse even for the fifth of July, which, falling on a Monday as it did, became an unofficial extension of the holiday weekend for most people. Jan saw three squad cars pulled over in front of a bakery where a bloodied man in a white apron was pointing down the street. The windows of his shop were shattered and the model of a wedding cake that Jan had seen on display there for years was gone.

Back at the General, Jan holed up with a cup of coffee to brood over her phone. Her first call was to the newlyweds, her seventy-year-old mother and her retired navy man, Ned.

"I didn't wake you, did I?" Jan asked.

"Heavens no. We're getting ready for a picnic."

"Oh."

"I know that tone," Claire said.

"I suppose you do, Mother. But it's nothing to worry about. I'll make other arrangements."

"I know about your other arrangements too," Claire said. "It's that job of yours, isn't it?"

"Have you listened to the news this morning?"

"And ruin my day?"

"There's been a riot at the hospital."

"And you're headed right down there, I suppose."

"I'm already down there, Mother."

"So who's watching the girls?"

"Leah."

"Leah?"

The last time Leah baby-sat, she disappeared with her boyfriend five minutes after Jan left.

"It was an emergency, Mother."

"Ned," her mother called out, "you can put that cooler away."

Which left Jan with the really bad phone call.

No matter what Eldon Hodges had warned her not to do, and no matter that the lieutenant had promised to get in touch with Felicia, Jan had made up her mind to call her friend as soon as she heard about Lyle. The only question was when. What finally put her over the edge was hearing the Little Admiral stick his head out his office door to tell his secretary, "Coffee." For Jan that single word, when spoken that way by a man, was something of a rallying call. As the phone connection went through, she prepared an apology for the earliness of the hour, but the call was snatched up before the first ring had died away.

"Lyle?" It was Felicia, sounding frantic.

"No, it's Jan Gallagher. Down at work."

A pause, possibly of confusion. Jan had never called her at home before.

"They're talking about riots on the radio," Felicia said, fighting for calm.

"That's what I wanted to talk to you about. Maybe at your place?"

"Tell me what's going on, Jan."

"I could be there in a half hour," Jan said, realizing as she said it that she'd never been to Felicia and Lyle's place, nor they to hers.

A dead spot occupied the line. The bell on Miss Pepperidge's carriage return dinged. Somewhere in the back of Jan's mind she knew the bell was part of a typewriter, not the secretary, but since at the moment Jan herself was feeling like little more than a cog in a gigantic, flaming wheel, it was difficult to keep such distinctions straight. Twisting completely away from Miss Pepperidge's desk, she hunkered down over her phone.

"Felicia—"

"Something's happened . . ." Felicia's voice cut in with a gasp, then broke apart. "H-hasn't it?"

"I really think—"

"He should have been home seven hours ago."

"How do I get to your place?"

"I can't wait here. I've been waiting here all night. You better tell me right now, or I'll get in a wreck on the way down there."

"He's missing," Jan said. "That's all we know for sure."

"What's not for sure?"

"Take it easy. We don't know that anything bad's happened."

"Jan, I'm looking down at my hand and it's trembling."

"I'm calling you a cab."

"I'll do it," Felicia said, turning testy.

"Everything's going to be all right."

"Don't say that," Felicia snapped, as if Jan was jinxing her.

"OK," Jan soothed. "OK. But try not to worry. I'll see you in a little bit but it better not be here. I'm not supposed to be talking to you. Let's meet at Scrubs and Eggs."

"Should I bring anything?" Felicia asked, now repentant.

"I'd say we've got everything we need down here."

Felicia laughed as if Jan had made a joke, which left Jan unsure what to say next. In the end they both hung on the line another ten seconds without speaking, then clicked off without a goodbye.

Since Scrubs and Eggs, a breakfast spot that catered to hospital employees, was at most a five-minute walk, Jan killed time by reporting to the Little Admiral all that she'd learned. Naturally she omitted the phone call to Felicia. With a slight limp, Eldon Hodges paced behind his desk, returning repeatedly to his office window to part the blinds as if on the lookout for a giant white whale that was the embodiment of evil. Nothing starboard yet. When Jan was finished, he dismissed her without turning away from the window, but before she reached the door, he stopped her with a reminder.

"Don't forget the chain of command, Gallagher."

"Is that the one around my neck?"

"Among other places," the Little Admiral said, waving for her to be gone.

BY EIGHT THAT morning the temperature was massing degrees for an assault on the record books. Jan's uniform's white top stuck between her shoulder blades, and her black trousers clung to her inner thighs. The interior of Scrubs and Eggs was as dim as the hospital's interior was bright. Perhaps that was its attraction. The air carried whiffs of the waitress's perfume and fried potatoes and strong coffee. Country heartache played on the jukebox, and the window air conditioner rattled as if on a death march to Nashville. Jan took shelter in a booth as far from the front door as possible without losing sight of it. She tried to ignore the fact that Burt, the owner and cook, had called in his two beefy cousins to stand guard by the door even though the streets were presently empty.

Five minutes later Felicia arrived, looking shot out of a cannon. So much for ordering up a taxi. She overran the entrance by several yards, stopped to regroup, then rushed forward. Her lovely brown face was puffy and sallow, her voice hadn't yet caught up with the rest of her, and her clenched hands were strangely stillborn at her sides. The transformation was startling in a woman whose slightly plump, sensual figure usually added a slow, calming grace to whatever she did. Banging in across from Jan, she pressed a hand across the front of her wrinkled white blouse, tried to speak, couldn't, and had to count several breaths before she was able to get anything out.

"How can he be missing?" she said at last. "He's always telling me that nothing will happen to him."

"Let's hope he's right."

"He usually isn't," Felicia said, lifting her chin as if preparing to be brave. "Not about things like that."

In response, Jan shared almost everything, holding back only on the fact that Lieutenant Harry Crenshaw was handling the case solo. It didn't seem as though that tidbit would help anyone. By the time Jan was finished, Felicia couldn't keep her right hand away from her lips and she hadn't blinked for over a minute.

"I've talked to the detective in charge," Jan assured her. "He's doing everything he can."

"We're talking about Lyle."

"They've dealt with these situations before."

"The police of this city have a reputation, Jan." Felicia's eyes slipped away uneasily. "In the black community, I mean."

There was more a sense of doom than rebellion in what Felicia said and Jan didn't know how to react. It was the first time either of them had ever mentioned race.

"I can't take a chance," Felicia said, staring at her hands as if she couldn't quite see them. "I'm going to have to do something. What about this one who's in custody? Is he saying anything?"

"He's playing tough guy."

"Can you get me in to see him?" Felicia asked, reaching across the table to touch Jan's hand. The contact set Jan's foot to tapping. "I work with a lot of girls from these gangs. Maybe I can find something out. He might be willing to trust me. Maybe I'll remind him of his mother or sister or something."

"Will you tell this Lieutenant Crenshaw anything you find out?"

"You really trust him?"

"He seems like one of the good ones."

"Then that's enough for me," Felicia said. "Deal."

"Now I guess we're supposed to say something brave to each other."

"My hands are shaking again."

"That's not what I had in mind."

"Sorry, Jan," she said, actually sounding sorry, "but it'll have to do."

"Then maybe we'd better get started before we get any sorrier."

They left just as the waitress arrived to take their order.

★ ★ ★

Jan led the way to Emergency Admissions for a peek at their log book. Deciphering the handwriting took some work, but eventually she located the names of three patients who'd arrived the night before with holes in them. One of the three was busy taking possession of the family farm, one had been sent home to think about gun control, and the third, a Rainy Penshorn, had been admitted overnight to station 41C in stable condition. The name Rainy clicked with what she'd learned at the Fifth Precinct and she tapped the log book to show they were making progress. That lasted until they got one of the clerks to check on the computer screen and no Penshorn, Rainy, came up.

"What do you mean he's not on the system?" Felicia demanded.

"They've probably given him an alias," Jan said, pulling her aside. "That's standard. If they put him in a bed last night, he'll still be there."

"How will we know?"

"By the cop who's hanging around."

That much she got right. Up on 41C, room 4122, a patrolman was making time with the nurses seated at the nearby charting tables. At the most he might have made a few seconds; none of the nursing staff were swooning, particularly not the ex-biker with Harley-Davidson tattoos on his forearms. The biker-turned-orderly was coming out of the patient's room with a breakfast tray as Jan and Felicia arrived. When the cop made a show of searching through everything on the tray, the orderly clued him in with a deep voice, "Your man's still in the bed."

"Freedom of speech ain't all it's cracked up to be, Harley."

Jan's arrival actually improved the cop's mood, for at last someone was paying attention to him.

"We're here to talk to the prisoner," Jan said, hoping to keep it simple.

"Nobody told me," he said, checking Jan up and down as if the shape of her ankles had something to do with getting past him.

"Do they tell you everything?" Jan asked, trying to keep it

friendly, although not too friendly. She could feel Felicia watching her and didn't figure that any fraternizing would increase the value of her stock.

"Look," the cop explained, "this is a murder suspect we're talking about."

Before Jan or Felicia had a chance to answer, a taunt came from inside the room.

"Let the foxes in, man."

"Quiet, you," the cop said over his shoulder.

"If you can't let us in," Jan said, "that's fine." She sensed a protest swelling in Felicia and had to hurry to play her trump. "We'll just tell Lieutenant Crenshaw you were too busy."

Felicia relaxed. To save face, the cop turned bored.

"Crenshaw?" the cop said. "Why didn't you just say so? But be careful. This guy's been playing grab-ass all morning."

That hardly looked possible, given the amount of gauze and wrappings pinning Rainy Penshorn's right arm against his chest while plastic tubing tethered his left forearm to an IV stand. On the other hand, even while flat on his back, the prisoner served up a lecherous grin and greeted them as if they'd been sent up by an elevator operator.

"Ladies, the pleasure is all mine."

"You got that much right," Jan said, positioning herself at the foot of the bed.

The patient made a pleading face at Felicia, who exhaled through her nostrils in response to his lounge act. That only widened his smile. The dusky brown face atop Rainy Penshorn's plastic neck brace had a pencil-thin mustache that made him look like the kind of lady's man ladies are forever swearing off. A regular contributor to the out-of-wedlock statistics. Some young woman who should have known better had braided his hair into corn rows with tiny barrettes, festive baby pinks and blues. He enhanced the lady's-man illusion by smoothly asking, "Would one of you foxes mind scratching my ankle?" He lifted his chin toward his left foot, which was handcuffed to the bedpost.

Without answering, Felicia rolled aside a stand and positioned a chair bedside, not close enough to seem intimate, not so far away as to seem intimidated. He found her unhurried, deliberate movements entertaining, and made an impressed face to show his approval of the floor show. In return, Felicia settled her eyes on his as if she knew all about him, from the way his mama had pinned his diapers to his taste in barbecue sauce and every stain lined up in between.

"Don't try messin' here, sister," Rainy Penshorn warned, taking a dislike to her measurements.

"You're a Seven, aren't you?" Felicia said, her voice so controlled that Jan had to fight a double take.

"What you know about it?" he asked.

"I know Latonya Adams, DeeAnn Moon, and Juju Lowell, for starters. Know their babies too. Maybe one of those babies belongs to you."

"Just the handsome, devilish ones."

"No doubt. Look, I want you to help me out with some business."

"I'll bet you do, sister."

"Cut the shit," Felicia said, her lips hardly moving at all.

The street talk didn't sound quite right coming from her, as if she'd read it somewhere but never pronounced it until now. Rainy Penshorn snickered at her effort.

"You know what happened last night?" Felicia asked, pointing a steady finger at him. She was doing better.

"It look like I home watchin' *Cosby?*"

"I mean," Felicia said, hand still raised, "do you know about what happened later, after you got patched up? Do you know about the man your homies grabbed?"

"You can't go hangin' that on me," he said. "I gots perfect alibis. Big ol' ugly cops all around me when that happen."

"Shut up and listen," Felicia said. "The man who got grabbed was mine."

"Then you probably a widow," he said, lowering his eyelids as if Felicia's troubles made him sleepy. "Sevens don't pretend to be bad guys. Sevens *is* bad guys."

"I want a name."

"You talkin' crazy."

"I'm asking for your help."

Something icy and submerged in her voice cracked open Rainy

Penshorn's eyes. He studied her before looking away in disgust.

"Shit," he said. "I don' know nothin' about it. They ain't even let me have a call." Of Jan he demanded, "When I get my call?" Back to Felicia, "So you might as well go askin' any Seven on any ol' corner. They knows more than Rainy Penshorn do."

"What if the cops offered you some kind of deal?"

"Felicia," Jan sputtered, stepping closer.

"Shit, yes," said Rainy, perking up. "I be out there scourin' the streets for you if they let me. You arrange that and you be gettin' a bloodhound."

"So now you think he might be alive?" Felicia said, satisfied.

"Hell yes. Sevens like to have they fun before gettin' down."

"All right," Felicia said, gazing so hard at Rainy Penshorn that he looked peevishly away. "If I meet any cops, I'll see what can be done."

"You do that, sister."

"But I'm telling you one thing right now, Mr. Rainy Penshorn. You pull any dirt on me and I'll make it my mission to see your mama crying over your grave."

"And how you goin' to do that?"

"Hire it done," Felicia said, which wiped his face clear in an instant. Jan's too, for that matter.

7

After Rainy Penshorn's bedside, Felicia's voice suddenly turned dreamy, night-sweats kind of dreamy, and her eyes appeared to be looking over distances too great for this world. The confrontation had sapped her strength and she drifted along beside Jan to the elevators and down to the lobby, where she had to sit down to gather herself.

"It doesn't necessarily mean what you think it does," Jan said, perching beside her. "Some rest will give you a new outlook."

"Jan," Felicia said, absentmindedly patting Jan's nearest hand, "I appreciate your help. I really do. But I've got to keep moving."

Rising, Felicia filed into the mostly vacant Administration wing with Jan right beside her. They paraded past the Little Admiral's office, where Miss Pepperidge ceased typing, and on to Personnel's reception desk, where they turned left and skirted a line of outer offices reserved for directors. Eventually they reached Felicia's work space, a square cubbyhole like Jan's, slightly larger, and with two file cabinets to Jan's none, but also with the same temporary cloth-covered partitions instead of walls. Social Services occupied the south quadrant of Administration's worker-bee area, a large open space without windows and no decoration beyond a trio of gloomy oils depicting General Jack's founding fathers. The portraits' long faces had been making the rounds from one unsuspecting department to another for years.

Sitting still at her desk, Felicia composed herself before saying,

"Some of the girls in the teenage pregnancy program might know something."

"What about the cops?" Jan asked. "They actually might be willing to cut some kind of deal with Penshorn."

"You see a cop," Felicia said, "you ask him. Me, I'm not going to hang my hopes on it."

Swiveling to the nearest file cabinet, Felicia slid open the middle drawer and let her fingers walk down the row of folders. Each time she hit a name she wanted, she lifted out the file and slapped it on her desk. Since it was a county holiday and the office space around them was empty, each *thunk* was amplified by the absence of competing office noises. By the time Felicia reached the back of the drawer, she had a teetering stack on her desk. She reached for her phone but stalled, sitting with her hand on the receiver.

"You going to be all right?" Jan asked.

Felicia hid her face in her hands, but then waved Jan off and started dialing. Tracking down the first sixteen-year-old mother took four calls, including conversations with a grandmother, boyfriend, sister, and public shelter. After all that, the conversation lasted as long as it took to mention the riot. There followed a long pause, as though Felicia was listening to a reply, but then she held down the phone plunger and said with resignation, "This is going to take some time."

"It's still a good idea," Jan said. "You keep at it. I've got some things to look into myself. You need me, I'll either be at my desk or over in Emergency Admissions."

As Jan left, Felicia was asking over the phone if a woman named LaRhonda was home.

THE EMERGENCY ROOM was eerily quiet, the way it sometimes got when heavy weather deterred all but the most serious ailments from coming in. At the triage desk there wasn't a single patient waiting for an opening in the ER. The nurse behind the desk's glass partition was trapped in a Stephen King and the nursing assistant was listening to his own chest through a stethoscope.

When Jan reached Emergency Admissions, the area was deserted, the clerks studious. *Cosmoplitan, People, National Enquirer.* Within a half hour she had twenty-seven names and phone numbers, or addresses if there were no phone numbers, of patients who had been waiting at the triage desk when the riot broke out.

Satisfied with her efforts, she doubled back to Administration and found Felicia a quarter of the way through her stack of files. A pile of crumpled papers was growing at her feet. Without interrupting her friend's labors, Jan sneaked down the corridor to see if the Little Admiral and his secretary had turned into pumpkins yet, or whatever it was that dyed-in-the-wool county bureaucrats turned into when they thought no one was looking. It turned out they vanished into thin air when no one was looking, leaving the lights on behind them. A note taped to Hodges's door informed any interested parties that he was in a meeting but that he was packing a beeper should anyone need to reach him. His note neglected to include the beeper's number. Jan got busy on the phone herself.

"THIS IS JACKSON County Medical Center calling," Jan said.
"Is that so."
"Would it be possible to speak to Jessica Littlebear?"
"She's dead," the voice said without a trace of remorse.
"Our records say she was just seen in our ER for a toothache."
"It killed her."
"When's the funeral?" Jan asked, realizing the woman was toying with her. "I've a few questions I'd like to ask the deceased."
"We're making arrangements."
Dial tone.

AFTER A DEEP breath:
"This is Jackson County Medical Center calling."
"Those tests finally done?"
"I wouldn't know about that, sir."

"These pills you give me don' be doin' jack shit. It still feel like I's pissin' flames out my pipes."

"I'm sorry to hear that, but the reason I'm calling was to ask if you witnessed any of the riot that occurred."

"Witnessed? I got stitches what proves how much I witnessed."

"Did you by any chance see a man being abducted?"

"Was he abducted from the men's room? 'Cause that where I was, standin' in front of a piss pot, bawlin' like a baby. When I heard all the shoutin' and bangin', I zipped 'er up and come runnin', 'cause it sounded like they was a fire or somethin', but soon's I step out I'm in the middle of some young hot blood barrelin' right along. He shoved me into a drinkin' fountain, which messed up my chin considerably. And I ain't payin' for a one of them crooked stitches you people put in there."

"Could you identify the young man who pushed you?"

"I ain't dead yet, lady."

"Is there anything else you remember?"

"Lady, what this got to do with gettin' my pills?"

OR, AFTER ANOTHER deep breath, a recorded message that howled, "I saw the best minds of my generation destroyed by MTV, low-salt crackers, and pharmaceuticals. Leaving a message is up to you." The beep at the end seemed less than promising but Jan left a request for help anyway.

AND THAT WAS how it went for the rest of the morning until Felicia appeared at Jan's elbow, tugging impatiently at her arm and saying, "I think I've found something."

"Slow down."

"I've got a girl name of Juju who definitely doesn't want to talk to me."

"What makes that something?"

"She's a Seven and she sounds scared."

"Right now, half the city's scared."

"I know this girl," Felicia insisted. "She isn't someone who scares easy."

"What are you thinking?"
"That we pay her a visit."
"We're just talking to her, right?"
"If we can find her," Felicia said, pulling on Jan's arm.

8

When Po' Rind phoned his sister Willie, he woke her out of a deep slumber. She'd just finished pulling a graveyard shift at Jackson General, where she was a hotshot nurse who made it rough on malingerers. Right away she had a sharp-edged question for him.

"Do you have the money I loaned you for a week about a month ago?"

Whenever Willie lectured him, she tried to sound white, as if setting a good example.

"I'm puttin' it together. Won't be long now. Not at all."

"Well, you let me know when it's all in one piece."

"That why I's callin', Willie sis. If you could see clear to lend a hand with a little somethin', I be payin' you back in nothin' flat."

"With what? Some of that old black magic?"

"Won' cost you a cent," Po' promised.

"Say," Willie said, ditching her whiteness, "isn't you gangsters s'pose to have nothin' but do-re-mi in yo' pockets? What you houndin' me fo'?"

"I keeps tryin' to tell you, this ain't 'bout"—the dial tone returned—"money."

On the call-back he got busy.

So even his own family was dogging him about his affiliations, but he had a positive kind of stir in his gut about this enterprise. Backing off a step, he decided this needed some studying, and a half hour later he had planted himself on a bus bench right on

Wabash Street, which cut between General Jack's two main buildings. It was the coldest bench he'd ever parked his bottom side on. The fact that it was one hundred plus-plus-plus degrees everywhere else in the city didn't chip any ice off that bench. He could feel Death sucking on his toes, it was so cold between those hospital buildings. Every few minutes he had to flap his arms and rub his hands together just to keep his circulation circulating. His sister Willie had to have antifreeze in her veins to put up with a place like this.

Because of the rioting, bus lines weren't running, which made his bus bench perfect camouflage. He could wait forever without appearing to be there for anything other than a ride home. That was essential. It meant that whoever was watching him from inside the hospital—and life had taught him there was always someone watching—would think he was a stranded traveler instead of someone plotting a prisoner's escape.

At one point during his wait a television crew shot some footage, positioning their fearless newscaster in front of a smashed plate-glass window. When Po' crept close enough to catch their drift, all he heard was blah-blah-blah about the siege of the hospital and the city. No mention of Rainy Penshorn. Just a lot of junk talk that made it sound as though those restless black people had trashed the place because they weren't getting Band-Aids fast enough.

He also sat there long enough to see three pregnant women arrive—separately. A van with a red cross on its side pulled up and a driver hustled inside with a small box. Visitors went in the front entrance across the street from him. Some got turned away, others got past the hospital cop at the door. A three-hundred-pound man leaving the hospital got stuck in a wheelchair and had to have three people pry him out; one of those tiny, two-door Jap cars had come to pick him up. The sight was enough to make Po' swear he was going back on one of those ruthless motherf–ing diets as soon as he got his respect back. He saw too many hospital employees to count step outside the front entrance for a smoke. When he spotted a priest going inside, he warmed himself by jumping up and flapping his arms.

53

Nothing caught his fancy until a transport van with iron-mesh windows showed up from the Jackson County Jail and two deputies led a pair of shackled convicts inside the hospital. And that's when it occurred to him: If Rainy was inside that place—and everybody knew he was—he had to have his own personal cop, and probably a city cop, not any county brown-shirt. The county boys seemed to mostly run the jail and sit around the courtrooms. But regardless of who was guarding him, the fact seemed promising.

An hour later, when a squad car pulled into the drop-off drive, Po' hustled across the street in time to ask the city cop getting out of it for some directions. The purpose of that was to make sure the hospital cop bulldogging the front entrance would see them conferring. Po' then cut to the curb as if waiting for a lift, but as soon as the city cop was far enough inside the hospital, Po' snapped his fingers as if he'd just remembered something important and made a dash for the entrance, timing it perfectly to miss the city cop, who was disappearing into an elevator.

"I need to talk to the officer," he said to the hospital cop at the door.

"Not right now, you don't."

"Listen, man," said Po', lowering his voice and checking over his shoulder to make sure they were absolutely alone, which they were except for some double-wide dude in a ponytail and hospital whites who was taking the cellophane off a pack of Camels, "I got to tell that officer something important."

The hospital cop shook his head in the negative.

"What I mean," Po' said in a stage whisper, "I'm his snitch."

"Nice try, but out."

"Hey, man, he tells me if I knows anything 'bout this riot shit to let him know, right? And he no more than splits than somethin' comes to me, right? So I's tryin' to earn my keep, right?"

"Out."

Po' checked over his shoulder again. Spotting no one but the ponytailed mountain tapping his cigarette pack against his palm, Po' opened up his pipes to say, "Ain't no sweat off my ass you don' get this Rainy Penshorn shit I'm remembering."

"Mine either," the hospital cop assured him. "Out."

Three times was usually the charm, and Po' had had his three, but he figured the fourth was free, so he took one last poke.

"Will you let me write him a note, man? This shit could be im-por-tan-te."

Considering that Po's literacy barely stretched beyond his name, it was a bluff, a stab at buying some confidence. The hospital cop stepped out from behind the little counter by the door and crooked a finger to beckon Po' closer. As soon as Po' stepped forward, the cop locked his hands on Po's left forearm, twisted it behind Po's back—spinning him around at the same time—and wheeled him through the automatic doors, which barely opened fast enough, and back outside without even a kiss-my-ass good-bye.

Po' was straightening out his clothes and pretending he'd wanted to be outside anyway, when he heard a deep voice rumble, "Want a smoke, friend?"

Turning, he found himself facing the ponytailed guy, who was standing in an alcove puffing on a ciggy. The dude was dressed up in hospital whites but had tattoos on his arms that said something or other. Probably biker shit, or at least the bikers Po' had known at county holding had been covered with the same kind of skull-and-crossbones doodads. Sensing something on the wind, Po' strolled over and accepted a smoke. After a drag, he said, "You work in this place?"

"Keeps me in leather, man."

"That's cool," Po' said, thinking it way past cool and into freezing. There was something down below zero at the center of this guy's eyes.

"You really a snitch?"

"No way," Po' answered, feeling his way. "Just trying to help a friend."

"Rainy Penshorn?"

"That's my man," Po' said, figuring he had nothing to lose.

"He's up on station forty-one C, forty-one twenty-two."

"How'm I gettin' up there?" Po' asked.

"You can't figure that out, man, it probably won' do you any good gettin' there, would it? They got heat on him upstairs too."

With that, the ponytail went back inside and Po' found himself whistling something sweet as he headed back to the Maxi man's place.

9

By noon the air felt heavy as a hearty soup; whatever nutritious particles it carried made Jan's eyes smart. The only people she saw on the street stayed in the shadows and in small groups. Rarely did she spot anyone foolhardy enough to be traveling alone.

They drove to the city's south side in Felicia's Sunbird. The shopping centers housed mostly chop suey joints, liquor stores, and check-cashing services—all closed. Juju Lowell's address was within hailing distance of the Savoy projects, which was as close to an international border as the city had. On one side of the freeway that sectioned off the Savoy projects was the ultrabuffed, buy-it-on-credit, build-a-space-station America; on the other side was all the junkyard-driven, black-market dealing, third-world America that could be shoehorned into rental property. Jan found herself feeling whiter and whiter with each passing block.

Juju's house number belonged to a corner stucco duplex that had round, plastered-over holes dotting its exterior, as if it'd been sprayed by something larger than a magnum. A moment passed before it dawned on Jan that the holes were the result of additional insulation, not bullets, being pumped into the walls. On the duplex's second-story porch a young man trained a pair of pink opera glasses on them.

"You don't have to come up there," Felicia said, trying to mean it.

"I want to help."

"I might learn more without you," Felicia said without convincing anybody.

"They already know I'm here," Jan said, nodding toward the lookout with the opera glasses.

Felicia nodded once in appreciation, opened her door, and disappeared into the heat and glare. Jan found herself hurrying to catch up, which she did just as Felicia rapped on the crooked front screen door. A bare-chested man appeared on the other side so fast that it felt as though he'd been waiting for them. Jan remained on the bottom step, wishing she was dressed in anything but a uniform.

"We ain't sellin'," he said through the torn screen. "And we ain't buyin'. So what you want?"

"To talk to Juju."

"Why the cop?" he asked.

"She's not a cop," Felicia replied. "She's a hospital security guard here for my safety."

Jan was the only one who laughed at that, and she did it to herself.

"Smell like heat," he said, sniffing.

"Let's forget her," Felicia said, "and talk about me. I'm the woman working on a holiday to try and help Juju have a healthy baby."

"That baby don' need healthy. It need mean."

"Maybe he'll be meaner if he's healthy," Felicia suggested, staring into the interior shadows. Her comeback hung in the air a moment before the man reacted with a chuckle.

"That pretty good. You the one tell Juju to keep her nose out of my drug bag?"

"I told her to stay clean. For the baby."

"My drug bag appreciate it," the man said, chuckling again. He turned away to bellow into the house, "Juju! Some goody-goody lookin' fo' you."

The man left Jan and Felicia squinting on the steps without an invitation to step in out of the sun. All up and down the block, the only shade was beneath cars or in between the tightly packed houses. Those trees in sight were curbside saplings that cast a shadow little thicker than a pool cue; maybe a quarter of them had been snapped off waist-high. Inside the house, Juju's name was shouted out again, followed by the squall of an upset child, followed by the slamming of a door and footsteps and voices that didn't stop bickering just because Felicia or Jan could hear them.

"I didn' tell her to come," Juju was protesting.

"Just see she don' come again."

Juju pressed close enough to the screen door for Jan to see her large eyes and glum mouth. Squirming in her strong arms was a diapered infant and looming behind her was the well-developed chest of the man who'd first answered the door. At six months pregnant, Juju was wearing a man's black T-shirt that hid her tummy behind a silk-screened red X, which was everybody's favorite letter that season, in honor of the late Malcolm X.

"There's a new program I need to tell you about," Felicia said. "We need to talk about it."

"Can't talk here," Juju said, making it sound against house rules. Her eyes, however, were more encouraging than her tone.

"How about if I take you to lunch?"

"Someplace cool?"

"It better be," Felicia said, fanning herself.

"My baby too?"

"A package deal."

"All right, then," Juju said, unlatching the screen. "Maybe I'll go."

"You ain't off to nowhere," the man said, pinching Juju's shoulder so hard that she flinched and clasped the infant against her chest.

Jan rocked back on her heels, but Felicia was right on top of it, saying, "I think you better let her come with me."

"Not without my say-so, she don'."

"You're keeping her here against her will, then."

"This girl ain't got no will but what I tells her."

A standoff until Jan piped up, "The police might think otherwise."

"You threatening me?" the man asked in disbelief.

"We're just trying to make sure you get that mean baby you want so much," Felicia said.

"You crazy," he said after a moment, maybe giving a compliment but also sounding relieved to be off the topic of the police. Pushing Juju outside, he said, "Go on, little mama, maybe you learn somethin' useful from women crazy as this."

"Hands off," Juju warned, resisting his shove but landing on the front steps nonetheless. She turned to glare and was poised to say something more, but thought better of it and spun away, saying to Felicia, "Come on, Ms. Smith. You better company anyway."

The man disappeared into the house, laughing, as Juju Lowell stormed past Jan without a glance. By the time they reached the car, the baby in Juju's arms was bawling in the heat, and opening the car door was like cracking a door on the sun itself. Several blocks passed before the AC cooled the car enough for the infant to quiet. Jan drew the back seat, and was ignored by the two women up front, which didn't rankle as much as it might have. It felt too good to be back in the relative safety of the car.

"That your man?" Felicia asked.

"Never mind 'bout that. What's this new program? And there better not be no classes involved."

"There is no new program."

Juju studied Felicia hard for half a block before saying, "Then why we drivin' along like this?"

"Because I need to ask for a favor," Felicia said, concentrating on the road but hitting every pothole anyway. Jan noticed Juju leaning away from Felicia as if suddenly afraid.

"You goin' to get me in trouble, ain't you?"

"You heard what happened at the General?"

"Heard," Juju sullenly said.

"My man's a guard down there and he got grabbed by some Sevens."

The young girl shrank away from Felicia as if she'd just seen a ghost, one whose skin pulsed between green and purple.

"He's a good man," Felicia went on, ignoring Juju's round-eyed reaction. "And I think you might know something about it, Juju."

"Don' know nothin'," Juju said.

"Haven't I always helped you?"

"Let me out at this next corner."

"I think you owe me," Felicia said, driving by the next corner.

"Don' owe nothin'."

"What if I paid you?"

"How much?"

"Five hundred."

"Huh," she scoffed. "That all?"

"A thousand."

"Huh. Think you can buy me, don' you?"

"I need your help, Juju."

"Can you promise you won't go to no cops?" It was as much taunt as question.

"I won't go to the cops," Felicia automatically answered.

Jan had to tell herself to be quiet.

"Are you a lyin' bitch?" Juju asked.

"I won't say a word to the cops," Felicia repeated. "Have I ever lied to you?"

"No," Juju said, mad about it. "You hasn't."

They drove another block.

"What 'bout yo' package in back?" Juju said, tossing her head toward Jan.

"She's bound by my promise too."

"That real cute," the girl said, not believing.

"Don't play with me, Juju."

"You go to the cops and my man'll shank me. Shank my baby too," she added, gently running a finger across the infant's forehead.

"You have my word."

Another block passed. Tears were edging down Juju's cheeks.

"What is it?" Felicia said, pulling over because, as Jan saw in the rearview, Felicia's eyes were wet too.

"They gots a man down in the basement," Juju hoarsely whispered. "I heard him cryin' in the night."

10

They had to drive nearly ten miles to find an air-conditioned restaurant that satisfied Juju's requirements for curly french fries and a salad bar. Not that she wanted any lettuce or carrots disturbing her plate, but the salad bar's presence seemed to reassure her that Jan and Felicia were taking her seriously. By the time they reached their table, everyone's eyes had dried.

"Are you going to tell your boyfriend that we know?" Felicia asked Juju.

"I ain't no crazy bitch, and you got my word on that."

"Are you going to stay there?"

"Ain't got nowhere else," Juju said.

"Let me give you the name of a shelter," Felicia said, sliding a card out of her purse and across the table.

"Why I be needing that?" Juju asked, eyeing the card as if it had six legs.

"Because I'm getting my man out of there."

"You said no cops."

"There are other ways," Felicia promised with an air of mystery, a rather thin air of mystery, it seemed to Jan.

"There be shit, too."

"I gave you my word about cops, but I don't think you'd have told me about that basement if you didn't want me to do something about it. Am I right?"

The reminder settled the girl down enough for Jan and Felicia to return to picking at their trays. Not Juju, though; she started packing it away as if thinking she might not get a chance to eat for a few days. They questioned her further, but she had one steely answer about what went on in the basement.

"I don' go down there."

When they dropped Juju back at her doorstep, she left without so much as a good-bye or even a closing of the car door. She was traveling too fast for that. Before she was halfway back to the duplex, the infant in her arms was bawling again, and by the time she disappeared inside, Jan and Felicia had started arguing about calling the cops.

"I gave my word."

"Who else is going to get him out of there?" Jan reasoned from the back seat.

"I'm not letting this house out of my sight," Felicia vowed. "What if they move him?"

"Why would they move him?"

"Maybe Juju spills something."

"So much for keeping your word," Jan pointed out.

"No one's smashing my mouth," Felicia said, defending the girl.

"You really trust her?"

"She told us about Lyle, didn't she?"

Jan couldn't argue with that and said instead, "So what are we going to do?"

"Think," Felicia said, putting the car in gear. "If we can."

THEY CIRCLED TWO blocks to come up on the backside of the duplex, parking a block and a half away. From there they could see the entire length of the duplex, as well as the alley that cut behind it. They couldn't see the front door, but then again, the lookout on the upper porch above the front door couldn't see them. A Jeep and a convertible were parked on its side lawn, if you want to call baked dirt with a few knee-high weeds a lawn. The vehicles appeared positioned for quick getaways through first-floor windows. By the time Felicia had turned off the motor and rolled down her window so that they could hear, a grin had seized Jan's face. She grinned when Felicia asked if she was all right. She grinned at a squirrel with a chewed-up tail, at a bumper sticker that said *Hip-Hop Nation,* and at a small green bug that scared her badly when it flew in a window and landed on the headrest in front of her face.

By then it was early afternoon. The sun was trying to squash the car into the asphalt, and Jan was beginning to feel heat prickles. It wasn't until she convinced Felicia to roll her window back up and crank on the AC, before they passed out, that Jan regained her senses and told herself to quit grinning. To get her mind off that, she tried paying attention to the surroundings. The few people out and about made a point of crossing the street to avoid the duplex in question. Cars driving down the street followed a winding course to avoid potholes. Rising heat waves made parts of the neighborhood fade in and out of sight. Conversation inside the Sunbird hit a drought. Ten or fifteen minutes easily passed between sprinkles.

"Say he's in there," Jan said. "What are the two of us going to do?"

"I've been thinking we might call Lyle's brother."

"What's he going to do?"

"I don't know," Felicia said, annoyed. "He served in Vietnam."

Minutes passed without further explanation.

"When are you going to call him?" Jan asked at last.

"I'm thinking."

"He might need some time to unpack his combat boots."

Felicia laughed harshly, without explanation, but then abruptly stopped to say, "Once you turn Lyle's brother on, it's hard to turn him off. So I want to make positive Lyle's in there first."

"How are we going to do that?"

"Look."

"I guess that beats asking," Jan agreed. "But don't you think they might notice us poking around?"

"Not if we do it when they're sleeping."

"You think they do that?"

"They're human, Jan."

"I was making a joke."

Minutes passed without a laugh track.

"Sorry," Felicia said. "I'm fraying a bit. All I'm saying is that we wait until late tonight and hope they don't sleep in shifts."

"How are we going to last that long? My back teeth are floating now."

"There's a little convenience store down the block. They'll let us use their bathroom."

"We can't be watching the house when we're down there," Jan pointed out.

"We'll take turns," Felicia said.

"I walk there alone?"

"And back too."

When Jan didn't respond, Felicia said that she was making a joke.

Felicia went to the convenience store first to pave the way. Jan moved to the front seat after her own excursion, which went without incident. The woman in the store let Jan call home from a phone with a cup beside it for quarters. Katie told her their grandmother was cooking their favorite for supper. Jan hung up before Claire could get on the line and complain about having to eat piggies-in-a-blanket once again. She almost dropped another quarter in the cup to call Lieutenant Crenshaw, but there was nothing private about phone conversations in that store, and she wanted plenty of privacy if she was going behind Felicia's back. Later, Jan and Felicia munched on bags of traditional stakeout food and washed it down with cans of traditional stakeout drink. They took turns napping.

Gradually the day's heat spike lessened and people abandoned their electrical appliances to gather on stoops and talk about what they'd seen on TV. The sun buried itself in the horizon. Bats dipped through the dusk, seeming like remote-control devices guided by kids. A squad car cruised by, shone a spotlight across the duplex, then sped off in a different direction. It seemed on remote control too.

They sat another hour. Two. Several blocks away the moon surfaced between the twin smokestacks of a trash incinerator built in that part of the city to generate jobs. Honest. Streetlights came on, crime-prevention ones that bathed everything in an amber-twilight glow. Jan had less to say. Felicia less than less. Under the cover of darkness—a phrase Jan had never imagined herself using—they leapfrogged to several different parking spots before settling on one a half block from the duplex and facing it. The new locale afforded them an unobstructed view of the front door.

From that short distance it sounded as though the duplex was a gigantic CD player and every window in it a speaker. Thanks to her daughters, Jan recognized the heavy rhythm as rap. At home she would have pulled the plug long ago, although by then she'd gone way past bothering to remind herself she wasn't safe at home. That point was driven home about ten that evening when the duplex's windows and doors flew open everywhere at once, or at least it seemed that way to Jan.

YOUNG MEN CAME pouring out of the duplex, tugging T-shirts over their heads, shouting questions, checking the chambers of handguns.

Jan counted seven of them, two maybe women. From a half block away it was impossible to tell gender under their baggy clothes. They piled into the Jeep and the convertible, murdered the gas pedals, and squealed directly past Jan and Felicia, who nearly knocked heads ducking below the dash. Then, quiet again, or as quiet as it got on that street. The boom-boom of rap music still rocked the duplex.

Felicia checked with Jan twice before unlatching her door and saying, "I guess this is it."

"You don't know they're all gone," Jan said, grabbing her friend's arm.

"Enough are," Felicia said. Fumbling with something beneath her seat, she came up with a revolver that had a barrel long enough to poke somebody's eye out if the bullets missed. "Th-this is for the rest."

"Holy . . . Do you know how to use that thing?"

"Generally."

"Are you going to use it?"

"I think so."

"Alone?"

"If I have to."

"What about Lyle's brother?"

"I'm going now, Jan." But Felicia didn't budge from behind the steering wheel.

"Will you at least give me the gun?" Jan said.

"I thought you'd never ask," Felicia said, awkwardly handing the pistol over by its handle.

With the transfer of the gun, Jan found herself exactly where she didn't want to be—in charge—but she had to admit, reluctantly, that it made a certain amount of sense. She was the security officer, after all. As if to prove her competency, she checked the revolver's cylinder to make sure it was loaded.

"You got a flashlight?" she asked.

"Glove compartment," Felicia said. She added in a small voice, "Am I going to get us killed?"

"No," Jan said ironically as she dug out a penlight with a beam powerful as a toy choo-choo's. "That's my job. And don't ask me if I'm any good at it."

Felicia promised that she wouldn't.

"You sure about this?" Jan asked, a hand on her door.

"I've never been sure of anything," Felicia said bitterly, opening her own door.

STARTING WITH THE side of the duplex hidden from the cross street, they crept along with fingers across their lips. The adjoining property was a condemned house whose windows were boarded up except where the plywood had been pried off. Between the two buildings was a narrow walkway shielded from streetlights. The shadows masking their expressions were probably a blessing.

Every first-floor window was screened off by either closed drapery or taped Sunday comics. The music pounding behind the glass made some of the loose panes vibrate. There were three basement window wells on that side of the house, and Jan, gun in one hand, penlight in the other, got down on her hands and knees to check each one. Although the beam from the dinky penlight didn't penetrate, making everything below appear murky and out of focus, she could see enough to make out a collection of old doors and bathtubs. The doors had all been relieved of their brass knobs; the tubs were the old kind with clawed feet. At one point the rap music cut out and Jan played dead for over a minute until Felicia suggested that maybe the CD had ended.

Rather than circle around the rear of the house, where the light from a back door spilled out on two abandoned dog kennels, they doubled back the way they'd come, turned left on the sidewalk, and passed the front door without craning their heads toward the house, although Jan's eyes rolled as far left as possible without nicking a cheek.

"Act natural."

"As what?"

With Jan concealing the pistol at her side, they made another left at the corner and followed the sidewalk until they were even with the first window well on that side of the house. For a few seconds they stood still, heads tilted together as if conferring although neither breathed a word. Jan was remembering the baby that Juju had carried back into the house. She hadn't seen any infants run out and jump into the departing vehicles, which meant the child must still be inside, maybe alone. Of course it was also possible the child's mother was inside holding down the fort. Jan didn't say anything about that. Who knew what Juju might be holding it down with.

Cutting across the pounded-earth yard, she got to work with the penlight. The basement window revealed more bathtubs. Bent over, she crept beneath the first-floor windows, working her way around some shrubs to the second window well. Doors without knobs down there. Felicia kept pace with her on the sidewalk, scanning up and down the street so incessantly that she had Jan doing it too. Expecting more doors in storage, Jan waved Felicia forward to a spot even with the last basement window, but when Jan got down on her hands and knees for the final peek, the scene sucked her breath away.

Beneath the octopuslike arms of an old-fashioned gravity furnace sat one last bathtub, a three-quarter-size one, and in the tub, with his knees bent, his head covered by a canvas bag, his arms tied behind his back—in that tub she saw a naked Lyle. Because of the hood, he didn't react to the penlight's weak beam and she couldn't tell much about his condition, except that he had open welts across his back. She crouched before the last window long enough to draw Felicia off the sidewalk.

"What?" Felicia hoarsely whispered.

Flicking off the penlight, Jan met her halfway, first restraining her and then forcing her back to the sidewalk.

"This isn't anything for us to handle."

"Tell me what."

"The thing to do," Jan said, turning Felicia back toward their car and pushing on the middle of her back, "is to get some trained people down here."

"He's in there?"

"He looks fine," Jan said. "And we'll get him out of there tonight."

The program seemed to be working. Felicia was cooperating even as she tried to get a glimpse of the last window over her shoulder. They covered half the length of the house without being observed and might have made it all the way if the draperies covering the middle window hadn't parted to reveal a wide-eyed toddler, barely able to see above the window ledge, gazing out at them. Jan tensed, expecting the child to sound the alarm by crying, but the kid didn't make a peep, which turned out to be the worst thing that could have happened. The child's stoicism triggered something inside Felicia, whose back stiffened. She pulled away from Jan's hands, gaining speed toward the front door with each step. The toddler silently watched her move across the lawn, but Jan wasn't as quiet. She had some second guesses to share.

"Lyle wouldn't want us getting shot."

"Let's try to oblige him," Felicia said without slowing.

"Maybe we *should* call the cops."

"No time," Felicia said, mounting the front steps and pounding on the screendoor. "Juju!"

When no one answered, Felicia opened the door, found the inner door unlocked, and entered. Jan followed with a hand touching Felicia's belt. She thought the first step would be the worst; each of the next ten steps proved that wrong.

The sweet stink of marijuana that filled the hallway seemed to come from the yellowed wallpaper. They crept past a fully lit living room furnished with an odd assortment of broken-down, legless sofas and new easy chairs with warranty tags still attached to the armrests. The second room back had a baby gate across it. As they passed the darkened doorway, the child within started bawling, high-pitched, crystal-shattering riffs that brought footsteps running from the rear of the house.

Felicia locked up, forcing Jan to step around her. She assumed her best target-range crouch just as Juju bolted through the doorway at the end of the hallway with an infant in her arms. She dashed two steps before skidding to a halt.

"You alone?" Jan said, her voice a little shakier than her gun, which was deceptively steady.

"Just me and these babies," Juju said, homing in on Felicia.

"How long until the others get back?"

"Don' know."

"Juju," Felicia said, "where'd they go?"

"Some kind of drive-by on Causeway."

"We're here to get my man out," Felicia said. "Not to cause you any trouble."

"Who else goin' to be troubled?"

"I told you no cops," Felicia said. "That didn't leave me much."

"Look like it don' leave me nothin'. How I supposed to make out?"

"Try packing," Jan said. "Where's the basement stairs?"

"You find 'em," the girl answered.

Jan edged past her as though she was armed with more than a baby, but Felicia put her hands on Juju's shoulders and told her the name of the shelter again, then hugged her to stop the both of them from crying. It didn't work. When they separated, she caught up with Jan and managed to say, "Are we doing this?"

"We seem to be," Jan answered, walking backwards to watch Juju collect the bawling toddler at the baby gate and hustle out the front door with two children and no bags.

"I'm crying again," Felicia said spitefully.

"As long as you're walking, that's fine."

The kitchen at the end of the hallway smelled of fried food and soiled diapers. A ceiling bulb brightly lit a scene where every door but the refrigerator's hung open. Plenty of chocolate breakfast cereals and angel food cake mixes in the cupboards. Three open microwaves on the counter, all containing the last remains of what could have once been a swamp creature. Felicia was brushing at her eyes and staring into a broom closet filled with golf clubs as if she didn't understand why it led nowhere.

"This way," Jan said, tugging her friend toward the back door's alcove. Around a corner they found a dark, descending stairwell.

"No lights," Felicia said, shriller than necessary, or at least shriller than Jan thought necessary.

"Slow down," Jan said, even though they were already standing still. She held her fingers across Felicia's lips until she nodded her understanding. "The best way to help Lyle is to keep our heads."

Felicia made a puckering motion with her mouth and eventually got out, "I'll try."

"Me too," Jan said, flicking the light switch at the top of the stairs. When no light came on, Felicia inhaled sharply. Jan hit the light switch again, same results.

"We're OK," Jan said, turning on the penlight.

The descent felt as though they'd joined Jacques Cousteau for a night dive. She wouldn't have minded having a camera crew along for company and thumbs-up signals. When they reached the ocean floor, they saw that the room on the left held stacked doors; the room on the right, antique bathtubs. Felicia shuffled so closely behind Jan that they bumped whenever Jan moved any direction other than forward. All that remained to check was a padlocked door behind the base of the stairs.

"Stand back," Jan said, raising the pistol.

"What are you . . ."

Jan squeezed off a round. The blast threw her right arm up, shook the penlight out of her left hand, and pulled a long vowel out of Felicia. Once everything had settled, they bounced their shoulders off the door twice before bursting into the room. Felicia stumbled forward to remove the canvas bag and take Lyle's head in her hands. By then Jan had found a light switch and turned on a bare overhead bulb. The sight that greeted them threw Felicia into a near faint.

The man before them wasn't Lyle. He wasn't even a man, more a boy, or a man-child.

Under the bright light that much was easy to see, once they yanked off his hood. The naked youth's hairline didn't recede far enough; his skin color wasn't black enough. The boy in the tub couldn't see that he wasn't Lyle Brown, though, not through his swollen eyes, and he may not even have known that he wasn't Lyle Brown, not the way his chin wobbled. Sitting there in his own urine, with burn blisters forming a crude heart shape on his chest and a hematoma making his forehead bulge lopsidedly—having lived through all that, he made several mushy, whimpery sounds that made it clear how grateful he was that someone thought he was Lyle Brown.

"Where's Lyle?" Felicia cried.

Jan said nothing, wishing she could take her eyes off the pulpy face before them.

"Where's Lyle?" Felicia said, shaking the man-child by the shoulders. He flopped like a rag doll.

"He doesn't know," Jan said, pulling her off.

"Where's Lyle?" Felicia demanded of Jan.

"We've got to get this kid out of here," Jan said. "He needs care."

She had to repeat herself twice before Felicia understood, or at least nodded as if she did. Although it was beyond Felicia to help untie the shoelaces securing the young man's wrist behind his back, she did come around enough to help stand him up and get his circulation going. He was far beyond modesty and did what he could to help move himself to the car.

They had to seat-belt him in to keep him from spilling sideways out of the front seat. Before climbing in back, Jan unfolded a city street map and covered his lap. Felicia skipped first and second gears, going right to third and killing the engine. Restarting it, she hit forty-five within a block and must have come close to blowing a tire on the potholes she plowed through. As they drove to the hospital, their passenger flinched at oncoming headlights, feebly lifting his one good arm as if to ward off blows. At the same time, Felicia repeatedly struck her thigh with a fist and said, "I can't." Jan didn't have the heart to ask for specifics on that.

11

Lyle prayed that keeping his captors laughing would leave all his parts attached right where he was used to finding them. His original plan had been simply to keep them talking, but since whatever he said had them in stitches, he went with that instead, even if their laughter pushed his brow right to the dew point. The only one who didn't find him funny was a woman who smelled of flowery perfume and who loved to poke him in the ribs while saying "too juicy," as if checking a carcass turning on a spit.

But he knew he had to keep himself pumped up. To get out of this, he had to somehow convince his guards that he wasn't a side of beef. Thus all the talking, more yapping than he did in a month at home. He just turned on his tongue and let it go.

After at least a half hour of rattling around in a car trunk with a tire iron and a basketball, he had been delivered to a garage. Oil and grease vapors gave the locale away, as did the cement floor beneath his bound feet. Except for the rush of freeway traffic that sounded overhead, he had no other clues as to his whereabouts. When manhandling him out of the trunk, they'd blinded his teargassed eyes with a flashlight and then blindfolded him before he could get his bearings. They'd used half a roll of duct tape on his wrists, which were bent behind his chair and numb from the tightness; the other half of the roll went around his ankles and felt sticky as a spider's web. He seemed to be sitting on a bucket seat removed from a sports car; anyone speaking stood well above him. The blindfold across his eyes was silky and perfumed, April in Paris.

At present he was alone with the woman, who hadn't jabbed him in the ribs for somewhere between ten to thirty minutes. The absence of clock time made the space between his breaths seem like minutes. What left him hopeful was the way the guards avoided using each other's names and the fact that they kept him blindfolded. All that implied a future in which he couldn't identify anyone.

"I ever tell you about my dog?" Lyle said to the woman. No matter that he couldn't stand mutts. Humans had pets, so he adopted a canine on the spot.

"Don' wants to hear 'bout no hound," she told him. He could detect the tiny *boom-tish-tish* of music escaping from her headset.

"How 'bout a glass of water?" Lyle asked, raising his voice so that she would hear him.

"You don' need no waterin'."

"Foot massage?"

"You way too juicy," she said without poking him.

"It was a joke."

"I probably be laughin' into next week. Now shut up 'fore I busts you."

He gave up on her. The low gears of her voice made it clear she could chop firewood with her bare hands. Quieting, he ordered himself to wait until the changing of the guard before any further attempts at proving his humanity. So far he'd had two other chaperons, one who delighted in ticking off the type of guns they might use on Lyle and one who spent all his time smooth-talking women over the phone. To be honest, neither seemed like a possible ally, but at a time like this, who wanted to be honest?

By Lyle's own reckoning, they'd now held him for twenty-four hours. The nearby freeway's volume had picked up twice, during morning and afternoon rush hours, he assumed, and now was barely more than a mosquito hum, occasionally punctuated by the baffles of an eighteen-wheeler. It promised to be another endless day. He'd nearly willed himself to sleep when a small electric motor clicked on and the clacking of a rising garage door made him alert. A car pulled into the garage, stopping within inches of his face. He could smell its motor. The fun-loving driver hit the horn, jolting Lyle halfway out of his chair before he lost his balance and fell backward. He found himself laughing uncontrollably.

A car door opened and a man ordered, "Get that piece of shit out of the way."

Lyle stilled.

Hands roughly shoved his bucket seat to the side.

The car pulled the rest of the way into the garage, dieseled, and died. Briefly the freeway sounds raced closer, and Lyle felt himself straining against his restraints. Then the electric motor started lowering the door and the impulse to flee died. Unconsciously he made an unmanly sound in his throat that he tried to pawn off as another laugh. No one cared, though. They were all conferring on the far side of the car. He heard four, maybe five voices arguing in tones too low to decipher. Then footsteps crunched on the littered floor as the group approached him. He imagined they were carrying a platter for his head. Unexpectedly, a voice crawled gently into his left ear.

"The accommodations to your likin'?"

Forcing himself to avoid looking toward the voice, Lyle said, "Room service was slow."

"I'll kick some ass," the voice promised. Raising his volume, he demanded, "Who's handlin' room service?"

"He got his glass of water," the woman said.

"That true?" the man whispered into Lyle's ear.

"It was overcooked."

"You complainin'?"

There was enough edge to the question to warn Lyle away from further smart-ass. Instead, he asked, "Have you decided when you're lettin' me go?"

To the room at large, the man said, "He always changin' the subject this way?"

" 'Cept when he braggin' 'bout the size of his pecker," said the guard who enjoyed naming weapons.

The woman grunted without humor.

"You yappin' over the size of your equipment?" the man in charge asked Lyle, feigning wonder.

"Not that I remember."

"You callin' my people liars?" His tone turned meaner.

"I must have been misunderstood. I thought we was talkin' 'bout the size of somebody else's pecker."

"Whose?"

"Don't remember," Lyle said, trying to cram respect and cooperation into the words.

"You wasn't talkin' up my long tom, was you? I hates it when people does that."

"Somebody else's."

"You implyin' my tom's not worth talkin' over?"

"Not at all."

The man crossed behind Lyle to speak sharply into his right ear. "You some kind of punk-ass fag?"

"No way."

"You got somethin' against punk-ass fags?"

Lyle said nothing until the man poked him in the ear and said, "Huh?"

"When we goin' to cut the shit?" Lyle asked.

"Right now," the man said. Snapping his fingers, he called out, "Where's that cat?"

Lyle heard two of his tormentors—the woman and the gun lover—shoving workbenches and toolboxes around as they called out kitty-kitty-kitty in childish, soprano voices. When he tried to wet his lips, his tongue only stuck to them as he remembered every cat he'd ever done wrong.

"How you feel 'bout cats?" the man asked, conversational again.

"Not so good," Lyle said, turning his head to the side as though he could see the man standing behind him. Soon the cat hunters returned with something that was hissing and spitting.

"There," the man said.

They dropped it on Lyle's lap, where it made a cornered sound, sunk its claws into his thigh, and hung on. Lyle tightened and bit his lip.

"He ain't goin' nowhere," the man whispered, close enough to startle Lyle, who was caught tensing against the cat's next move. "He can't see," the man added with satisfaction. "He's a blind ol' cat." He let that fact sink in without further comment.

"Born blind?" Lyle asked.

"You might like to think so," the man in charge said. Then his voice quickened. "I wants a favor from you."

"Or I'm a cat?"

"That's it. I wants you to autograph something."

"What am I signing?"

"He's a stickler," the woman said.

"He pissin' up his pants," said the gun lover.

"What you think, bro?" the man in charge asked someone farther away.

"Look dry to me," an unfamiliar voice answered.

"He do, don' he." Into Lyle's ear, the man in charge whispered, "You don' want no disrespect. That it?"

"It ain't high on my list."

"Turn off the lights," the man ordered over his shoulder. "And bring me a flashlight."

Footsteps. The garage went dark and a light appeared front and center.

"Now take that scarf off this man's head."

Fingers unknotted the back of Lyle's blindfold, exposing his eyes to a powerful flashlight bulb. He saw white spots pirouetting. The rest of the room was shadows, even the cat crouching on his lap.

"Close them eyes," the man snapped.

Lyle complied. The flashlight went away. He heard footsteps and the crinkling of paper.

"Open 'em."

A sheet of blue-lined paper was being held a foot from his nose. The flashlight beam now poured over his shoulder to light it. There was printing on the paper and after a few blinks he could read it:

> WE HAVE YOUR MAN. YOU WANT HIM BACK,
> GIVE US OURS.

They brought the flashlight around front again, forcing him to close his eyes.

"We sendin' that to General Jack. You understandin' you been 'napped?"

"I do now."

"Any troubles with that?"

"What if they won't trade?"

"You be wishin' you white."

"White?"

"White 'nough for them to think you worth swappin' for. You ready to sign this?"

"Not with my hands behind my back."

"Cut 'em loose," the man disgustedly ordered. "You must be the same niggers I told to get me somethin' white. Next you be tellin' me you forgot your green when you grabbed him."

Denials all around. They used what felt like tin snips to bite through the duct tape wrapped around his wrists. He brought his arms forward one at a time, shaking them out to get some blood past his wrists.

"Can I move the cat?" Lyle asked.

"Just so you don't drop him."

Lyle carefully unhooked the cat from his thigh but let him remain on his lap.

"What should I write?"

"That you breathin' and that we mean motherfuckers who know our business."

The pencil they put between his fingers felt big as a two-by-four. He dropped it twice before getting down what had been dictated.

"Bust your ass signin' it," the man in charge said.

"They'll know it's me," Lyle promised, signing his name with the same tight scrawl he used to endorse paychecks. "Now what?"

"You keep that cat company."

Everyone but Lyle thought that was pretty funny. Even the woman laughed.

PART II

12

Within twenty-four hours of the initial riot at the General, the news anchors of two of the three networks were in town. The anchor of the third network was rumored to be on his way out of a career. Thanks to the efforts of other cities, the type of footage they played on the evening news was already far too familiar to the nation. A traffic accident triggered one scene. The refusal to cash a personal check ignited another. The biggest mob looted a shopping mall that consisted of a grocery store known for its price gouging, a liquor store that specialized in Tokays, and a gun shop renowned for its back-room specials. There were too many rumors about what started that one to ever learn the truth.

The National Guard arrived shortly after the news anchors. They were there to help enforce a dusk-to-dawn curfew imposed by the governor.

Day or night, the sky held at least one hovering helicopter.

The TV reporters' favorite metaphor for the spreading riots was "the fire storm." Their favorite adjective for law enforcement was "beleaguered." It happened to be ratings week for the local stations, so they pulled out all the stops: twenty-four-hour action centers, help lines for the totally freaked out, and hourly reports from the governor's mansion. Everyone with any history of being a community leader had to beat off the cameras. One independent station had footage of a teenage boy bicycling away from a burning pet shop with an aquarium across his handlebars and a pair of spaniel puppies inside the tank, standing on their hind legs. The station was the envy of its competition and played the clip regularly.

On the second day of the riots the FBI was called in to deal with Lyle's abduction. The networks all appreciated the lift it gave their coverage.

13

Special FBI agent Kyle Ford had a face chiseled out of network rhinestone, a semilustrous rock quarried from the back lots of NBC, ABC, and CBS. Looking into his eyes made Jan feel as though she was leaning over two gallon buckets of blue paint. She had yet to catch either bucket blinking. A sun-bleached blond with a surfer's genes, his skin had been dipped in something coppery. The kicker was his belief in the power of fine tailoring and the way central casting had padded his shoulders. After the shoulders, the rest of him was sleek as an adder overdue a meal. A gold chain bracelet on his left wrist looked ready to fall off.

"I have a favor to ask of you, Officer Gallagher."

"Fire away," Jan said, trying to avoid looking too cooped up in her cubicle even though that's exactly where she'd floundered through Tuesday, July six, when a special-delivery ransom note had arrived addressed to Rainy Penshorn, and through most of Wednesday, a good deal of which Jan spent convincing Felicia not to go public with news of the note. Not yet, anyway, not before the authorities had a chance to ply their trade. And now it was Wednesday afternoon and here were the authorities, arranging press conferences and building bridges, as they were prone to say.

"Would you mind having a cup of coffee with me?"

She wouldn't mind but she checked her wristwatch and held up a beat before telling him so. Three times he'd already come and gone from the Little Admiral's office; by the fourth visit she knew it was the agent thanks to the flutter in Miss Pepperidge's breath. On the walk to the cafeteria, he made small talk and Jan made small answers. It looked as though it was going to be a first-name basis, particularly once he vowed to be totally honest with her. Agent Ford sprang for the coffee but wasn't quick enough to pull out her chair. Except for a food-service worker filling salt shakers, they had the cafeteria to themselves. The Styrofoam cups before them steamed, as did the city outside the large window to Jan's left, but by the fourth day of the current heat wave, the hospital's air conditioners had finally caught up and even overshot the mark. The room was almost chilly.

"Do you mind if I ask you some questions, Jan?"

"It's going to be awfully quiet if you don't."

He smiled to show he'd been trained to recognize wit. "How badly do you want Lyle Brown back?"

"Very," Jan said, matching his gaze. "He's a friend."

"What do you think we should do to get him back?" he asked, blowing on his coffee.

"That a trick question?"

"Hardly. I'll listen to anything brilliant."

Jan burned gray cells a moment. To accomplish that without blue-eyed interference, she had to look out the window. Down below she could see an overweight ambulance attendant straining to shove a patient's wheelchair up a ramp and into a van.

"I don't know," Jan said. "Give them whatever they want, I guess."

"And then what? After we gave up Rainy Penshorn, I mean."

"I'm not following," she said, rolling the coffee cup back and forth in her hands.

"Do you think that will be enough?"

"You tell me," Jan said, her hands stilling. "You're supposed to be the expert."

He rocked back on the rear legs of his chair and stared into his coffee cup as if reading the grounds. His eyes took on some gray. Nothing serious, just a minor shading.

"Do you have any objections to working with the FBI?" he asked.

"Should I have?"

He grinned, boyishly, she supposed.

"I've got to reach a decision about you, Jan." He was watching her again.

"In regards to . . . ?"

"In regards to Lyle Brown's life," he said, pushing his coffee cup aside. That left nothing but Jan's cup between them. She kept a hand on it.

"So ask your questions," she said.

"Problems with the FBI?"

"Nothing major," she said. "I don't trust you as much as I did when I was a kid, but then there's not much I do."

He nodded as if he could live with that and said, "Why did you sue the county?"

That much honesty caught her off guard and she answered truthfully, or as truthfully as she could. "Maybe to give them what they deserved."

"That all?"

"To prove a point."

"Nothing else?"

"Maybe because I didn't know any better. What is this, anyway?"

He smiled faintly, approving of her spunk. She'd quit warming to that routine shortly after puberty.

"I'm trying to figure out if you always go by the book, Jan. Or if sometimes you make it up as you go along."

"That all depends on what book we're talking about." Her heel began to tap.

"I need a promise," he said, leaning forward on his elbows. "What I'm about to tell you can't leave this room."

"And if I don't promise?"

"Then you'll have done all that you can to help your friend Lyle Brown."

"Which is nothing?"

He reached for his coffee, blew on it, sipped it. He didn't say anything, only watched her over the curve of his cup.

"It stays in this room," Jan said, not liking it.

He let his blues work on her a minute before speaking so low that she had to lean forward to catch the words.

"We're not giving up this Rainy Penshorn for your man."

There wasn't any give to the words. Jan's heel stilled.

"What?"

"We can't afford to. He killed a man. Two cops witnessed it. If our laws mean anything, we can't do it."

"What happens to Lyle?"

"We do it once," he said, "who knows what we'd be opening the door to."

"What in the hell about Lyle?"

He nodded as if she had every right to be outraged.

"Even if we act in good faith," he said, "we don't know that they will. They've kidnapped a man, Jan. That's heavy stuff if they go down."

"What you're saying is that Lyle's dead."

"Not at all."

"Then what?"

"I'm saying there's no book to follow, Jan, and that I need your help."

"Why me?"

"Because a Lieutenant Crenshaw with the local heat tells me you're the only one who might be able to help us turn this around. I need someone who has contacts with these gangs, because from what I hear, everyone the cops talk to has lockjaw."

"The only gang I know anything about is Spanky's."

"What about this guy you rescued out of a basement?"

"I didn't find him. Felicia did."

"Exactly," he said, resting his case.

"Hey now," Jan said, raising a hand for him to slow down. "Wait a minute. You want help from Felicia, you better talk to her."

"I already have. She's got an attitude about my employer."

"Was that before or after you mentioned you weren't making a trade?"

"We didn't get around to that topic."

Jan's eyes narrowed. "You want me to, is that it?"

"No," the agent firmly said. "When the time comes, I'll take care of that. I don't want you to say a word to her about it. Is that clear?"

86

"Overly. So what *do* you want me do?"

"I want you to help her."

"I'm sure," Jan said, glancing away, then back. "I suppose you have something in mind?"

"At this point I wish I did," he said, taking a renewed interest in his coffee cup. "About all I can tell you is this: We need something fast. The number of people running over the crime scene took care of any leads there. One of your guards saw Lyle Brown being tucked away in the trunk of a dark sedan, maybe an LTD driven by Sevens. You can imagine how much help that's been. We've tried matching the names of known Sevens to the make of car they drive. So far nothing. We've had Forensics paying close attention to the trunks of any recovered stolen cars matching that description. The only good news is that we haven't found Lyle's body. The gang intelligence unit with the city PD has rousted some Seven safe houses plus a couple of the heavy hitters at the gang's top. You'd think they were all churches and ministers. This is what it comes down to: For now we'll pretend to go along with whatever the kidnappers want. We've got a negotiating team in the wings and a SWAT team polishing their scopes. But all of that doesn't bring anybody home, not unless we know where the hostage is. So we wait."

"For?"

"Instructions from the kidnappers. But I don't think that's going to be enough to crack this. If we're going to save Lyle Brown's life, we need a tip."

"What about the note?" Jan said. "That must have told you something."

"That they know how to spell."

"Christ," Jan said, staring down at her untouched coffee. "I'm not going to lie to Felicia."

"I wouldn't call it lying."

"You've got a longer word for it?"

Special Agent Kyle Ford shrugged, keeping any longer words to himself.

"OK," she said with a deep breath, "let's say I'm officially part of the team. Then what?"

"Actually," the agent said with a wink, "it'd probably be better if we're not so official about it. Your friend might not be so open if she thinks we're working together."

"My soon-to-be ex-friend," Jan corrected.

"She won't hold it against you once we have Lyle back," he predicted. "But to do that we need to know anything she learns from her contacts. No matter how insignificant, pass it on."

"I don't think Felicia's doing much more than staying in bed, if you want the truth. She's taking this ransom note hard."

"Then you better get her up," the agent said, sounding as though it was time to strike up the band. "She may be our only shot at this."

"Other than giving the kidnappers what they want."

"Not an option," he reminded her.

"Right. I only hope you'll try to remember one little thing while you're upholding the law."

"I can try," the agent said, trotting out a smile.

"Lyle's the one you're here to save."

The agent nodded, minus the smile, and held out a business card on which he'd penned a beeper number in red ink. His handwriting had a backward slant, but at least he hadn't held off on the bad news. She took that as a hopeful sign.

14

When Jan called Felicia to tell her they needed to talk, Felicia said, "Aren't we?" She sounded genuinely puzzled.

"Just stay put," Jan said, "I'll be right over."

Fighting a street map all the way, she eventually found Lyle and Felicia's address. The neighborhood was storybook neat, even if the fences were more often wire than white picket. With all the faces she saw being black, she found herself trying to hide behind sunglasses. At the side door of the bungalow she pounded without results, although a full saucer of fresh milk placed on the top step made it feel as though someone was home. The prospect of losing sight of her car and the street made her uneasy, but she worked her way around to the rear of the house anyway. In back there was a flagstone patio shaded by a grapevine-covered arbor. Beyond the stone lay a small vegetable patch laid out in straight rows and free of weeds. A black man in a wheelchair was misting the plants with a yellow garden hose. At his side stood a small wrought-iron table with a telephone whose cord ran into the rear door of the bungalow's other half.

"Excuse me," Jan said from a respectful distance.

"She's home," the man announced without turning. His voice was a gruff baritone. "Knock loud."

She did, and a minute later she was still knocking when the man spoke up from directly behind her.

"She won't answer."

Her breath caught and she spun about, intending to demand

to know if he always sneaked up on people or if she was a special case. That was before she saw the blindness of his eyes, which drifted involuntarily from side to side, and the emptiness of his pinned-up pant legs. Not knowing what to say, she said nothing.

"She's in there with that stray cat she feeds," he disgustedly said, dipping his chin toward the door. "Won't come out."

"Well, I need to talk to her. Are you close to her?"

"Not particularly," he said, arching his head back slightly as if it helped him see her. "I'm Lyle's brother, Haywood. You that white thing been helpin' out?"

"How . . ." But Jan didn't bother to finish the question, realizing that she sounded white even as she asked it. Looking away, she said, "I am."

"You bringing news?"

"No," she said, knocking on the door again.

"It bothers you, coming down here where it's all black, don't it?"

"So what if it does?" Jan said, having heard enough.

"Now that's an attitude I can 'preciate," Haywood said. "Step aside, lady. I'll get us in there."

Lifting a string and attached key from around his neck, he rolled up a wooden ramp at the side of the steps and unlocked the door. Inside, the kitchen was spotless but smelled stale. The television voices rumbling in another room might have been from the next world, the one that comes after this one, not the one adjacent. Through the doorway to the living room Jan spied Felicia frozen in a wing chair, dressed in a robe, bathed in TV light.

"She was all right for the first day or so," the brother said, without bothering to lower his voice, "but the bottom fell out after you helped her rescue that punk. Then came that ransom note. That put her low, too low, you ask me."

"She say something?" Jan asked, uneasy about whether Felicia could hear them.

"That just it. She sits there with that cat and won't hardly speak. We had some piece of work from the FBI out here and 'bout all she could do was dry sob."

"Has she talked to anyone?"

"Cat, maybe."

"Great," said Jan. "Is she getting any sleep?"

"I've told her to," he said, defensive about it.

"Food?"

"Told her that too."

Jan inhaled another breath before turning to Lyle's brother. "Have you got anything to help her sleep?"

"Lady," he said, "I gots a medicine chest full of shit."

"So," Jan prodded when he didn't budge from the center of the kitchen, "do you make house calls?"

"How you going to get her to take it?"

"The same way my mother did," Jan said, lowering her voice. "Without telling her what it is."

Haywood rocked the wheels of his chair back and forth before abruptly spinning about and leaving. Halfway to the rear door, he stopped to say without looking back, "I suppose you think I should be thanking you for coming." He never bothered to say it, though.

For half a minute after the brother's departure, she kept her hands braced on the edge of the kitchen sink as if it might help with the weight on her shoulders. Rousing herself, she opened a window, put water on to boil, and pointed herself toward the living room, where she turned off the volume but let CNN's twenty-four-hour news roll on. Felicia never glanced away from the screen. Her shadowed and droopy face looked about to slip into her lap; her eyes could have used an exorcist, but, in contrast to her haggard expression, her posture appeared poured in concrete. Under the bathrobe, she remained dressed in the same white blouse and dark skirt as when Jan had last seen her. Trapped on her lap was a yellow tabby. Felicia had a death-lock on its neck with one hand and gently patted its back with the other.

"I'm making you something to eat," Jan said.

After a moment, Felicia's eyes tracked to the left and located Jan's face. Being looked at by those eyes made Jan feel like a TV screen herself.

"And then I think you better get some rest," Jan said.

"I can't."

Back to that refrain, the same one she'd repeated as they rushed the naked boy-man to the hospital. Jan squatted down until she was at eye level with Felicia.

"Why not?"

"If I go to sleep," Felicia said, "somebody will die."

"Well," Jan said, "at least something to eat."

Felicia's premonition spooked Jan enough to almost forget about doctoring any tea, but another half minute of watching her friend transfixed before a muted TV cured her waffling. She brewed a cup of sleepy-time that, when spiked with a capsule from the brother, knocked Felicia out. Freeing the tabby from her grasp made her fitful, and Jan dared no more than to roll her down to the floor, making a bed for her there. She then retired to the patio with Haywood.

"Now what?" Jan asked.

"Kick some ass," he said, meaning it figuratively, of course.

"You got somebody in mind?"

"That ain't nothing for you to worry about."

"Look," Jan said, "I'm trying to do everything I can." She steadied herself with a breath. "So are a lot of other people. If you've found something out, I'd say you'd better share it. For Lyle's sake."

At least that last part wasn't a lie, and if she had to tell someone what plans the FBI had, it would be Felicia, when she was stronger, not some stranger with an attitude.

"I'm working my side of the street," the brother answered. "You do yours."

"All I'm asking is that you share whatever you find out."

"Lady, if the people I be talking to think I'm into sharin', they won't be putting out."

"I've got access to resources you don't."

"I know about those resources," Haywood said with a snort. "I ain't no stranger to no U.S. government." Picking up the garden hose, he was about to open up the nozzle but stopped to ask, almost naively, "You really want to help my brother?"

"I do."

"Then hit up that punk you and 'licia found. He'll know something."

"They've been trying," Jan said.

"No!" he said. *"You* talk to him. Not some cop. Not some window dressing from the F-B-and-I. You. You saved his ass. He might have something for you, because it sound to me like he a boy what got reason to talk."

End of conversation. The telephone rang and the brother ordered her to leave. Picking up his receiver, he said into it, "Hold on a minute, man," then carried the phone inside his half of the bungalow as if Jan would eavesdrop on him. His secretiveness made her mad, especially since she lingered on long enough to prove him right.

THE ONE THING she hadn't done in the past two days was talk to the naked kid they'd rescued. It hadn't been a high priority, given all that had been going down. One time she'd stopped by the MICU but he'd been sleeping deeply. A second time the attending doc was examining the patient and she didn't have enough patience to wait. But what Lyle's brother said made sense, and an hour later she was back at the General in Medical Intensive Care Unit 1.

"He's gone," the charge nurse said.

"He could barely talk," Jan protested.

"That's right."

"And you let him go?"

"Against medical advice," the nurse answered with a resigned shrug that said they'd done their best to reason with the boy.

"What about the cops?" Jan said. "I thought they had a guard over here protecting him. Couldn't they hold him?"

"The police told us that he wasn't under arrest and there was nothing they could do."

Jan brought a hand to her forehead. "When did all this happen?"

"This afternoon."

"Did you get a name on the patient?"

"We got three," the nurse said, consulting a clipboard. "But we finally settled on Isiah Lawrence. That's the one his mother told us when she picked him up."

"Thanks," Jan said, writing down name, address, and phone number from the nurse's discharge sheet.

15

Lyle's guards were half his forty-one years, if that much, and had taken to calling him Dad. The little pricks were constantly sticking a cigarette up his nose and lighting it or dumping a cup full of ice down his back. Ho-ho-ho. Then, within five minutes of some cheap shot, they'd turn right around and ask him some aw-shucks question, like had he ever flown. They wanted to know what it was like, really like, up above the clouds. He caught himself feeling protective of them. Ten minutes later he wanted to kick their butts. They were so far out of their league that they were bound to do something foolish, something that everyone but him would live to regret. Among other things, he knew from listening that they'd watched way too many gangster movies.

Except for the pranks, he soon enough had the routine down cold. They weren't even experienced enough to know they should be constantly shuffling him to new locations in the middle of the night.

The day shift kicked off with the woman guard turning on the TV and dropping a bag of fast-food breakfast in his lap. Three biscuits filled with egg, ham, and cheese. No potato cakes. The guard claimed they were evil and wouldn't have anything to do with them. The woman was also on a first-name basis with every TV talk-show host who had ever interviewed a pervert.

"Which one's your favorite?" Lyle asked her one morning.

"Dad, I got an oil rag fo' that mouth of yours."

He'd interrupted her running dialogue with Phil Donahue, but later, during some totally unrehearsed testimonials for a pain reliever, she cooled off enough to grow curious.

"Favorite what?" she asked.

"Talk show host."

"Ain't none my favorite."

"OK, which you hate most?"

"That a tie too."

"I was on Donahue once," Lyle said, making it up word by word.

"You?" she hooted. "What Phil want you fo'?"

"Reincarnation."

"I 'member that one," she said, flashing serious. "Don' 'member you."

"They didn't have time to get me on."

"S'pose you was the only black man," she said.

"Don't remember."

"Trust me, Dad. What kind of nigger you reincarnate from?"

"Average kind."

"Least you got that straight."

That ended her conversation for the morning, but afterwards she at least quit poking him in the ribs and saying he was too juicy.

Each day between Phil and Sally, she cut the tape off his ankles, tipped him out of his bucket seat, and pushed him toward the john, the door of which she left open.

"So we ain't got no secrets, Dad."

Twice the blind cat was curled up behind the toilet bowl and scared a yelp out of Lyle as it tore out of hiding. The woman thought that almost as funny as his behind-the-back routine to wipe himself.

For exercise, she let him do deep knee bends until Sally was done interrupting her guests and Joan was about to start. Then it was back to his seat, fresh tape for his ankles, and no further action until hours later when Oprah was wrapping up. At about that time a door somewhere behind Lyle opened and the next shift entered with Lyle's supper, a bag of burgers, fries, and a cola half siphoned off.

Evening meant the lady's man, who spent the first half of his shift on the phone apologizing for missed dates and the second half lining up new ones.

"Hope you're taking precautions," Lyle told him during a breather from his scheduling.

"You know how I can tell when some old cud ain't gettin' any?"

"How's that?" asked Lyle.

"He always be talkin' up precautions. Ain't no precautions ever snagged any squish-squash."

"You maybe got a point there."

"Damn straight, I do."

"Any other advice?" Lyle asked.

"Not fo' free I don'."

"Think I'm gettin' out of here alive?"

"Not fo' free you ain't."

"I could see it wasn't for free," Lyle offered.

"I'm blood-related to these people, Dad. Don't even think 'bout it." But his voice quickly dropped to a whisper for a follow-up question. "How much?" Before Lyle could name his bank balance, the lady's man burst out laughing. "Don' pee your pants, man. It ain't goin' to happen, not for a zillion dollars. You want to know why?"

"No."

That answer only stretched the guard's laugh out longer. Proudly he told Lyle, " 'Cause the two little motherfucks runnin' this biz are the meanest downtown motherfucks I ever met. And that's no motherfuckin' lie."

Before Lyle could push it any further, the guard was back on the phone line sweet-talking some young thing named Taneisha.

Another trip to the john, a finger of peppermint schnapps for a nightcap, and that pretty much wrapped up the evening. Lyle knew the next shift had arrived by the sound of rusty brakes outside.

With the graveyard shift came high-rpm gun talk. The blast-happy guard on that watch galloped along with the late-night westerns, rooting for the Injuns or bad guys and getting short when they finally were ten toes up and the singing cowboys gathered around the campfire for some harmonizing. About then the guard usually started threatening to shoot the white cap off every one of those sissy motherfuckers. He also had a thing about educating the older generation, which included Lyle.

"You know they was black cowboys?"

"Not in Hollywood," Lyle said.

"You got that right, Dad."

"Would you really blow me away?" Lyle asked.

"If I had to, I'd shoot so many holes in you there wouldn't be nothin' but holes."

"Why would you have to?"

"Maybe get ordered."

"Wouldn't bother you?"

"Be a waste of bullets. That'd bother some. Say, you know what you 'mind me of, all bound up there?"

"No."

"Some nigger being shipped from the Gold Coast. Them slavers kept your way-back granddaddy bound up just that tight. You think that over and see if you feel like workin' for the man."

"I'll do that."

"Don' be givin' me that yes-sir shit," the guard snapped. "I see through that. That shit's old as pimpin', and I don' want to hear none of it. You tell me what you really thinkin' or I'll save everybody a whole lot of trouble and give you six new assholes right now." He laid the oily barrel of his gun against Lyle's temple.

"I'm thinkin'," Lyle said, "it ain't no white man got me tied up right now."

The gun barrel pressed harder for a moment. Lyle squeezed his eyes shut behind his blindfold. But that eternity passed. With a laugh that changed into a curse, the guard holstered his piece and headed toward the john, throwing over his shoulder, "You probably like it if I would."

After that exchange, John Wayne's volume was turned up to an ear-splitting level, but it didn't attract any complaints from neighbors. By then Lyle figured that the nearest neighbor had to be several blocks removed. He was either in a warehouse district or some string of abandoned tenements waiting for a passing firebug.

The only excitement came early on the third evening while

the Don Juan guard was in the middle of promising the moon and part of Mars to some sweet young thing named Doresha. He must have been using his own cellular phone because in the background another phone started ringing. The second phone sounded for maybe five minutes before the guard told Doresha he hoped she'd be wearing plenty of zippers, blew her a kiss, and hung up.

"Huh?" the guard said into the other phone. "I'm right here. That where I been. . . . What you mean they tried bustin' Rainy Penshorn out? . . . If they'd had me along, that wouldn't a been happenin'. . . . So what if someone do bust him out? . . . What I supposed to do with Uncle Tom here? That what I mean. . . . Shit, 'course I know how to use my imagination." Hanging up, he stomped over to Lyle and said, "You lucky I don't use some precautions on you, Dad. Damn lucky."

16

Back at her desk, Jan had to dry her hands on her slacks three times before dialing the number she'd been given for Isiah Lawrence. A toddler picked up the other end on the fifth ring. An adult eventually wrestled the receiver away from the child and Jan asked to speak to Isiah.

"Who's calling?"

"Jan Gallagher. I'm one of the women who helped get him to the hospital."

"This is his mother and I thank you for what you did, but he can't be coming to the phone right now. He's not even supposed to be out of the hospital, but he don't listen to nobody."

"When do you think I could talk to him?"

"I don't think that would be possible at all," the mother said. "My son's one boy got to learn to keep his mouth shut. God bless you, ma'am, and good-bye."

Which left Jan staring at the address she'd copied down. The boy appeared to live in one of the south-side projects, where she wouldn't be going by herself. Pocketing the slip of paper, she picked up the phone again to call home but her dialing was interrupted by Eldon Hodges huffing down the corridor with Victor Wheaton, Security's evening supervisor, opening doors for him. Hodges made Wheaton wait outside the last door, though, his office door, as he went inside to use his hush-hush phone voice, the one reserved for hospital administrators and revered ancestors.

"What's happening?" Jan asked, doubting that she'd actually be told, but as soon as she stepped out of her cubicle, Wheaton was glad of the company.

"Jerry Cody caught one kind of low."

"One what?"

"One bullet." Wheaton said it as if she was dense.

"Now what's going on?"

"Three misunderstood guys tried springing our prisoner."

"And they shot Jerry?"

"Actually," Wheaton said, warming to his story, "no." He loved telling about anything that had gone wrong in his adoptive country. A Canadian by birth, he'd moved south because his wife was from Detroit, a city that never failed to bring a sneer to his lips. "The well-trained cop guarding the prisoner opened up just as Jerry came around a corner."

"How'd these three guys get in?"

"Through the ER. Claimed they'd been in a car accident, then took off as soon as they got sent to a waiting room. One of them encountered some bruises," he said, turning modest. "The other two won gold medals in the hundred-yard sprint and haven't been seen since."

"Victor," the Little Admiral called out, and Wheaton was gone. Jan didn't mind; she was too busy cutting toward the Emergency Room, the most likely stopover for someone who'd made the acquaintance of some bruises.

THE ER WAS listing but not capsized, as it had been on the night of the riot. Yet of all the bruises she found being treated, none were receiving the star status reserved for anyone arrested on the grounds. She was almost ready to give up when she spotted Jackson Martin disgustedly snapping off a pair of surgical gloves, which the guards wore to protect themselves from IV users and lice buses. Flinging the gloves in the trash, he headed out of the ER in search of fresh air. She caught up to him in front of the triage desk and followed him outside the hospital, where they found themselves alone except for the bugs popping against the hospital's exterior lights. In the yellowish-green entrance lights, Jackson's black skin took on a bronze cast, and he watched Jan with eyes that could have been poured in a foundry and cooled on the moon.

"What happened to the one they caught upstairs?" she asked.

"The fool trying to free Penshorn? A few stitches and the cops hustled him off."

"FBI involved?"

"Moving and shaking."

"Which way were they headed?"

"They had me on lice patrol," Jackson said, referring to the drunk tank. "Have to ask Huey. He drew the prisoner."

"Huey?"

"None other," Jackson grimly agreed.

Jan thanked him and turned to leave but found Jackson holding on to her elbow.

"What you getting into here, Gallagher?"

He spoke guardedly. She waited until he let go of her arm before answering.

"Trying to help Lyle out."

"The talk I'm hearing, it's too late for that."

"But what if it isn't?"

"Then this is probably one case where it actually is better to let the hotshots do what they're paid for."

"What if they're not so hot?"

He shook off that suggestion, wagging his head as if reminding himself he had it right the first time. "It probably doesn't matter, and the safest thing for you to do is let somebody else find that out."

"You positive?" Jan asked.

"No," Jackson said, amused by her contrariness. He went back inside without saying more.

Jan remained alone for a minute, staring into the emergency room entrance as though locked out. Going back in, she veered away from the ER and headed for her cubicle in the administrative wing. The Little Admiral's door was half closed, with Victor Wheaton behind it saying yes sir, yes sir, yes sir. She tuned that out and tried calling Detective Crenshaw, only to be told she'd get a call-back as soon as possible but not to hold her breath. Giving the dispatcher her home phone, she left for the day. It was five past six.

WHEN SHE OPENED the back door to her house, she found everyone, including her mother Claire, waiting in the kitchen.

"Is the whole city really going to explode?" Tess, the youngest, wanted to know.

"Did you nab 'em?" asked Katie.

"You're not going to be on TV again, are you?" asked Amy. During Jan's trial for sexual discrimination her face had regularly embarrassed Amy by showing up on the local news.

Even Leah took off her headphones to ask, "They mail in an ear yet?"

"That's enough," Jan said. "This isn't some sideshow. There's a man's life at stake here. A man I happen to know. I want you all to go to your rooms and think about that."

"Laying down the law, Mom?"

"Get going."

"I heard they're calling out the Marines."

"Now."

"There was a fight at softball today," Katie announced, proud of it, as though she too had a part in the drama.

"About what?" Jan asked, slowing her herding motions.

"Who's descended from monkeys."

"We all are, and I hope you know it. Now everyone get moving. I want to talk to your grandmother."

Under protest, the girls filed to their bedrooms at the back of the house, which left Jan with her mother, who looked secretly pleased, as if she was about to get the real goods on what was happening on the street. But when Jan sat down across from her with a worried look, Claire's face took on some lines of its own.

"Now what?" Claire asked.

"They're not doing too well with all this, are they?"

"The girls?" Claire said. "They're all wound up, and that's a fact."

"They don't seem to think it's real."

"I'm with them there," Claire commented.

"It feels like I should be talking to them . . . or something. This isn't some game. People have gotten killed."

"Pretty hard to talk to them from here," Claire observed.

"But what should I tell them?"

"I don't know. Just don't lie to them, I guess. That's the main thing."

"What do you mean by that crack?"

"Touchy," Claire said. "What I mean is, you shouldn't make something up to make them feel better."

"Why would I do that?"

"Because you're a do-gooder. And do-gooders don't have any sense of when to tell it like it is."

"You're really building my confidence, Mother."

"You asked," Claire said, then softer, "Just do the best you can. If you ever meet anyone who can do more, let me know."

So Jan waved the girls back out to the living room, sat them all down on cushions, ordered the TV off, and informed them they were going to talk about the riots. Her daughters faced the TV as if trying to will it back on. Their concentration on the tube only grew as Jan gave them a little lecture about different races, slavery, and getting along with people regardless of their color. No one raised their hand during the question-and-answer period. She scrounged up the atlas and pointed to Africa, Europe, and Asia. Leah, ever helpful, drew their attention to Antarctica. Jan did a quick review of the Civil War, segregation, and civil rights. Tess asked Claire if she was old enough to have lived through all that.

"Older," said Claire.

"Any other questions?" Jan asked.

"What if I like rap?" Leah said.

"Play it in your room."

"Can I date one?" Katie asked.

"You better not," Amy quickly warned.

"One what?" Tess said.

"You're not old enough to date anyone," Jan said.

"That's not an answer."

"All right," Jan said. "When the time comes, you'll have the same rules as for dating a white boy."

"Honesty, courtesy, and no car," Leah recited.

"What about tattoos?" asked Amy.

"No more tattoos," Claire said. "Leah has enough for everyone, thank you."

"And no gangs," Jan added.

"Can I change my name to Lakatie?" asked Katie.

"When you're eighteen."

"What if someone's mother is black and their father white?" asked Tess.

"What do you mean?" Jan said.

"Well, what color are they?"

Jan looked to Claire for help, but Claire was studying her lap.

"They're black," Amy said without doubt.

"But that doesn't make any sense," Tess complained. "Not if they're half white."

"No, it doesn't," Jan agreed, "so maybe it'd be best if you tried not to think of them as any color at all. Just think of them as people."

"That's what they're always telling us at school," Tess said with a frown.

"That's what's wrong with school," said Leah, the dropout.

Claire said, "What do you mean by that, young lady?"

"That you can forget about what color people are all you want, but there's plenty of people who aren't going to forget you're white. Then what are you going to do?"

"What's she mean by that, Mom?"

"I guess she means that not everybody wants to get along," Jan said. "And that's a good thing to remember too."

AROUND AND AROUND they went, excited and confused, until almost nine, when Lieutenant Crenshaw finally returned Jan's call. Not wanting an audience, she ordered everyone back to their rooms before picking up the phone and quickly getting to the point.

"Do you have somebody down there who tried to spring Rainy Penshorn?"

"Not here," Crenshaw said. "The FBI put him back out on

the street. They're hoping he can turn something for them."

"Did they question him?"

"What I heard, maybe more than they should have. Didn't buy them a thing. Listen, Jan, we're processing a load of brick throwers so I got to run, but let me give you some advice an old-timer once shared with me. If you're going to be a cop, you got to know when to duck."

"Like right now?" she asked.

But he was already ducking.

17

They were sewing the top of Po' Rind together because he and two of his homeboys had got it into their thick heads to free Rainy Penshorn before something worse happened to him. South Africa wasn't the only country with accident-prone cops, and there were so many Golds hauling bullets engraved with Rainy's name that they couldn't all manage to keep shooting themselves in the foot. Even a Gold might get lucky. But Maxi, the head g-ster in his 'hood, wasn't buying, so Po' tried the pitch on two friends, how they should all do some serious work on their reps and whatnot. The adventure turned to shit damn fast. Before he knew what was going down, cop cannons were *ba-whoom*ing and some hillbilly hospital cop was whanking him over the head with a club. Two or three times the club went *ka-thunk* without any rhythm. The rest was all part of the history that never gets in the history books.

The damn doctor threading the needle above Po' wouldn't even touch him without those plastic gloves on, as if he was afraid to leave any prints, which left Po' suspicious they were planting some kind of spy shit in his head. The goddamn chief of police would be listening to every word he said, track him with satellites, tune in to his private thoughts. Po' sent out a trial *Fuck you* just in case. Shortly thereafter, he could hear a tiny beeping above his ears, and the lights started flickering on and off, though that last touch might have been the guard playing the shitty little tricks some cops love so much when no one's watching.

They had him in this small, square room at the county hospital, the General, a cell with a tiny screen window in the door and a remote camera suspended from one corner of the ceiling. He thought about doing something X-rated for the camera but appeared to have fractured his funny bone along with everything else and let it lie. All he could see through the screened window was cops, so he didn't bother looking more than once because he sure as hell knew how a policeman looked, smelled, and tasted. He'd once bitten a sergeant on the ankle. Tough, old meat. Maybe a rookie would have better flavor. Maybe not. It was all in his rap sheet.

A nurse unbolted the door, entered with a guard, and without once looking him in the eye asked him a ton of questions. He said no every time there was a pause but still got stuck with the long needle, like he knew he would. The next highlight was an armed escort to X ray, where his doc was still wearing those plastic gloves.

"No fracture."

So it was back to his cell for the big wait, the one where they don't tell you anything and only peek in every once in a while to wrinkle their nose like you just dropped out the rear end of some junkyard dog. Po' spent the time pressing his fingertips to the top of his head, trying to feel if they'd left anything sticking out beneath the dressing. He'd heard stories about the county. All he touched was the fishing line they'd stitched his split head up with. The only human voice he heard for the next several years, other than the turd-bug in the cell next door singing in Spanish, was the voice of the nurse telling him to quit poking at his wound or he'd end up with an infection and then he'd be sorry. She didn't step into the room but called it through the screen window.

When they finally came to retrieve him, there were three of them, all white as moonshine—two city cops and one hospital number whose name tag read F. Huey. They handcuffed him and delivered the usual cop shit about not trying anything funny. Po' refrained from telling them about his fractured funny bone.

"Ain't I s'posed to get a call?"

"They giving these guys calls now?" one cop asked the other. Po' had heard cop humor before and yukked it up with the other cop, who right away wiped the smirk out from beneath his skimpy mustache.

"This way to the 'lectric chair, Rasmus."

Po' had heard that one before too. Keeping it friendly, he said, "You wouldn't know what they put in my head, would you?"

They hustled him out of the cell without an answer. That was when the long night began to go strange. They marched him away from the doors leading outside the hospital, going instead down a back hallway crowded with rickety wheelchairs and broken machines that looked as though they once had sucked things out of people. The mean-eyed hospital cop led them to an elevator that took them down. It was close enough on that elevator to know that one of the three officers didn't wipe his ass the way he should. It was also close enough for the hospital cop to plant an elbow in Po's ribs.

"Lose something?" Po' asked.

The hospital cop dug in a little deeper while watching the elevator's light indicator.

"Aren't you going to ask about your buddies?" the cop behind him said. His breath warmed the back of Po's ears.

"What buddies?"

That was as hilarious as it got.

The hospital cop took back his elbow and led them off the elevator into a lower-lower level, one way down below the street. It definitely didn't resemble any jailhouse route Po' had ever sampled, and he considered himself something of a connoisseur. They steered him down halls lined with gurgling pipes; they pushed him through doors whose heavy metal latches belonged on a submarine; they stopped him in a two-story-high room that contained a row of story-and-a-half boilers or pumps or whatever, all humming away at their jobs, which probably involved pumping blood and lungs and shit all over the hospital above them. The room was dim, with bare light bulbs hanging down every ten feet or so. The smell of oil and grease made him think of tools he didn't want to see.

Po' found himself wishing for one brave thought, wanting to throw at least one get-back in their faces, the way it got done on a theater's big screen, but all he could come up with was that he'd do whatever he had to. He wanted to get out of that hole alive. Something was shaking in his boot and it felt like his foot.

They waltzed him past three machines to the fourth light, beneath which sat an old school chair complete with a writing arm carved up with hearts and arrows and such. He didn't quite fit but they pushed him down into the chair anyway.

Then arrived some more of the big wait.

The cops stood around cracking their knuckles and admiring a spot about two inches in front of their crotches where they probably imagined their peckers would reach if hard. The hospital cop burned so much gas looking mean that his eyes crossed. Nobody but Po' talked, and all his talking was in his head. He went on about how hot and close it was in that big room with all those working machines throwing off heat and noise, so much noise that no one would ever be able to hear what went on in that place.

He finally slept. Something that doctor gave him brought that on, no doubt. The night must have passed, or maybe only a minute. Down there in that basement he had no way of knowing.

Finally, a blond guy in a light-blue suit and red tie entered the room carrying a briefcase. After a short confab with one of the cops, the one with an eagle tattooed on the inside of his forearm, the newcomer buzzed slowly around the chair Po' was stuck in, looking for a place to land. With the chair barely holding him up, Po' didn't make any generous offers. Instead of watching the plainclothes cop's revolutions, Po' concentrated on a screened-in office cage straight ahead of him. There was a pinup-girl calendar on the wall in that office; its top sheet was nailed down and Po' could read the year in red numbers—1956. Way before he was born.

After two or three orbits, the new cop dragged another school chair out from somewhere behind Po' and set it directly in front of him. The new man was a pretty boy, with enough blue eyes to make Po' sweat. Taking his suit coat off, he arranged it carefully over the back of his chair. A gold chain bracelet slipped down to his bony left wrist. Rotating his chair so that it faced Po's, he sat without dusting off the seat. A tough guy.

"It doesn't matter what my name is," the new cop said, all manners, "but I want to know about yours. Did your mother really name you Pork?"

If they knew his name, that was bad. Po' hadn't laid it out for anyone, which meant some cop had made him and also meant they'd probably gotten a two-wheel cart out to haul up his file.

"Yes, sir," Po' said, voice raised to be heard above the machines. "She did. After twelve other Rinds she ran out of naming power."

"I'm told you're a Seven."

"Mister, I'll be a seven, eight, or nine. Any number that makes you happy."

"Sounds like you're planning on being cooperative," the cop said, twisting his bracelet as he spoke. He sat just inside the ring of light with Po'. His high forehead was shiny, his blue eyes now in the shadows of his brows. The man's voice was cordial enough to let Po' know he was in trouble deep.

"I'll do my best."

"Let's start with what brought you down to the hospital tonight?"

"Visitin' my aunty."

"Her last name?"

"Gibson," Po' said, a half second too late to convince even his aunt. Sensing that, he poured it on, saying, "They hacked out part of her stomach and some other stuff too while they had the lid open. She called me up and ask for some smokes, so I brought 'em down. But when I gets here, all hell broke loose in that hall. What that all about, anyway?"

The cop in front of him grinned to show he enjoyed a good yarn as much as the next fellow. He said, "Were the other two guys visiting your aunty too?"

"What other guys?"

"I thought maybe your aunt's last name was Penshorn."

Blink. Blink. "Not that I remember."

"Because the room you were trying to visit, that room belonged to a Rainy Penshorn."

"Well, I sure ain't got no aunty named Rainy." Talking with his voice raised was making him hoarse, and that thing they'd planted in his head was starting to ache, which didn't make dodging questions any easier. "I don't s'pose you know what those docs threw in up here?" He pointed to the top of his head.

"Government secret," the cop said, at least not pretending it was nothing. "What I can't figure is why you're down here trying to bust Rainy Penshorn loose when you're already holding Lyle Brown."

"Who Lyle Brown?" Po' asked, paying close attention.

"The hospital guard you Sevens are trying to trade for Penshorn."

"Mister," Po' said, beginning to understand why the Maxi man had warned him off Rainy, "there's hundreds of Sevens out there, maybe thousands. How am I gonna know what they all up to?"

"What we're looking for," the cop said, fiddling with his bracelet, "is someone to help us find Lyle Brown."

"You askin' me?" Po' said, straining to sound flattered.

The cop in front of him nodded at someone to Po's left. An instant later something whooshed past Po's ear, making him jump and nearly fall sideways out of his chair. Looking to the side, he saw the hospital cop patting his billy club in his palm like it was some kind of friend. Mr. Bad Cop had arrived.

"What do you want to do with your life, son?"

"Do?" Po' said. "I dunno. Maybe move to Los Angeles."

"Well, you're talking to your ticket, but I want you to take this seriously."

"I'm diggin' in," Po' promised. "What you want?"

"For starters, what I'm looking for is somebody to hustle themselves out on the street and let the right Sevens know we're ready to deal for Lyle Brown."

"I know how to move around out there."

"But will your heart be in it?"

"You'll think it's Valentine's Day," Po' promised.

Nobody picked up on that line, though. They all just let it deflate until the cop in charge snapped his fingers for his briefcase. The uniformed cop with the underwear problem carried it to him. Setting the briefcase on the floor, the head guy popped it open and lifted out a thick, coppish kind of dark-green folder. Reaching into an inside pocket of his hanging coat, he pulled out a pair of reading glasses for that judicial look that reminded Po' of his step old-man who put on the same kind of half glasses whenever the need arose to address Po's bottom with leather. The old bastard hadn't been able to read a lick but knew his leathers.

"Recognize this?" the cop asked, holding the folder up like a scorecard.

Po' had been asked that same question a good deal as a juvenile delinquent, so he knew better than to let them smell blood. He dummied up like a pro.

"It says in here," the talking cop said, lowering the folder and leaning forward to tap Po's knee with it, "that you're currently on probation following conviction for armed robbery. Any idea what that means?"

"My ass is pork chops?"

"They're sizzling," the cop agreed. "I want to start hearing some answers."

"I'm a talkin' fool, mister."

"Who'd you come down here with?"

"Two g-sters name of Twink and Archie," Po' said, lying on the fly. "Don' know they straight-time handles."

"Why come down?"

"Pay Rainy a visit. We was buzzed, saggin', and baggin'. Thought we might do some work on our reps."

"Whose idea?"

"Think you'd have to say it hit all us at once."

"I'd say there's more to it than that, son."

"Wish there was," Po' sadly answered. "But it was just some bad ol' crank and some dumb-ass talk that got us down here."

For once a cop appeared to believe him when he was spreading out the truth, or else the cop had something ten tons heavier on his mind. Either way, the cop made one of those jumps cops are always making.

"Where's Lyle Brown?" the cop said, all coy about it.

"Mister, I never heard that name except when you just spoke it. And that you gotta believe."

"Is he still alive?"

"How many times—" Po' started to cry out.

112

A billy club wedged across his throat interrupted his train of thought. Without waving the stick away, the cop with the gold bracelet put his nose so close to Po's that they could have been dogs at a fence, except that one nose wasn't black enough. Meanwhile, the two free cops, wanting to make a contribution, latched onto Po's shoulders so that he couldn't flop. The cop in front of him was talking so fast the spittle flew from his lips, but the words didn't register, not the way the blood was pounding in Po's ears. Everything started to get light and floaty. Then there was a rush of air into his lungs and the billy club went away.

"I don't want any more shit," the cop in charge was saying. "All I want is for you to listen how it's going to be. Got it?"

Po' coughed and nodded.

"Maybe you were wondering why we brought you here instead of the station?"

Not anymore he wasn't.

"You're down here," the cop said, "so that nobody will know you got collared, so that you can go back out on the street and find out where Lyle Brown is, so that we can bust down some goddamn doors and save his ass before this whole city goes up in flames. How we doing?"

Po' assured him they were doing fine, that there was nothing he wanted more than to cooperate because anytime someone even mentioned his going back to jail he couldn't shit straight for days. The cop in charge liked his attitude so much he put an arm around Po's shoulder and led him out of the machinery room. Except for a short pause at the door to undo his handcuffs and let him glance back at what he'd escaped, Po' was embarked on a whole new profession—Mr. Snitch.

18

In the morning Jan found Haywood stationed on the patio, one hand on the yellow garden hose, the other pressing the phone receiver to his ear. She kept her distance until he was done shouting over the phone. After slamming the receiver down, he squeezed the hose nozzle tight, raking squash leaves with its spray.

Jan raised her voice to say, "I tried talking to that boy."

"Sound like you didn't try hard enough," he said, letting the squash plants have one last blast.

"His mother wouldn't let me talk to him."

"Then I better have a word with her," he said, throwing the garden hose aside and rolling toward the house.

"Not without Felicia," Jan said, holding her ground.

"You saw how she was," Haywood said, stopping before her.

"Maybe some rest helped."

"Only thing make her better is getting hold of Lyle."

"We'll need someone to talk us past this boy's mother," Jan said. "And I doubt that's you."

"What's this *we* shit?"

"Who knows *where* the boy is?" Jan asked.

That brought Haywood up short. "You trying to use some kind of *voice* on me?"

"I'm trying to tell you that it's not worth going over there without Felicia, so I'm not going over without Felicia, so maybe we better go see about going over there *with* Felicia."

Haywood's mouth contorted, but in the end he pushed himself to Felicia's back door, muttering, and let them in. Felicia had moved from the blankets Jan had laid out for her into the bedroom, where she lay facing the red numbers of her digital alarm clock. Her eyes were open but not blinking. Jan perched on the edge of the bed and put a hand on Felicia's leg.

"It's morning."

"That's good," Felicia said after a moment. Her voice was clear but listless.

"Are you hungry?"

"I just ate," Felicia said. "Got to keep my strength up, you know."

That sounded hopeful but when Jan checked over her shoulder, she found Haywood shaking his head as if their exchange was pitiful. "She ain't been out of that bed," he said.

"Do you want a shower?" Jan asked Felicia. "To help you get up and going."

"Going where?"

"Haywood's suggested we talk to the boy we rescued. I think it's a good idea. We might learn something that could help Lyle."

"Then let's go," Felicia said, sitting up without warning. She'd slept the night in her blouse and skirt, and her hair was a series of peaks and valleys.

"First we have to get you feeling better," Jan said.

She guided Felicia down the hall to the bathroom and listened at the door until the shower was turned on. Returning to the kitchen, she put water on to boil, toasted some English muffins, and scrambled eggs with cheese and green olives, which was as close to a usable vegetable as she could find in the house. Haywood was underfoot all the while.

"You're handy with a phone," Jan finally said to him. "Why don't you see what you can find out about this Isiah we rescued. He lives over in the Oak Hills projects."

"You tellin' me what to do?"

"Only because we're such good friends."

"Don't get smart," the brother said. "There probably only two or three hundred Isiah's running around over there."

"Isiah Lawrence."

"That ain't much," he said, moving toward the back door, "but at least it's something. I'll see what's shakin'."

For the rest of the morning, Jan had Felicia to herself. Occasionally she could hear Haywood through the center wall of the bungalow, but the words weren't distinct and she was too busy reminding Felicia to chew or put down the cup she'd been holding for five minutes to pay much attention to the brother. As the morning advanced, Felicia crept out of her shell. It wasn't anything Jan said that brought her around, for Jan couldn't think of much beyond "Everything will be all right," which sounded so simpleminded she soon quit saying it. Whatever restored Felicia's willpower had to have come from inside her.

"I'm not being much help, am I?" Felicia said after changing into jeans and a dark knit shirt.

"You're doing fine."

"What are the police telling you?"

"That they're doing everything they can," Jan said. It wasn't until after the fact that she realized she'd said it without the slightest hesitation. Now wasn't the time to reveal what *everything* included and what it didn't.

"Did you say something about that boy we found?" Felicia asked, making prolonged eye contact for the first time.

"That I think we should talk to him."

"I don't know if I can."

Jan didn't push it and within a half hour Felicia had convinced herself they'd didn't have much choice. That's when her training as a social worker kicked in, or maybe it was just good common sense; either way, she didn't call the Lawrence family cold. She made three other calls first, starting with a preacher who referred her to another preacher who gave her the name of a mother whose daughter had been helped out of a scrape or two by Felicia. She explained to the mother that she wanted someone to vouch for her to Isiah Lawrence's mother, and that was how when Felicia finally called the boy's home, she had a longer, more fruitful conversation than Jan had. Haywood had rejoined them in the middle of all the phone calls, but hearing Felicia in action, he had nothing to say until Felicia was finished talking.

"Count me in," he said.

"She told me to come alone."

"Then who going to ask the hard questions?"

"They're scared people."

"That kid knows something," Haywood said. "You can count on it."

"You can't shout it out of him," Felicia said.

"Poison for poison."

"Can I say something?" Jan asked.

"Not to my ears," Haywood told her.

"Felicia," Jan said, "I think you better take us along."

"But the mother said—"

"You may need our support," Jan said, overriding her objections.

"What if they won't let you in?" Felicia said.

"Tell them I helped save their boy's life. Tell them Haywood is Lyle's brother. That ought to buy us some goodwill."

"You keep saying *us,*" Felicia said.

"She got it half right," Haywood said.

"Which half?" Felicia asked.

"My half," Haywood said. "No way I'm trusting anything what's white."

"Listen to you talk," Felicia said. "I never heard of you trusting any other color either."

"Somebody got to do the sayin'."

"As far as concerns me," Felicia said, "Jan's on our side. If there's any half won't be going, it's your half. You'll only spout something out you shouldn't."

"But that may be exactly what we need," Jan said, which quieted all objections, including the naggy ones she had been keeping all to herself.

BEFORE LEAVING, FELICIA loaned Jan a change of clothes, since her uniform wasn't going to help open any doors. She ended up in a lavender blouse and white slacks whose waist had to be safety-pinned—Felicia had two dress sizes on her. Then followed an argument over whether a hat would help matters. That was when Jan knew it wasn't just her uniform they were worrying about.

The color of her skin must have ranked right up there too, although neither of them asked her to drop out. She suspected that was because both of them were afraid they might need help with the other one. In the end they decided on a billed cap that was white with blue crossed tennis rackets on the front.

They drove a van specially equipped for the handicapped, Felicia behind the wheel, Haywood's wheelchair locked into place on the passenger's side, Jan in back. The closer they drew to the projects, the more often Felicia said, "Are we all right?" She repeated it so often that Jan and Haywood quit answering.

"On the street," Haywood said while they were stopped at a signal light, "they call this boy Jump. I learned that much over the phone."

"He'd been jumped, all right," Jan said, watching the road from over Felicia's shoulder. They'd already left the neighborhoods where pride of ownership kept the homes looking like cupcakes and had moved into an area where the gingerbread man had long since flown the coop. Felicia's eyes kept darting to the side mirrors as though somebody might steal the back of the van.

"Usually he the one doing the jumpin'," Haywood said. "He some kind of b–ball player, one they claimin' got a future. That probably what landed him in that basement."

"Basketball?"

"His future. I'm hearin' he might be Gold and them Sevens grabbed him for some kind of get-back. Drugs got to be at the bottom, and they wanted the best example they could get."

"So what are we asking him?" Jan said.

"Basics. Do he know where Lyle is."

"You just said he wasn't a Seven."

"So?"

"How's he going to know?"

"Lady, don't matter what color he flies, after what them Sevens done to him, he motivated to know. He got some cuz or friend of a cuz or some trash-talker some cuz know from juv cen or rat city, or whatever. News buzzes."

"All right," Felicia said, raising her voice above both theirs, "we lay our cards on the table. That to your liking?"

Haywood snorted and said, "This kid only shit on them cards."

"Then what?" Felicia said.

"We're all ears," Jan added.

"Simple," Haywood said. "We offer this punk money. He ain't no NBA millionaire yet."

Felicia started to object but swallowed instead. Jan didn't raise her voice at all. They pulled into the project's parking lot arguing about who would make the pitch. It wasn't much of an argument since Haywood was the only one who really wanted the job.

19

It was early Thursday morning when they released Po'. He hit the street running, literally, to catch a number 13. The buses were running again, on a limited schedule and with police escorts. Claiming it might blow his cover, the big shots wouldn't spring for a taxi, so he rode public transportation, pretending all the while that he couldn't hear any homing device buzzing and crackling on the top of his head. The other passengers played along too. It was too early for any Seven who knew anything to be up, and since he didn't have anywhere safe to lie low, he rode buses and dozed for several hours. Near noon he got off near the vacant lot beside the Top Hat Liquor store. Three clean cars were parked on that weedy patch, and the four or five brothers who were socializing greeted Po' with a glad hello and the hooked-finger Seven sign.

"What's happenin', Po' man?"

"Got nothin' happenin'."

"Then how come you got the top of yo' head taped like that?"

"LaDonna tried out her new phone on me."

"You affordin' a phone?"

"Not me, man. LaDonna. And she ain't got it plugged into nothin'. It just sittin' there on the table to admire. That all."

"Like decoration?"

"That it."

"Shit, I could a made prime use of that cash."

"That what I say," Po' answered, rubbing a hand over his head as if in painful memory.

"I hear you, man. Say, you know that Big Bark and Catfoot huntin' fo' you?"

"That right?" Po' said, sounding uninterested as possible. At least Big Bark and Catfoot, the real names of his partners in the failed bust-out, appeared to be lying low without bragging on their exploits. That much was good, but considering his new profession, Po' wasn't exactly eager for a reunion with his old friends. Instead, he glossed over their interest in finding him by switching topics. "Say, you hear 'bout this Lyle Brown? The hospital cop been missin'?"

"Who ain't?"

"What they mean sayin' some Seven snatched him?"

"Who else got balls 'nough?"

"I'm secondin' that," said Po', ready to be on his way, since no one was giving off those little signs indicating they were in the know. But he wasn't ready quite yet. This snitch business made for a thirst, so he pulled on an offered bottle or two before departing.

"You hear that buzzin' sound?" Po asked, tapping the side of his head.

"That the twentieth century, man."

"That too scary for me," said Po', edging away. "Think Big Bark's down at the blue house?"

"Good guess."

"Then I's off."

"Don't be turnin' yo' back on no Golds."

"They still rattlin' 'round these streets?"

"Took a shot at Johnny Toots over on Causeway."

"Hit him?"

"Mostly."

"Ain't nowhere safe?"

"Nowhere the sun shines ain't."

"And quite a few places it don't," Po' said, walking backwards down the street.

HIS NEXT STOP was as far from the blue house as he could get on foot. He picked the Triangle Park farther down Claremont Avenue for some more of the same.

"Here come Po'."

"Hide the women."

"Food too."

"Ain't no women fool 'nough to be with you dogs," said Po'.

"They heard you comin'."

"Like that hat, Po'."

"That hat look mo' like a bandage to me."

"You seen Big Bark or Catfoot?" Po' asked. "They supposed to be wantin' me."

"You know Big Bark don' come near here no mo', not since he got popped behind the fountain."

"That right," Po' said. "Forgot. Say, you had the po-lice-men houndin' you over this Lyle Brown shit?"

"Anybody who anybody been pulled on that one," said one man.

"Oh yeah?" said another. "They missed me."

"What they mean," Po' said, "trying to say some Seven snatched him?"

"Maybe they right."

"Yeah?" Po said, arching an eyebrow in disbelief. "Who got balls that size?"

"Don' know 'xactly, but it have to be a Seven."

"Listen," Po' said, leaning closer, "I caught somethin' whoever got that Lyle Brown should know 'bout."

"That straight?"

"As my dick."

"I seen that dogleg."

"Listen, man, this is serious shit. You know that."

A moment of weighing Po's eyes, then, "Talk to the Milkman. I heard he's knowin' something."

"That one of his ad campaigns? Or fact?"

"With Milk? You never know. But he is on that information highway, you know that, Po'. Just don' tell him I sent you."

"That right. I never seen your lips move."

SINCE HE DIDN'T know where to find the Milkman until later in the day, he hoofed over to LaDonna's place. She'd changed the lock on him again and wouldn't answer the bell. Not until she didn't come screaming out of nowhere as he pushed in the bedroom screen did he figure the coast was clear. He collected the few clothes he kept there and swept off his shelf in the medicine cabinet. All that fit in a diaper bag once he dumped out the rattles and other shit. A quick once-through of dresser drawers and cupboards didn't turn up any cash, which only meant that LaDonna had some new hideaway. The month was too new for there not to be money, but he didn't have time to tear the place apart proper and anyway, maybe she was hiding it at one of her sisters' places. She'd pulled that before.

Going into the bedroom closet, he lifted out the laundry basket, dumped it upside down, and began filling it with whatever looked like cash. He selected the new cordless phone, a baby monitor, a CD player, a TV with a screen smaller than his hand, and from the kitchen he grabbed up a toaster oven, electric mixer, and a set of carving knives that LaDonna was all done threatening him with. Then he sacked out for a nap that got interrupted some time later when a key jiggled the front lock. He left the same way he'd entered—through the back screen window.

AT THE PAWNSHOP the bearded guy behind the counter acted as though everything was broken, the same way he did whenever Po' brought in a haul. For once Po' took his first offer, which left the clerk stunned, as if he'd overbid. He counted out nine twenties in a grumble.

On the way to the doc's office where his cousin worked, Po' mailed the pawnshop stub to LaDonna, just to be fair. At the doc's office, he motioned his cousin, the receptionist, into the hall.

"What ran over you?" she asked.

"Justice."

"Got you good," she said, stepping to the side for a better look. "You still runnin' with those hoodlums?"

"No way. Got me a job as a minister's assistant."

"Now you addin' lying to your list of accomplishments?" But she was smiling.

"I was wonderin' 'bout an X ray of this thing," Po' said, pointing at his head.

"Look like you already got it fixed."

"Down at the General don' count."

"How you going to pay?" she asked, no longer smiling. His last two visits had gone on her tab.

He lifted the twenties from his shirt pocket.

"Oh, Po'," she said, disappointed, "I thought you was all done payin' cash for things."

But she peeled off four twenties and told him to take a seat with everyone else. The X ray failed to reveal anything that didn't belong in his head, not that the proof helped to relax him. They could make things so small these days. After his X rays, he went back to riding the bus until he figured the Milkman would be on duty at Aunty Thea's convenience store.

20

Jan pushed Haywood's wheelchair and let Felicia lead the way. The Oak Hills projects, known on the street as Shotgun Mountain, were a flawed maze of WWII barracks sprinkled in a fairy ring around a pair of thirteen-story towers. The city fathers had gotten the temporary barracks for a patriotic song after agreeing to throw up the towers. In the years since the city had sung that song, the barracks had sagged, rotted, and frequently been mistaken for kindling.

The faces they passed were either black, mulatto brown, or Southeast Asian brown. They proceeded from the parking lot and its open-air auto mechanics past a playground teeming with child energy and up a sidewalk lined by ancient oaks that offered the only protection from the sun along their route. Haywood did all the talking.

"Don't go naming any prices," he said. He said it twice, in fact.

The yard in front of the unit where Felicia stopped had a clothesline strung with light blue sheets that hung limply in the heavy air, but there wasn't anything limp about the woman in the gray shift who answered the door. Somewhere between age forty and sixty, she looked fit enough to take a mule to forty stump-filled acres and make it bountiful. Her hair was pulled back in a bun; her brown face was round and her cheeks full.

"Mrs. Lawrence," Felicia said, "we're only here because—"

"Mrs. Malbarth," the woman corrected. "Elvera Malbarth."

"But you are Isiah Lawrence's mother?"

"Oh yes," the woman said without offering any explanations for the name mutations. "Who the man in the wheelchair?"

"Lyle Brown's brother."

"And the gal pushing him?"

"The woman who helped me rescue your son."

"Aiming for all our heartstrings, that it? Well, I'm giving you five minutes, not one tick more. Am I understood?"

"Yes, ma'am."

"My boy's still recovering from what they done to him."

To get Haywood inside, Mrs. Malbarth flagged down two passing boys in high-school letter jackets. They carried the wheelchair up the steps easily as a glass of water. For their efforts, Mrs. Malbarth directed them toward the kitchen, where a woman was cooking better than she could sing. The house was filled with wonderful whiffs of spicy food that cloaked an underlying scent of medicine.

"I'm tasting home ribs," Haywood said, turning gracious.

"Save your butter," Elvera Malbarth said. "Isiah's back this way."

THEY FOLLOWED HER to a small back bedroom whose contents fit together tight as a puzzle. There was a double bed, a cot, a straight-backed chair, an AC wheezing in a window, two dressers, and a nightstand covered with prescription bottles. That didn't count people or pets. An old woman in her nightgown sat up in the bed; a gray, long-hair cat with milky-white eyes was stretched out on her lap. Isiah Lawrence occupied the straight-backed chair on the near side of the bed. He wore a satiny bathrobe whose sleeves hadn't kept up to his wrists for a year or two. The swelling in his eyes had gone down but his lips remained chapped. To see his guests he had to tilt his head back and squint. The ceiling light was on but it was a low-watt bulb that left the room dim.

"These the people what saved you from those friends of yours," Elvera Malbarth said. "The friends what mistake you for an ashtray."

"No friends of mine," Isiah Lawrence muttered.

The bedridden granny spoke up then, patting the green chenille bedspread and saying to Felicia, "Sit with me, child."

Felicia lowered herself to the edge of the bed, right next to Elvera Malbarth, who remained standing, arms crossed. Since Jan couldn't push Haywood's rear wheels through the narrow door, Haywood sat halfway in the bedroom, Jan behind him. Then followed a pause long and graceful as the *Kitty Hawk*'s maiden voyage.

"Do you know who I am?" Felicia asked at last.

"Know," Isiah Lawrence said.

"And about what happened to my man, Lyle Brown?"

"It on all the TVs," the mother said when her son didn't answer. "He know."

"We're trying to reach the people who have him," Felicia said.

"I ain't no Seven," the boy said. "Don't know nothin' 'bout your man."

"Save that jive-ass for the neighbors," Haywood piped up, patient for as long as he could stand it. "I'm here to tell you we can't count on no white cop to save no black ass, and if Lyle Brown my brother, then black got to be the color of his ass. So don' go tellin' me the phone line busy, hear?"

The way Elvera Malbarth was swelling up, Haywood's stump speech would have been their ticket out of there if not for a toddler who had sneaked up behind Jan and, frightened by Haywood's demands, started bawling. The child's operatic wails started Felicia sniffling, which flustered Elvera Malbarth into swallowing their marching orders and stretching out her arms instead.

"Hand that child over," she told Jan.

As Jan reached for the little girl, the child's eyes popped wider and her decibels went for the room's glass. The child started kicking, which caused Jan to nearly drop her on Haywood's head. Elvera Malbarth couldn't comfort her either. That honor went to Isiah Lawrence, who scooped her onto his lap with his good arm. Only then did the child fall silent, clinging to the lapels of his bathrobe and burying her face against his chest. Not until the child started nuzzling did Jan see that she was the boy's daughter.

"That about enough for one day," Elvera Malbarth announced.

"I hear their man's dead," her son said, not about to let his mother do all his talking.

Felicia's head panned so slowly toward Isaiah Lawrence that it looked as though she was fighting the motion all the way.

"Don't be telling us no lies," Haywood said. "We come prepared to pay hard cash for the truth."

"It appears to me," Elvera Malbarth said, looking fire at Haywood, "that you got what he knows for free. Now out, 'cause you done talkin' insults in my house."

"I'm talkin' five C-notes," said Haywood.

"Boys," Elvera Malbarth called out to the kitchen, "come and take this nasty thing away."

Jan stepped aside to let the two letter jackets at Haywood, who didn't shut up all the way out of the house. Felicia stayed behind long enough to apologize, "You'll have to excuse us, Mrs. Malbarth, but we in harm's way." To Isiah Lawrence, she said, "Are you meaning what you're saying about my Lyle?"

He looked away rather than answer.

"You answer her," Elvera Malbarth said.

He cursed under his breath before saying, "Maybe it not true. They sayin' every kind of thing out on the street."

And that's where they left it. Jan had to drive the van home because Felicia couldn't manage to unlock its door, her hand was shaking so bad. All the way back Haywood chewed them out for having such nice manners. Once at the bungalow, he went inside, swearing he'd handle everything himself. All Felicia said was, "I think I'd better lie down." She ended up back in the same fetal position that Jan had found her in that morning. For a minute she lay there without speaking, then she jumped up and unplugged the clock. Climbing back into bed, she stared at the stalled timepiece as if she'd finally done something to help Lyle.

WITHIN THE NEXT hour Jan had told Felicia a half-dozen times that she didn't believe Lyle was gone. The first time she'd said it, she fumbled the last word, having no idea how to say it, but eventually she'd settled on "gone" and had stuck to it ever since. She sat beside Felicia without touching her. At first she'd rested her hand on her friend's leg, but Felicia lay so still, almost inanimate, that Jan soon withdrew her hand, feeling unsure of herself and, worse, foolish. That was when she put a cork on the clichés. At least she felt vindicated for not having sprung the whole truth on her friend.

She could hear Haywood on the other side of the bungalow, roaring over the phone. The words were indistinct, the tone familiar. Whenever he quit delivering insults the house became so still she could hear cars passing by. A half hour later a door slammed, and she made it to the living room window in time to spy Haywood rolling himself down the front sidewalk toward a Datsun pickup. A huge black man in an orange jumpsuit got out from behind the wheel and met Haywood at the gate. He had the impassive face of a drill sergeant, and whatever Haywood was saying didn't soften his expression one bit. Not until money passed hands did he transfer Haywood to the pickup's front seat. He picked Haywood up from behind, as if handling an awkward stick of furniture, and seat-belted him in. Folding up the wheelchair, he tossed it in the back of the pickup, next to an old refrigerator tipped on its side. Haywood was jawing all the while.

THE REST OF the afternoon Jan trod lightly around the house. She changed back into her uniform and made a call home. At least her girls hadn't tied Claire to a chair yet. A little before six a car door closed and she parted the drapes in time to see Haywood dropped back into his wheelchair by the man in the orange jumpsuit. As Haywood rolled himself up the ramp to his half of the house, Jan hurried out Felicia's back door to greet him.

"You don't look encouraged," she said.

"You still here?"

"Somebody has to watch Felicia."

"I guess," he said, backing down a bit. "I went to talk to Sevens, all the good it did me. The punks I found all got a bad case of the dumbs."

"Does that mean you're able to stay with Felicia tonight?"

"What for? She ain't the one been kidnapped."

"I'm worried about what she might do."

"So go on, git. I never thought we needed your hand in this anyway."

"You'll check in on her?"

"I ain't got nothing more to say to you," Haywood answered, but he rolled himself around Jan and toward Felicia's door.

By the time Jan got home she had an urgent message waiting from Agent Ford. When she called his number, the agent answered on the first ring, his voice breaking apart over a celullar phone.

"We're tailing one of the boys who tried springing Penshorn, and I think he's about to lead us to water. What I need is someone who can ID Lyle Brown."

"That's me," Jan said, taking down instructions on where to meet him.

She gave any daughter or mother between herself and the door a peck on the cheek and was soon driving to a mall clear across town. Nobody passed her on the way.

21

Po' rode buses until five, when the Milkman punched in. Slipping into Aunty Thea's Milk and Stuff Superette, he inspected snack foods until he was sure the coast was clear. The only other customer was an old man leaning heavily on a cane and carrying a can of tuna toward the front counter fast as a tortoise might. Satisfied, Po' aimed for the dairy case. Three times he knocked on the frosted glass door farthest to the right. When he opened the cooler door, a voice issued out from behind the one-percent half-gallon cartons.

"What size rock you after, man?"

"Need a word. It Po'."

From inside the cooler a mittened hand parted the milk cartons, a steady eye peered out, a suspicious voice said, "Out back."

Po' bought a marked-up half-gallon anyway, its price being the Milkman's rent. Leaving the carton on the counter, he went outside to circle around back and sit by a Dumpster that Aunty Thea should have had emptied last week. Five minutes later the Milkman, still wearing his work clothes—parka hood up, felt boot liners on—joined him, looking friendly as Po's parole officer.

"You smell like cops," the Milkman said without sitting down.

" 'Course I do," Po' said. "Had them breathin' on me most this mornin'."

"And *now* you need a word with me?"

"Someone say you might know dirt 'bout this hospital cop been missin'. I overheard somethin' they might need to know."

"Someone told you wrong," said the Milkman, but he didn't head back to his cooler, either. He squatted down on his haunches so that he was only a head taller than Po'. "Leave it here and anyone needs it, I'll pass it on."

"Needs faster than that," Po' said. "What I heard them cops say, someone been talkin'."

"So what the heat plannin'?" the Milkman said, turning confidential.

"Big headlines."

The Milkman removed his mittens to blow on his hands before saying, "I don' know nothin' 'bout this shit. Goods like you dealin', there only one man to be tellin' that to."

"You think?"

"Man, I know. And don' be tellin' ol' Z.Z. I sent you."

The Milkman pointed in warning at Po's nose before returning inside and leaving Po' more alone than he'd ever been in his entire life, which was plenty after subtracting social workers, foster parents, and counselors.

There wasn't any creature from the black lagoon had anything on Z.Z. Rip. The man had enough respect to propel himself past the moon. He wasn't *a* Seven, he was *the* Seven, the one you went to when desperate for a mad dog to settle a dispute. Po' knew he could never look in Z.Z.'s all-knowing eyes and tell a straight lie. Yet that's where he appeared to be headed. Time was running out. Sooner rather than later either Big Bark or Catfoot would start talkin' up their adventure. They'd wonder out loud how Po' got away when the last they saw of him a hospital guard was trying to tune his skull. Then people on the street would start remembering his questions. They'd recall how he drifted on so quick and tried to act too cool. They'd know he had a new profession. Maybe all that had gone down already, which left him but one option: Los Angeles.

DEPARTING THE MILKMAN'S back door, Po' hopped a city bus to a suburban mall, where he searched for a hardware store to buy a plain old screwdriver, a pair of pliers, and some rubber hose for siphoning. The closest he found was a specialty shop called One Universe which sold him a gadget that included a screwdriver and pliers, along with thirteen other tools he'd never heard of and never would have a use for on this planet. It cost him fifty dollars, no rubberhose included. It did come with a handcrafted leather carrying pouch that could be worn on his belt but which he stuffed in his diaper bag along with all his other worldly possessions. He'd have to pick a hose up off some lawn, 'cause he sure couldn't buy gas all the way across the country. Back at the bus stop he read the schedule and discovered he had at least a forty-five-minute wait before the next arrival, when he would have to get on board or risk looking suspicious to whatever mall cops were lurking about. Taking a seat on the bench, he surveyed the rows of parked cars before him.

A half hour later a Bonneville, whose color of scarlet had an appealing shimmer in the evening light, pulled into a handicapped parking spot right before him. A woman in high heels got out and wobbled for the doors of a mall restaurant, looking as though her handicap came in bottles from Kentucky. Five minutes later she had yet to return. Po collected his diaper bag, sauntered over to the Bonneville, and made himself to home.

Forty minutes later he was topping its tank off at a truck stop on the interstate. The road pointed west into a setting sun that burned so red Po' realized for the first time in his life that it was on fire. On the way out of town he had shouted good-bye to everyone that mattered by rolling his window down when the freeway curved by LaDonna's place. If his luck held, he might take a breather in Vegas; otherwise, it was a straight shot to LA and a new life in his own little witness protection program.

His luck held about as well as it had for most of his life. He didn't reach the end of the gas-station drive before three unmarked cop cars boxed him in. There wasn't any need for the I-forgot-to-pay routine, not when the cop climbing out of the nearest car was the snappy dresser who wore the gold bracelet and liked to do all the talking. It was then that Po' knew he hadn't been anywhere near as alone all day as he'd felt.

The cop climbed in the front seat with his gun drawn, which

struck Po' as overplay but he raised his hands just the same. Sliding in back was a small white woman dressed in a hospital cop's threads. She had glossy black hair and didn't once take her eyes off the cop up front, which gave Po' the impression she didn't trust the head cop any more than he did.

"Need to talk to someone out this way?" the cop asked, minus a hello.

"This ain't the way to your office?"

The cop's eyebrows crashed together and he reached across the front seat, cupped a hand behind Po's head, and pulled him forward until their foreheads nearly touched.

"Can the shit, son. I want to know what you've got."

Po' saw right away that a lie was called for. Most days it was like that. The truth didn't get much exercise.

"You'll let me go to LA?"

"Buy your ticket."

Po' nodded as if he believed him and said, "It's slippery. Word is, they keep movin' him."

"Who's they?"

"The lid's down tight on that."

The cop snapped his fingers as if he didn't already own Po's complete attention. "Let's not forget the alternatives."

"I'm not sayin' my hand's empty," Po' added. "But, mister, there's some things it's safer to run with."

The cop didn't act impressed, and Po' understood it was his job to leave him wowed. He also knew better than to answer right away. A lie would come out fast, but any facts would travel slow, as though they were pulling a hook up his throat.

"I maybe might have a lock on where they plannin' to trade for Rainy."

"Go," the cop said, all concentration.

"I'm hearin' Triangle Park where that footbridge cross the freeway."

"How?"

"Mister, I 'bout got my ass burned findin' out where."

"All right, when?"

"They enjoyin' stringin' you along too much to figure that out yet."

"Well, that's your next project," the cop said, patting Po' on the shoulder as if they were some kind of pals. His voice took on some edge, though. "And you better hope you find out before we do." Making a forward-ho motion to the cars surrounding them, he said, "We'll ride with you. Who knows, you might get this loaner back before they call in the FBI."

No one laughed but Po', who cut the chuckles short, wishing the woman in back would say something so that he wouldn't have to keep repeating "I don't know" all the way back into town. She didn't talk, though, not until one of the unmarked cars trailing behind put a red flasher on its dash. By then they'd already penetrated the outer suburb's industrial parks.

"I think we're being paged," she said.

Checking over his shoulder, the cop up front ordered, "Pull over."

Once they'd stopped, a short-legged man from the car following them jogged up to them in the twilight. Into the cop's open passenger window the runner said, "They just got ransom instructions."

"What specifics?" the cop seated beside Po' said, an eager crispness entering his words.

"How to connect up with them on the Lake Shore Causeway."

"Nothing more?"

"A time."

"How long have we got?"

The man checked his watch. "An hour plus twenty-eight."

"I want every available surveillance team on the ground. Dispatch them to a city park called the Triangle." To Po', "Where's that at?"

"Claremont and sixty-something," Po' answered, feeling a shiver work his spine. A city cop should know the Triangle.

"Tell them to concentrate on the footbridge over the freeway." Snapping his fingers, he turned back to Po'. "What freeway passes there?"

"Lake Shore," Po' said, grateful that it did but weak about the one chance in two or three zillion that his lie wasn't a lie.

"That's it, then," said the cop, pumping his fist as if the cards were all his. "Everything's long distance until my signal." To the inside of the stolen car, he added, "We move back to one of the radio units."

He had to wave his pistol before Po' came around enough to oblige.

22

When Lyle's blindfold started slipping, all bets were off. The scarf folded and tied around his eyes loosened up the third night after the gunslinger freed his hands, and just his hands, for some calisthenics. It was the sit-ups that got him in trouble. Each time the back of his head rubbed the cement floor, the blindfold shifted.

Later, after his hands were taped back up and he was dropped back in his seat, sleep came a dozen times. When he stirred in the morning, the outer corner of his blindfold had slipped even farther. Through the remaining thin layer of red he had a gauzy view of the garage cluttered with engine parts as well as a look at the woman now guarding him. Her body was a major chunk of work, a figure that looked like five or six stuffed laundry bags tied together. The bathroom scale must have gone the limit when she stepped on. She had a nose that was mostly nostril and a 'do that was plastered to her scalp with treatment and arranged in paisley spit curls. When she drew near enough to drop Lyle's breakfast on his lap, her pores looked big as craters. Picking her out of a lineup would be no problem, and he knew it was only a matter of time before they knew he'd become a liability.

Shortly after the noontime news the automatic door went up and the two ringleaders pulled an orange Toronado into the garage. Moments later, Lyle got a solid look at the both of them: short, boxer ugly, jailhouse muscles. A few years older than the others, they had a way of sizing people up as if measuring the distance to their chins. If they were brothers, the family tree had some pit bull in it.

Today they'd brought a visitor, a young guy dressed in a bathrobe and needing a hand out of the rear car door. He shuffled toward Lyle in slippers. Around the eyes his face was puffy as rising bread, and he pressed a hand against his rib cage with each step. In between steps he wheezed, sounding as if rice paper and balsa were rubbing inside him. Drawing close enough for Lyle to smell Bengay, the kid lifted a hand toward Lyle's forehead and that's when it happened.

Lyle blinked.

The hand hung in midair and for an instant Lyle's eye locked up with the kid's swollen eyes, only sheer red scarf separating them. Then the kid's hand continued upward, his fingers tracing a path across Lyle's forehead and down his nose. His touch wasn't light, like a torturer's might be; it was rougher, as if he wanted to make sure Lyle was really there in front of him. Unexpectedly and without comment, he pulled on the blindfold as if testing whether it was secure. The tug moved it back into place. Once again Lyle was safely blind.

"Haven't they done any carvin' on you yet?" the sick kid asked, jabbing a finger against Lyle's brass name tag.

Lyle didn't have enough spit to answer.

"We dullin' the knives up," the head talker promised.

"S'pose they feedin' you steak and caviar?" the sick kid said, again jabbing Lyle's tag.

"B-burgers," said Lyle, unable to remember ever stuttering before.

"He's plump," the head man agreed. Then, without warning, he flew into a rage, screaming at the woman guard, "Turn off that blah-blah-blah." Once the TV voices went away, he added conversationally to the sick kid, "We wanted you to see this."

"I 'preciate it."

"You want us to do some cuttin' on him, just say the word."

"Not to *this* one."

"I hear you, man," said the head guy. "I hear you. We goin' to get this *all* square. You, Little Donny, everything. Don' sweat that." Then loudly to the guard, "This guy been givin' you trouble?"

"Only his past lives," the woman answered.

"Good," the head man said as if her answer made perfect sense to him. Poking a finger into Lyle's throat, he went on, "We got some work fo' you."

There was a click followed by a whir that ended with another click.

"Say this shit the way I do," the head man said. "Start when you hear the click."

And then they got down to work. Minus the clicks, Lyle repeated the following for a tape recorder:

"This is Lyle. I'm all right. But you have to set Rainy Penshorn free to get me out of here. Follow these instructions: Put Rainy Penshorn in a car with only a driver. Drive south on the Lake Shore Causeway between the McKinley and Merrimack exits at ten sharp tonight. Watch for an orange Toronado traveling slow in the far right lane. Follow him. When he stops, you stop. Not too close. Your driver meets their man halfway. He tells you how to find me. Don't fuck up or I'm fucked."

Turning off the tape recorder, the head guy said, "You really will be, man."

THAT NIGHT THEY transferred him to a car whose backseat felt big and roomy as a Toronado's might, but he didn't feel surrounded by orange, however that might feel. The woman guard and the womanizing guard were up front, ragging on each other about who should be driving. The woman got the wheel and must have nearly broken it off the steering column, the corners they were taking. Forty-seven turns later, they pulled over. The woman got out and padded past Lyle's door on what sounded like gravel. She opened the car's trunk, lifted something out, moved away.

"How long's this going to take?" Lyle asked.

"Don' sweat it, man. If it takin' too long, you'll know 'cause you dead."

The woman returned and the other guard hit a button to lower his window.

"All set," she said.

"We got a couple three minutes," the man told her.

With the window down, Lyle could hear traffic on a nearby freeway and high overhead a jet. The sounds of freedom. A long time later the woman opened his door.

"Just cooperate," she told him, "and we all done pokin' you."

She walked him across twenty yards' worth of gravel and pushed him down on a folding chair. There was a breeze and there were bugs on the breeze. One batted against his cheek; after that, he made sure his mouth was shut. Something hummed above him, probably lights. Something flapped too, sounding like bats with six-foot wing spans. Maybe they'd carry him away. Outside of the car's AC, he could smell the lake. The rushing sounds of the freeway were directly in front of him, so close it felt as though he might get hit.

"Stay put, Juicy," the woman said and left him sitting there.

He heard the car doors slam but didn't hear them drive off. So they were sitting in the air-conditioning waiting for whatever was going to happen to happen.

23

They stuck Jan behind the steering wheel because she knew Lyle by sight. They shoved Po' Rind in back, behind the driver's seat, to play Rainy Penshorn. On such short notice he was the only believable stand-in they could lay their hands on. Agent Ford didn't bother reminding her that they weren't trotting out the real Penshorn.

"Ain't you got some professional nigger achin' to prove hisself?" Po' asked.

"You're it," said Agent Ford, who was crouching behind the passenger seat with a pistol filling one hand, a two-way radio the other, but no knife between his pearly white teeth.

They were all cozy in an LTD equipped with AC and a motor big enough to make a bootlegger blush. The foot feed was hair-trigger, causing some false starts until Jan got the hang of it. Agent Ford maintained constant radio contact with two unmarked cars several blocks behind them and with the welcoming committee setting up shop on the side streets leading to the Triangle Park, where—Po' continued to swear—the trade was going down. The closer they drew to the park, the faster Po' swore. At first he directed his oaths to the agent, and later to Jan, but since neither of them would answer, he started making vows to himself too. In fact, everyone on board was talking. Jan moved her lips silently, and Agent Ford code-talked over his radio, sounding like a sports weenie all wrapped up in the pennant race. At intervals he relayed the standings to Jan.

Traffic was sparse due to the curfew. Jan stayed in the second lane from the right, seeing orange Toronados that turned out to be blue Hondas, red Escorts, and two-tone Saturns as she passed them. She called out the McKinley exit at one minute past ten, and a half mile later she found an orange Toronado that stayed an orange Toronado. Falling in line behind it, she flashed her brights and found herself close enough to read a reflective bumper sticker that said *Get Yours*. Agent Ford had to tell her to back off.

"Bottom of the ninth," Ford broadcast over his radio.

"I only see a driver," Jan reported.

"What you expect?" Po' asked. "You ain't dealin' with no fools." He made it sound as though that honor was all his.

"Just follow him," the agent said. "Their rules until you see Brown. Can you get a license number?"

She eased closer again, read it off, dropped back. Agent Ford relayed the letters and numbers over his two-way, translating it into the name of a Venezuelan shortstop and his batting average. Minutes later he was informed their man had stolen that batting average.

"What if you scare him off?" Po' asked, chuckling over the plates.

"We'll blame it all on you," the agent told him.

Po' was the only one to laugh at that, and not for long.

They exited on Merrimack, drove south for a mile, west on Lexington another mile, a quick turnaround on a cul-de-sac named Primrose, where the Toronado's headlights briefly lit up the tense lines of Jan's face. Then back to Lexington, still convoying west.

"Not the way to the Triangle," Jan observed.

"Of course not," the agent said.

Po' had now grown watchful and silent. In the rearview Jan caught glimpses of him sliding down on his seat every time a car pulled beside them at a signal light.

Then came a dime-turn south onto a residential street, four squealing rights around a block, four more rights—same terrorized block—and a heavy foot back to Lexington.

"This is it," Ford said. "Stick with him." And into the radio: "He's rounding third."

They hurtled beneath streetlights, returning to the causeway. Jan quit talking to herself, needing all her concentration for the taillights ahead of them. At the Lake Shore Causeway they headed south, the direction of the Triangle. When Po' started in with his what-ifs again, Agent Ford did something that took his breath away, then continued talking baseball into his radio.

Jan kept the distance to the Toronado steady even though they were now cruising at over seventy miles per hour, passing everything on the road. They passed the city's pro football stadium and the exit for a well-known Bible college. They hit a long stretch of car dealerships whose floodlights made the inland side of the causeway gleam like midday. The Toronado signaled an exit.

"He's getting off," Jan reported.

"Their rules," Ford reminded her.

"This is too early for the Triangle."

"Ain't no fools," Po' said.

At the end of the off-ramp, they turned left, crossed back over the causeway, and hung a left on a service drive that ran above an incline of riprap leading to the lake. Far out on the dark lake were the green and red running lights of boats, but in closer to shore the water was black and still. They drove north, the only other traffic being a turtle hiking down the center strip. After a mile, the Toronado pulled onto the gravel shoulder. Jan followed suit thirty yards behind him. The driver of the Toronado lit up a cigarette before finally getting out and coming halfway back to the LTD, casually taking a seat on the guardrail overlooking the causeway and the car dealerships on the far side. Puffing on his cigarette, he appeared to be taking in the scenery.

"Nice," Agent Ford said.

"What should I do?" Jan asked.

"Go talk to him. See what he wants."

"Is that safe?"

"I'm back here if he tries anything."

"I guess that's better than having you with me."

"Go," Ford said, unamused.

Outside the car it was hot and buggy and the nearness of the lake didn't comfort. When she got close enough to make out the man's features, she couldn't see anything but a dark ski mask with white circles around the eyes and mouth. It made him look astonished. When she stopped ten feet shy of him, he flicked his cigarette away, sized her up, and said, "You a cop?"

"Don't worry about what I am," Jan told him. "Where's Lyle?"

"You got Rainy Penshorn?"

"Back there. Where's Lyle?"

"Look across the way," he said, waving toward the causeway. The gesture had a rehearsed limpness to it, but the rest of him was coiled, a tautness in his thighs, a twist to his neck. He wore a nylon windbreaker with flared shoulders and an army of zippers. His right fist was buried in a deep pocket.

On the far side of the freeway stretched an Oldsmobile dealership whose floodlights reflected off all the marked-up windshields; above the lot, American flags the size of bedspreads were stirred by a breeze limping in off the lake. Just in front of the first line of cars for sale, at the very end of the line, a tied-up man sat on a folding chair. He was black, had something red around his head, and wore a security uniform from the General. With nearly a hundred yards between them that was all she could tell, except for the fact that a dark sedan was parked on the street twenty to thirty feet to his left. The man in the chair swiveled his head from side to side, always returning his attention to the sedan.

"We don' want no typical cop shit," the man on the guardrail said.

"How am I going to know it's Lyle?"

" 'Cause we get any typical cop shit," the man said, "there's snipers got you in their sights right now."

There didn't appear to be any vantage point for a marksman, save out on the lake. If the Sevens had a navy, now was a hell of a time to learn of it.

"You won' see 'em," the man assured her.

"We're not turning your man over until I know that's our man."

"That's cool," the man said and lifted something from a coat pocket. She crouched, nearly ran, but then saw he was holding out binoculars.

"Set them on the rail."

"We think alike," he said with a chuckle.

He placed them halfway between them and backed off. The bulky binoculars were powerful enough to make it seem as though she could almost reach out and touch the car dealership. She found herself admiring the front grille of a Cutlass. Lowering the binoculars to check how far off she was, she raised them and scanned to the right ten or fifteen feet. It was Lyle, all right. Blindfolded, hands tied behind his back, still in uniform, he appeared alert and uninjured, and he wasn't talking to himself, which was more control than Jan could lay claim to. They were parked a good five miles from the Triangle Park and the cavalry.

"What now?"

"You bring ol' Rainy to me. Me and him drive off. Five minutes pass. I call my homies over there and tell—"

A shot rang out behind them. Jan twisted in time to see the flash from a second shot in the backseat of the LTD.

"Motherfucking . . ." The man leaped off the guardrail and was digging into another pocket.

A car door behind Jan opened. She flattened to the pavement. Po' was shouting, "It's a trap, man! A trap!"

The man near Jan jerked an automatic out, shouting, "Dead meats, lady. Your man's dead meats." But he didn't shoot, just took off running.

That left Jan alone, facedown on the pavement. To one side, Po' was hopping down the riprap leading to the lake. To the other side, the ski-masked man was sprinting toward his open car door. Before the Seven reached the Toronado, Jan picked herself up, ditched the binoculars, and broke for her car. On the way she heard a splash from the lake as Po' Rind dove in, and she also heard a squeal as the orange Toronado fishtailed into the night.

She found Ford crumpled up in back, gun still in hand but the hand looking limp and lifeless. The rest of him was alive, though. He was broadcasting orders when she arrived.

"Close the gap. Close the gap." And to Jan: "Hit it!"

"Lyle's across the highway."

"Follow the one we've got," he said through gritted teeth.

The door Po' had escaped out slammed shut on her takeoff, and the agent fought through a moan to shout for a description of Lyle's whereabouts. Jan slowed enough to yell details over her shoulder. By then the Toronado's bouncing red taillights were a quarter mile ahead of them. Ford broadcast Lyle's position and ordered follow-up. Twice, he made pained, sucking sounds that had Jan afraid to look in the rearview.

"You need a hospital."

"Drive."

She put on a show. By the time they reached the first overpass, she'd cut the Toronado's lead to a block. Swinging left onto the overpass, she ricocheted off a curb and never looked back. Airborne twice, sideswiped once, several one-eighties, and once, thanks to an open fire hydrant, a complete three-sixty.

Fortunately the Toronado was having adventures of its own. One-way streets the heart-stopping way. Sufficient red lights to string a Christmas tree.

They streaked deeper and deeper into the city, and several times it seemed to Jan as though the man in the Toronado had a destination in mind. He fought to make specific streets rather than going helter-skelter with whatever the traffic allowed. After causing a semitrailer to jackknife, she hoped he made it to his hole-in-the-wall soon. Each time she thought Agent Ford had blacked out, he startled her by shouting something into his radio.

Near downtown the Toronado took out the wooden gate of a parking ramp and headed up. Jan ran over the gate's arm seconds later. The two unmarked cars trailing behind broke off to blockade any exits.

Jan squealed around eight tight corners before reaching level four and hitting the brakes hard enough to make Agent Ford gasp. Dead ahead the Toronado was trying to play hide-and-seek amongst the long-term parkers. Its orange paint job and rear bumper sticker made finding it almost too easy.

Within a half minute she had a string of squad cars behind her. Cops were crouching behind open doors everywhere. By then the two unmarked cars reported there was only one way to drive in and one out of the facility. Everyone was feeling pretty good.

It took fifteen minutes' worth of bullhorn and stalking to figure out they were a little premature on the self-congratulations. The Toronado was empty. They needed another five minute to discover why. Up on the top level of the ramp they found an identical orange Toronado, right down to the bumper sticker and stolen license plate in back. Neither car had a front plate. The second car was parked at the edge of the ramp, close enough to the next building for a man to jump the gap. Except for a ski mask, this Toronado was empty too.

PART III

24

On the Friday morning after the FBI tried tricking the kidnappers, Dr. Graham Knox was last seen leaving Jackson General, headed toward the hospital's parking ramp. A cool front had blown in overnight, sweeping away the heat and smell of indigestion that the city had been wrapped in for days. The doctor was moving at a brisk pace and whistling a Haydn symphony. Haydn for gallbladders. Bach for appendices. Wagner for bowel obstructions. He wore a white lab coat that was weighted down with five beepers. The three in his right waist pocket included one for his physicians' group, one for the local children's hospital, where he was on call, and one for a suburban clinic he was a partner in. His left waist pocket held two more beepers, one for his wife, the other for his broker. At the moment he was headed to the children's hospital for an emergency consultation on a juvenile nephrolithiasis—kidney stones. He felt a bit like a white knight to the rescue and liked the rush.

His age was thirty-five; his head full of sandy, curly hair; his jawline fit for nobility. When he took the ramp stairs two at a time, he never noticed the pair of young men who slipped into the stairwell behind him and pulled nylon stockings over their heads. Just as the doctor opened his Saab's door, they grabbed him from behind. The doctor's first thought was *I didn't order this.*

"Nice and easy does us, Mr. Doc-tor," said a voice in his ear. "You is a doc-tor, isn't you?"

"A surgeon."

"That ought to do. We be takin' you for a ride."

"But I'm due in surgery."

"Not anymore, you isn't."

"But where are we going?" the doctor asked as they lifted his car keys right out of his hand and shoved him into the back seat.

"The evenin' news," was their only reply.

AT ROUGHLY THE same time Jan was busy pacing herself, hoping to make it through a conference with her boss, Eldon Hodges, the Little Admiral himself, although calling a meeting with him a conference wasn't quite accurate. "Seance" would have been a better word choice, but it also had to be admitted that words generally failed her when it came to the man. Still, his small eyes were overtaken by a distant, misty look whenever Jan entered the room, as if he was about to attempt calling forth a bygone era, a time when women knew that pedestals were for stepping onto. As for Jan, being in the same room with the man for more than five minutes usually raised a rash on the back of her neck. At the moment, he was trying to blame her for something Felicia had done last night, the night when Haywood had promised to be with her, the night when Jan had been busy chasing orange Toronados and Agent Ford had been collecting flesh wounds.

"And then she came back with a gun," Hodges said, sounding suspicious that Jan had supplied the firearm.

"Where is Felicia now?" Jan asked for the third time.

The two of them were alone in Hodges's office, which was about as alone as you could get, as far as Jan was concerned.

"She came back with a gun," Hodges repeated. "That was after we had already removed her from the prisoner's room."

"Did she get Penshorn to say anything?"

"Only that he intends to sue us."

They'd been at it for close to a half hour by then, which made it slightly past eight A.M. Jan had pieced together this much: At about seven the previous evening, Felicia had attempted to visit Rainy Penshorn without getting past the policeman at the door. By the time hospital security arrived, she was screaming at the cop and had to be escorted out of the building. Much later that night, at a few minutes before three, she had returned with a gun. What she'd done with the gun remained unknown. The Little Admiral entered a fog bank whenever Jan raised that point. Just as Jan was about to tackle the question once more, there was a soft knock on the door, followed by Miss Pepperidge peeking inside the dim room.

"You might want to check the news," the secretary said.

"What now?"

"There's a breaking story," the secretary said, shooting Jan an accusatory glance before withdrawing.

The Little Admiral swiveled about in his well-padded chair, slid open the door on a credenza, and solved a mystery that had been bothering Jan for some time, namely, what he did while holed up in his office for hours on end. Hidden behind his desk was a twenty-four-inch color console. The first channel he turned to showed a reporter stationed on the granite steps of City Hall. The wind was buffeting the collar of the reporter's trench coat but couldn't make a dent on her sprayed page boy. The Little Admiral unplugged a set of headphones and the reporter's voice filled the room.

"The man," broadcast the reporter, "apparently represented himself to the mayor's staff as a community leader, claiming that he headed a coalition with a plan for ending the unrest on our streets. Prior to his arrival, and unbeknownst to the mayor's staff, he had also announced a press conference in the mayor's office. In the confusion that followed the arrival of the press, the man handcuffed himself to a desk and then delivered a statement."

The TV picture switched to a crowded room with people milling about in the background and reporters flinging out questions. Everything quieted as the man began to speak. He was a black man in sunglasses, but it wasn't until the camera pulled back enough to show more than a head shot that Jan saw his wheelchair and realized that the sunglasses hid Haywood's face. At the moment he didn't appear worried over Felicia's whereabouts. Behind him stood the large man in the orange jumpsuit who'd chauffeured him about yesterday.

"I called you down here," Haywood announced, "to let you know that the mayor, the city police, and the FBI ain't doing nothing about finding my brother, Lyle Brown, who was kidnapped five days ago while on duty down at Jackson General. That's the first thing you need to know. They all got to answer for his life.

"That the bad news," Haywood said. "The good news is that my brother's employer, Jackson County Medical Center, is offering a fifty-thousand-dollar reward for his safe return. So I hope the mother—"

A bleep drowned out the rest of his statement as the scene shifted back to the reporter on the City Hall steps.

"We've learned that the man has been cut loose from the mayor's desk and taken into custody. For now the mayor has refused to comment, other than to say that he has been working behind the scenes day and night to insure the safe release of the man's brother, Lyle Brown, a security officer at the county hospital. For now, it remains tense both here at the center of our city's government as well as on our streets. This has been Sandy Crawford reporting live at the scene."

The picture cut back to the studio news anchor, who cut to a commercial break for laundry detergent. Jan and the Little Admiral sat there staring at whiter whites until Jan found enough voice to say, "Is there really a reward?"

"What I want you to do—" Hodges said, sputtering to life. But before he could finish his thought, if that's what it was, his phone console rang and he snatched up the receiver. "Hodges here." He listened, frowning, which was perhaps his best expression. "What?" More listening, less color to his splotchy cheeks. "When? . . . I see. Well, I'd recommend that we notify the FBI immediately. . . . Yes, I can handle that. . . . No, I don't. . . . Have you been keeping abreast of this news story at the mayor's office? . . . I see. . . . Yes, I can understand why you might feel that way. I'll keep your office posted on all developments."

Hanging up, he turned his back to Jan, and poured himself a glass of water from a stainless steel pitcher atop the credenza. He drained the glass, poured another. Jan sat waiting.

"There is no reward," Hodges said, his back to her.

He drank his second glass of water, set it down, and turned on her as if fortified.

"Now they appear to have kidnapped one of our doctors," he

said. "We've just received an anonymous threat and the doctor in question is not answering calls to his pager. That means I've more pressing matters than the mess I called you in for. If you're willing to take custody of Felicia, we'll just forget it all happened."

"How tidy."

"I believe," Hodges plowed on, "that was Lyle's brother we were just watching."

"Looked like him," Jan said.

"Perhaps you could say something to him, if you can manage it. He's only complicating matters with little stunts like the one we just witnessed."

"No doubt," Jan said, making a point of remaining seated.

"Was there something else?" Hodges asked.

"Who's the doctor?"

"Need-to-know basis," he said.

"The same people who snatched Lyle?"

"That's not your concern, Gallagher."

"Right. So what am I supposed to tell Felicia?"

"That we're doing everything we can to help her."

Simpleminded as it sounded, maybe that was what she should tell her friend.

25

They had Felicia in a cell whose only stick of furniture was a low metal cot. The closed-circuit TV monitoring the room showed her back, so it was impossible to know if she was sleeping or simply staring at the padded wall. Her accommodations were part of the Crisis Intervention Center, which adjoined the General's emergency room and handled the mentally ill or emotionally disturbed patients who needed attention before whatever was short-circuiting in their heads or hearts sparked a fire.

As far as Security was concerned, the Crisis Center was one of the hospital's hot spots, which explained why Jan was on a first-name basis with Gladys, the psychiatric nurse handling Felicia's care. During Jan's years as a regular security guard, she had been radio-dispatched so often to Crisis that she also knew that Gladys had been divorced three times, married four. The only thing the nurse had quit more often than holy matrimony was smoking. Today Gladys was wearing her soothing pastels, as she called them, a peach blouse and willow-green slacks, pure serenity except for the pack of smokes resting beside her dimpled elbow.

"How long's she been like this?" Jan asked, using Gladys as an excuse for not looking at the TV monitor.

"Since I came on at seven, poor dear."

"Say anything?"

"Not to me."

"You know who she is, right?"

"I've heard the whole dreary story," said Gladys. "She's in

shock. We see it sometimes when a person suffers a loss."

"But she hasn't lost anybody. Not yet, anyway."

"She's terrified she will. Probably feels guilty about it too."

"Guilty?" Jan asked, her vision now drawn to the TV monitor despite herself.

"People make up things they should have done. Or said. They try to find some way they could have prevented it, whatever *it* is, and usually end up blaming themselves. How well do you know her?"

"Well enough to say I would have never expected anything like this."

"That's what I mean," Gladys said. "The feel I have for her, which granted isn't over much time, but anyway, she seems stunned that she even tried what she did last night. People do some daffy stuff under stress. Things they'd never normally do. They're temporarily someone else. They become suggestible and liable to do who knows what. That's the bad news. The good is that she should eventually go through a recovery stage and get back to normal."

"If we ever get Lyle back," Jan said, looking for something wooden to knock on and having to settle for a pencil. "What are the chances of keeping Felicia here for a while? To settle her down."

"She's refusing to stay, and you know the law, Jan. If she doesn't appear to be in any imminent danger to herself or anyone else, there's not much we can do. There's no history of mental illness that I know of. Do you?"

"No, but she was waving a gun around. Can't that count for something?"

"Good Lord, no. Besides, it wasn't quite as dramatic as all that. When they caught her trying to sneak in, there was a struggle and it fell out of her purse. She acted as though she'd forgotten it was there. Took four of them to carry her in here, I'm told, though she quieted down really quick."

"What if she wants to stay?"

"We can probably arrange a room in the inn, but I wouldn't count on that. She seems determined to leave, which is probably a good sign. Something on your mind, Jan?"

"Every minute of every day. What I'm wondering, is she ready to go home?"

"Is there anyone there? What she probably needs most is some hand-holding."

"She'd be alone."

"Then I'd say it depends on what she says when she decides to say something."

"Should we go see if that's now?" Jan asked without rising from her chair.

THE NURSE UNLOCKED the door to the holding room and led the way inside, telling Felicia in a rise-and-shine voice that someone had come to see her. No reaction. Although Gladys sounded kindly, she also kept a respectful distance from Felicia's hands and feet.

"Are you ready to talk to a friend?" Gladys asked.

"I want to go home," said Felicia, voice clear but monotone. One look at her eyes said she hadn't been sleeping; they were ringed and hollow.

"Felicia," Jan said, "how do you feel about staying here a night or two and resting up?"

"I want to go home."

"That might be hard to manage right now," Jan said, squatting so that her face was level with Felicia's. "I think it'd be best if you were around people, and there's no one at your place."

"Haywood," she said.

"He doesn't seem to be around," Jan said without mentioning where he might be—city jail with a sawed-off handcuff on his wrist.

"I want to go home."

"OK," Jan said, regrouping. "How about if you come to my place for a day or two? Would that be all right?"

"I'd rather you came to my place."

"I think you need to have someone with you for a while, Felicia, and I can't stay with you. One of us has to keep on top of things, and right now I'd say that's me. But at least you'll have company at my place."

"Have you asked them?" Felicia said after a pause. She'd never met Jan's girls, only heard the stories.

"I don't have to," Jan said. "They'll be happy to have someone new to pester."

An hour later they were on their way with an antianxiety prescription in hand. Gladys told Jan the pills, a form of Valium, might help or might not, but that it definitely sounded like a good idea for Felicia to be around a normal family for a while. Jan didn't comment on how much normal Felicia would be getting with her clan. Conversation on the way home was skimpy.

THE FIRST THING they heard upon entering Jan's kitchen was silence. There was no such thing as pin-drop silence in a house with four girls under eighteen, and at the moment there was the low *boom-ta-boom* of Leah's stereo from the back bedroom, but nothing else was making much noise. The three youngest daughters plus Grandmother Claire were frozen around a game of Monopoly at the breakfast table. Everyone saved their breath for a double take at who had just walked in the door. It might have been unusual for Jan to show up in the middle of the day, but not that unusual. The process of elimination, along with the slackness of jaws, said Felicia was the X factor. Marvin Gardens was about to be integrated. To cover up her embarrassment over her brood's reaction, Jan turned chatty.

"Hello to all of you too," she said. "This is my friend Felicia from work. She's going to be staying with us a day or two until things calm down a bit at her place. That means she'll be with us long enough for all of you to close your mouths and think of something pleasant to say."

The mouths closed shop one by one until reaching Amy, who stood with her fists clenched at her side and her face aghast. Her mouth twitched until she lurched forward, blindly shoving the kitchen table aside. Hotels and motels went flying as she stormed out of the room in near tears. She stopped only long enough to blurt, "Mother, how could you?"

Everyone's mouth was open again—Jan's the widest—and it quickly grew quiet again, except for Leah's stereo. Young Tess saved them all from themselves by popping up and declaring, "I get all her hotels."

"Not if Felicia wants to take her place," Katie said. "Do you, Felicia? She owned all the railroads."

Felicia tried to laugh, but ended up by turning away to wipe at her eyes.

"Maybe later," Jan said. "I think she's kind of tired right now. Why don't you guys help Claire fix up the guest room while I get Felicia settled."

"Guest room?" said Claire.

"I'll show you, Grams," said Tess, leading the way to the basement, where they kept a daybed tucked away beneath an abandoned hamster cage, rolls of surfing-Santa Christmas paper, and a stack of single shoes whose partners had abandoned them. Katie lingered behind until Jan shooed her toward the basement too.

"The one making a scene was Amy," Jan said, pulling out a chair for Felicia. "Do you want me to make excuses for her?"

"I'd rather you didn't."

"All right," Jan said. "I won't, but I don't want you thinking she's always a bad kid."

"OK, I won't. Do you really want me to stay?"

"Yes."

"And you're not going to ask me about what I was trying to do last night?"

"You were trying to help Lyle," Jan said. "That's all I need to know."

"The strange thing is," Felicia said with an amazed shake of her head, "I didn't even remember I had the gun until it fell out of my purse. I just wanted to talk to Penshorn alone. See if I could get through to him that way."

"There's some things I should tell you about," Jan said, fingering a five-hundred-dollar bill from the Monopoly board.

Felicia sat down and nodded to go ahead. Jan started with Haywood's visit to the mayor and ended with the unknown whereabouts of one of the General's doctors. She skipped over everything that had happened the night before when she'd gotten as close to Lyle as a pair of binoculars. She didn't have the stomach for that. Felicia's eyes crimped together as Jan talked about Haywood, as if she was trying not to picture it. She didn't ask any questions, not even about the make-believe reward. When Jan moved on to the second kidnapping, Felicia's chin slowly lifted and when Jan was finished, she said, "At least Lyle won't be alone."

"Is there anything I can get you?"

"Just Lyle," Felicia said.

"You need anything, just let my mother know."

Jan turned Felicia over to Tess and Katie, who were already squabbling over who would do their guest's bidding. Before leaving she went to the bathroom to warn Amy that there'd better be no repeat performances. She said it through a locked door, which was probably a good thing for both of them.

BACK AT THE General everyone in Administration was moving hurry-up as though a civil defense siren was wailing in the background, although the only audible sound was the hum of the fluorescent lights. After calling hospital information to make sure that Agent Ford wasn't still in a bed recovering from the gunshot wound to his shoulder—he wasn't—she paged him three times without results. She reported back to the Little Admiral, who looked at her as if he couldn't remember their last conversation. She saw executive administrator Averilli come and go from Eldon Hodges's office, a first. Averilli rarely traveled to other people's offices except by memo. The Little Admiral's phone console was in a constant state of agitation and curious office workers were forever coasting by in pairs, casting sideways glances toward Miss Pepperidge, who sat typing all afternoon as if her next keystroke might save the world.

It wasn't until three that afternoon that Special Agent Ford stiffly cruised into Hodges's office, his pager in plain sight on his belt. He didn't look any the worse for wear, except for a slight slowing of his pace. Jan had to wait to catch him on the rebound, falling into step beside him when he left Hodges's office.

"What's going on?" she said.

"Nothing we can't handle."

"What do you want me to do?"

"Wait by your phone."

"For what?" Jan asked, stopping in her tracks.

"Further instructions," he said without turning.

It was shortly after that that investigative reporter Sandy Crawford received an anonymous tip that there had been another kidnapping. She appeared in the General's main lobby within twenty minutes of the call. Jan timed her.

26

Po' hit the water flutter-kicking, windmilling, even biting, for all the good it did him. He'd never swum a lick in his life. That was all right, though. He'd rather go out sucking lake water than cop bullets. So he sank forever into the darkness. He held his breath and thought his dying thoughts, which turned out to be of LaDonna, who'd always said he'd end up hugging the bottom of something wet. He said a pitiful little bedtime prayer drilled into his head by one of his foster parents. Before reaching the end of the prayer, he started glugging. Gagging, he thrashed his way to the surface, a distance that turned out to be roughly five feet. The real lake hadn't dropped off anywhere near as fast as the one in Po's imagination.

Wading back to shore, he pulled himself onto a riprap boulder, figuring it wouldn't do him any good to run. That homing device was planted so deep inside his skull they'd be finding him wherever he went. He might as well save himself some effort.

An hour and plenty of sirens later he was still hanging on to the same rock. Apparently all that dirty lake water had screwed up the electronics they'd been using to track him.

He stayed put another half hour trying to decipher his options. Five minutes would have been more than enough time for all that he came up with. Everything he thought of ended up canceling itself out for one dangerous reason or another. The more he thought about it, the more he felt like throwing himself back into the water, except that having given the lake one shot at him, he wasn't inclined to give it another. The only person deserving another shot at him seemed to be LaDonna. That much made sense.

Dragging himself up the riprap, he pointed himself toward the city. If nothing else got accomplished, he intended to straighten that girl out about him and lake bottoms, but before he'd hoofed it halfway to her place, avoiding any headlights coming toward him, he knew there was another reason he was going there. She had a head on her, that LaDonna did, and it was the only head he could think of that might be willing to help think him out of troubles this deep. His own brain had too much soggy electronics in it to be much good.

AT ONE IN the morning LaDonna didn't answer her door none too friendly and it took a major campaign to get beyond her peephole to the door-chain stage.

"I know you?" she asked.

"I been to the bottom of that lake," Po' said. "Just like you said I would be."

"You do look like some kind of wet rat."

"Don't be nickel-and-dimin' me now. I come to you in my hour of need."

"Spouting Bible too. My, my."

"Anybody been around askin' for me?"

"You the forgotten man, Po'. Not a soul. You not going to start crying 'bout it, is you?"

"My head whirlin' like a cop light, 'Donna. Don' know what to do. What to say. Where to go." Realizing he should be feeling dizzy, he braced a hand against the wall. "What I'm needin' is some solid advice. And there ain't no one I trust to give it to me straight but you. I guess you know that much."

To get inside, he thought he might have to pass out too, but before he started slumping, the dead bolt clicked and the door opened the length of a brass safety chain. LaDonna was wearing a blue terry cloth bathrobe, held together at the neck by her chunky hand, and she gave him her fish-market once-over, not believing his story a whole lot more than the sign over the red snapper that said *Fresh*. A baby whimpered from the bedroom, causing LaDonna to speak faster.

"What kind of jam you stuck in now?"

"The kind best talked 'bout behind closed doors."

With a sigh, she let him in. He followed her to the couch, taking the opposite end rather than trying any knee-to-knee stuff, not yet, anyway. But it felt so good to be somewhere comfortable and familiar that he just sort of held himself a while. LaDonna went back to coo to the baby before Po' could get started on his woes.

"You spell it out," she said, returning with the baby, his daughter, in her arms. "And I'll tell you what I think. Then you on your way. We got an understanding?"

He was so busy watching her lips that it took a moment for the words to sink in. He'd discovered some long time ago that it generally helped a good deal to stare at a specific part of LaDonna as if hypnotized. That way she couldn't get at him with her eyes, and also, concentrating on her lips or throat or hands, it somehow broke down her resolve. When it dawned on him what she was saying, he lifted his vision to her lovely earlobe and said softly, "If that's what you want, sug'."

"And don't try that old hound-dog look either," she said, shifting the infant to the shoulder away from Po' and sitting on the far end of the couch. "Now, what's got you begging at my door? I ain't got no money for you. I ain't got nothing you can hock, 'cause some low-down broke in here and took anything that was worth anything. Whoever it was was the same size as you. Took all your clothes, razors and all. Ain't that something? So, exactly what is it you after, Mr. Po' Rind?"

"Just like I said," Po' answered, giving her earlobe all he was worth, "some advice."

That got to her. She spent some time complaining about how he knew that it would get to her, but he kept staring at her earlobe, wearing her down. Finally, she told him to start dishing out his lies so that she could say what she thought and tend to her baby, who was making fussy noises on her shoulder.

He told her.

He talked to her earlobe for maybe five minutes solid, taking her from the messed-up attempt at springing Rainy Penshorn to his dive into the lake, without skipping over hardly anything brave along the way, although he did gloss over breaking into the apartment he now sat in. Reaching the part about making a grab for the cop's gun, he shifted his vision to her eyes and found them closed tight. He hadn't expected that. Usually she was studying him the way she did crawdads on ice. It unsettled him considerably to see her there all defenseless, and he shifted his sight back to her earlobe fast as he could. Wrapping up, he peeked and saw her eyes were beading on the edges, and that was when a sick feeling started creeping up his throat. Even the baby was quiet.

"You only got one choice I can see," she told him after a minute or two.

"I don' like the sound of that."

"Go see Z.Z."

"I don't know . . ." Po' said, shying away from it.

"Who else going to lend you a hand? Cops? You know what goes with that hand. Family? This sound beyond them, Po'. You in way deeper than your mean ol' mama. No, it sounds like the only one got it in him to get you out of this is Z.Z."

"I been tryin' to have a word with that man for weeks. Ever since I got thunked and that deal went dirt. They blamin' me for all that. Which is what sent me down to spring Rainy in the first place. Tryin' to earn me back my name. So why the Z going to help me now all of a sudden?"

"You a Seven, ain't you?"

"Not by much, I don't appear to be."

"What else you got going for you? That's what I'm saying. I'm thinking you'd better cash in on it while you can."

Po' chose that moment to try sliding down the couch, but before he could lay a hand on her knee, she spoke again.

"You better start moving now."

He sat there, hand in midair, for about as long as it had taken him to hit the bottom of that lake—forever—and when he looked up her eyes were still slammed shut tight. The fact that she couldn't bear to look him in the face made what she said seem all the more right. The only person who could help him was Z.Z. Rip, head Seven.

Withdrawing without touching her, he shuddered, thanked her

for telling him what he should have known, and dragged his feet toward the door. She never said a thing to stop him but did have one last word of sad advice.

"And don't go playing Mr. Smooth when you get over there," she said, fighting a sniffle, " 'cause you a whole lot bumpier than you know."

He looked and now found her watching him, so naturally he gave her a thumbs-up sign and told her not to worry. She just shook her head and left him standing in her living room.

"You know the way out," she said, taking the baby to the bedroom.

The hardest thing he'd done that day was not follow them back.

HE WANDERED SIDE streets for another hour, trying to work up a song and dance that would get him close to Z.Z., but whatever he composed only sapped his strength and forced him to sit down on the curb to catch his breath. A lie would never do. Z.Z. fed liars to his pit bulls. Yet the only possibilities were all flat-out lies. In the end, he worked up the best tune he could muster and hoped his mouth wouldn't go dry whistling it.

The Tangerine Club, where Z.Z. held late office hours, had taken over a space that before suburban flight had been a Mob restaurant. It was housed in a two-story red brick building whose upper floor had held a bookie operation. Still did. Z.Z. Rip believed in tradition, even if he had to make it up himself. The club was always open, never packed. The doorman saw to that. His breath was at the crossroads of Chili Pepper Avenue and Tabasco Sauce Drive, and anyone who belonged at the club called him Onions. Po' knew that much.

"Onions, I got news for the man."

"Give me a name," the doorman said even though he'd passed Po's name on several times in the last month.

"Po' Rind. You can tell him I know who did it."

That was a lie, of course, but he was hoping somebody's name would come to him at the proper time.

"Did what?" Onions asked.

"Did the money, man."

"Always somebody showing up with that news," Onions said, picking up his intercom phone. "Round back with you."

Po' circled the building to the alley door that had a camera mounted above it. Several minutes passed. He never moved a muscle but in his throat. When the door finally opened, he was primed but never got a chance to gush.

"Z.Z.'s been wantin' a word with you," a huge bodyguard known as Fat Cakes said, frisking him as he said it.

He got pushed through the gourmet kitchen, where a chef dicing carrots followed them with his eyes. The lounge beyond the swinging service doors had low lights and tables set for dinner. No customers, though. The only people present at close to three in the morning were Z.Z.'s private secretary and two more bodyguards. They sat at an arrangement of sofas and love seats covered with blue suede and positioned around a coffee table with a large floral arrangement dead center. Nobody paid any attention to Po's wiggling. They were all watching Z.Z., who was strolling around the furniture arrangement, talking real slow into a portable telephone. He always spoke slow, letting his audience know he could make them listen for hours if he wanted.

Z.Z. Rip was a tall, handsome man with light brown coloring, a knobby, shaved head, and tiny ears. He possessed a gangly physique, all elbows and knees, that demanded, and got, the best tailors. Tonight he was in a flat black suit, lavender shirt, and shiny silver tie. His only jewelry was a diamond stud in his left nostril. The two-carat rock made his eyes seem all the darker. The story of how he got the name Z.Z. Rip had a body count of three.

When he'd finished on the phone, he telescoped the antenna, stepped up to the floral arrangement, and plucked a red carnation that he attached to Po's top buttonhole.

"Have a seat, Po' man."

Fat Cakes nudged the back of Po's knees with a straight-back chair taken from a dinner table and pushed him down, keeping a hand that felt webbed on Po's shoulder. Z.Z. lowered himself to the arm of the nearest sofa, rested a hand on Po's other shoulder, and did some digging with his eyes. Po's bones started vibrating. Then Z.Z. gave him a little smile and everything got still and heavy as a judge's gavel about to fall.

"You hear about Johnny Toots getting it on the causeway?" Z.Z. asked.

"I know who did the money," Po' said.

"Don't matter who did that money, Po' man. What matter is whether you rested enough to help set right what they done to Johnny."

"Plenty rested," Po said.

"That good, 'cause I been hearin' 'bout another matter, one what probably lost you plenty of sleep." Z.Z.'s smile widened enough to add a chill to the air.

"What matter that?" Po' respectfully asked.

"That matter of how tight you becomin' with the heat."

"Ain't nothin' tight there."

"We been hearin' diff, Po'. Very diff. And you know what we say 'bout that kind of diff, don't you?"

"Didn't you hear?" Po' said, trying to stand but not making it more than a couple of inches before Fat Cakes shoved him down. "How I messed up that fake drop-off for that hospital cop? Didn't anybody tell you 'bout how I saved that?"

"Maybe you better fill me in on them details," said Z.Z., leaving one hand on Po's shoulder.

"They stuffed me in that car 'cause you give them such short notice on the trade for Rainy," Po' said. "That was smart of you."

"Glad you think so," Z.Z. said, losing his smile.

"So I was supposed to be Rainy, 'cause they ain't plannin' on lettin' him go, you ask me, and they didn't have time to find nobody else the right color."

"I'm sure."

"So when you tried to trade that hospital cop for Rainy, you was only goin' to get me."

"If that much," said Z.Z.

"That right," Po' agreed, " 'cause I had to do some talkin' on the go. Had to tell them where the trade was goin' down, they had me in such a tight spot."

"So you admittin' that you ratted?"

"No such," Po' said. "I didn't know where you was intendin' to trade 'em. I only made it up 'cause they was fallin' on me hard as bad ol' crank. See, they caught me makin' a run for it, and they

169

didn't like that 'cause I was supposed to be workin' for them, but I couldn't take the smell, so I . . ."

"Take a breath, Po' man. Take a breath."

". . . so I decided it be best if I try my hoe down the road a piece. And that just what I was doin' 'til they nabbed me on 'count of that beeper they sewed in my top after they caught me down at the General tryin' to pop Rainy—the real Rainy—loose so's I could get my respect back after losin' that money that you say don't matter now anyway. I didn't have no way of knowin' you had other plans for gettin' Rainy, but when I saw the trap those dogs was layin' for you, I wrestled that pig's gun away. He tried puttin' holes in me. Burned my hand, I had the barrel so tight. I jumped for it, called to our man it was a trap, and hit the water with bullets thick as I don't know what around me. And I hid in that dirty ol' lake for an hour or two and then made my way here, 'cause by then . . ."

"Get this man a glass of water."

". . . I didn't know which end was up, but knew you the only man could tell me. So help me God."

There was a long pause. When Z.Z. lifted his hand off Po's shoulder, Po' nearly reached out to put it back. Z.Z. checked in with the bodyguards and his secretary around the coffee table, all of whom shook their heads as if they'd heard better stories on *Sesame Street*. Finally, Z.Z. returned his attention to Po', speaking so soft that Po' had to strain to catch every word.

"So the cops weren't plannin' on tradin' for Rainy," Z.Z. said. "That what I'm hearin'?"

"You sure is."

"Who weren't they plannin' on tradin' with?"

"Why, you."

Z.Z. shook his head no and kept his eyes dead center on Po. "They weren't not tradin' with me, Po' man. Who you think that leave them?"

"Don' know," Po' said, having to wet his lips with his tongue. "But you can bet I didn't tell 'nother soul 'bout none of this. Figured you'd want to be the first. All I'm hopin' is maybe you can help me out of this mess. I got cops lookin' for me in my dreams. Maybe you could send me out west or somethin'."

"Po' man," Z.Z. said, draping an arm around Po's shoulder, "you way too valuable for that. I don't want you worryin' 'bout a thing. Old Z.Z.'s developin' a plan. You in it."

That was when the head Seven smiled his famous smile, the one that woke mothers out of deep sleeps to worry over their sons. In fact, Po' had a flash of his own old lady. She was grabbing her pillow tighter, refusing to wake up. Just when he could have used her, too.

27

When Jan arrived home that Friday evening everyone but Amy and Felicia was seated at the kitchen table having supper. The spread included roast chicken, mashed potatoes, gravy, scalloped corn, and biscuits. Claire's Sunday dinner menu. The tablecloth was out. A daisy centerpiece meant that Jan would be hearing from Mrs. Donaldson two doors down about the sanctity of her flower garden. As for her daughters, they sat primly at the table, napkins on their laps, all wearing dresses except for Leah, who had at least removed the floppy Renaissance hat she'd been living under for weeks. There weren't even any TV voices filtering in from the living room. The illusion of civilization lasted until Claire spoke up.

"Amy won't come out of her room."

"Won't let us in, either," said Tess, cheerful about it.

"That's right," Claire said. "Barricaded herself in."

"And what about Felicia?" Jan asked. "How's she doing?"

"Sleeping," Claire answered. "I had to slip her a couple of those pills you brought home."

"She didn't want them," Tess said, still cheerful.

"Some nonsense about how she couldn't sleep," Claire said, "or someone would die."

"She was all tired out," said Katie, the resident mother hen. "Poor thing. Is there any news about her husband?"

"Boyfriend," Leah corrected, always keen to flout tradition.

"Nothing," Jan said, raising her voice enough to quiet everyone. "Now, I'm going to have a word with Amy. The rest of you stay out here and count your blessings."

"Out loud?" asked Tess.

"To yourself, please," said Jan, heading for the living room, which didn't have a stray toy or dress in sight. She even lifted the davenport skirt but found nothing stuffed beneath it. The power of houseguests. Back at the rear bedroom on the right, the one shared by Amy and Leah, she listened a moment, heard nothing, knocked.

"Go away." A stubborn, teary voice.

Jan put a hand out as if to push her way in, but thought better of it, saying instead, "We can talk this way."

"Mother, I can't believe you brought her here. In our home. Daddy would never have let it happen."

"Is that where you're getting all this nonsense? From your father."

"We're not her friends."

"I am," Jan said. "And if you're lucky, someday you will be too. You think about it."

Having made her point, she withdrew before Amy managed to push any of her buttons. Back in the kitchen she was greeted by questioning stares.

"She's thinking about it," Jan reported.

Leah was about to assess Amy's thought processes, but Jan warned her off it with a glance and asked Claire to please pass the biscuits.

FOUR MOUTHFULS LATER the telephone rang. There was the usual red-alert scramble, but Katie, being nearest the receiver, beat out the competition. She answered, listened, and courteously asked whoever was calling to repeat him- or herself. She listened harder before abruptly holding the phone out to Jan.

"For you. I think."

"Work?" Jan whispered.

Katie shrugged in ignorance, so Jan took the receiver and decided on her office voice.

"This is Gallagher."

"You know how many J. Gallaghers there are in the book?" It was Haywood. There was no mistaking the indignation.

"I hope this isn't your one call," Jan said.

"No, they let us colored people use the phone often as we want these days."

"In jail?"

"Don't play around with me."

"You are in jail, aren't you? After seeing the mayor."

"They too embarrassed to keep me. Give me a ride home and told me to keep my nose clean. I told them that impossible, considering where I has to stick it."

"So why are you calling every J. Gallagher in the book?"

"To find 'licia," he said. "She's not home and I need her."

"She's over here," Jan said. "Resting, I might add. Lightly sedated."

"This ain't no time for that."

"Did you put her up to that business last night?"

"She ain't never let me put her up to nothin'."

"Well, last night, when you were supposed to be watching her, she tried to get in to see Rainy Penshorn and ended up in a holding cell for her troubles."

"You makin' that up?"

"They had to take a gun away from her."

" 'Licia? Hold on now."

"You saw how she was the other night," Jan said.

"There ain't no time for this," Haywood complained. "There work to be done. Or has everyone forgot 'bout my brother?"

"What's going on?"

"My little TV show payin' dividends, that what. I finally heard from the head Seven hisself, Z.Z. Rip. He wantin' a word, you see."

"Why's my toe tapping?" Jan asked.

"I need someone to get me there."

"What's wrong with the guy in the orange suit?"

"After the mayor's office, says he won't take me nowhere but a landfill."

"What makes you think this Seven you talked to has anything we need?"

"Name some other choices?"

"You got me there," Jan admitted. Lowering her voice and turning away from the dinner table, she said, "Is this going to be safe?"

"As polyester. What's it matter to you?"

"I'll give you a ride, if there's something to this."

"You?" Bottomless disbelief.

"Do you want help or not?"

"This got to be the low point," Haywood said. "How soon can you get over here?"

Leaving instructions to let Felicia sleep as long as possible, Jan changed into jeans, running shoes, and a beige blouse. Before leaving, she left further instructions to keep Felicia away from Amy.

SHE MADE IT to Haywood's a half hour before sunset. He was waiting on his front sidewalk, wearing his mayor's office outfit, sunglasses and all.

"We got to shake it," Haywood said by way of greeting. "If we going to get there before lights out, that is."

Meaning before curfew, which didn't get any argument from Jan.

"Where to?" Jan asked once seat-belted into Haywood's van.

"City park."

"No way," Jan said, letting go of the steering wheel.

"Relax, Gallagher. Ain't no reason for muggers, rapers, or chunk salesmen to be in there on a night like this. With this martial-law shit they ain't got no one to do their business on. Fact is, empty as it going to be, that park probably the safest place in the city."

"That almost makes sense," Jan said. "Do you really think we'll find something out?"

"Fifty-thousand-dollars reward will do wonders for Lyle's next birthday."

"There is no reward," Jan said.

"They don't know that."

Jan started the engine and said, "They will someday."

175

* * *

CITY PARK WAS a ten-minute drive. Pulling into an empty parking lot above the Cawsy River, which cut the park in half, they arrived just as the sun was getting tangled up in a ridge of spruce trees. It looked big as three suns and red as some filmmaker with a lump in his throat would make it. Once lowered to the pavement, Haywood couldn't resist slamming his door. The retort silenced every cricket and frog within hailing distance.

"So they know we here," he told her.

A bike path curved away from the river, over a hill, and down an incline to a small pond with an A-frame pavilion at one end, cattails at the other. Dusk's beard was getting long by the time they reached the pond. The evergreen needles on the hills around them seemed to be breathing red in and out, and the pond had an eerie pink glow that Jan didn't have time to worry about, not with all the growing shadows that bore watching. Haywood talked all the while, cranky about every word, as if feeling an obligation to help Jan relax. She would have told him to shut up if the time or two he'd paused for breath hadn't been way too quiet for comfort.

"Used to come down here as a boy," Haywood said. "Catch tadpoles out of this ol' pond. Dragonflies too. I was big on them. Smell of it now, there must be some bodies dropped in there these days. Kissed my first girl not far from here. Paid her a quarter. Ran out o' funds, or she'd have let me go further. Our mama wouldn't let us come over here for nothin', so we always on the sneak, me and Lyle. He was always 'fraid, so I'd have to bully him into it. We played Tarzan all 'round here. Back then we thought we could be just like white boys. Got chased by lions, rhinos, and alligators all over these hills. Once saw a . . . Why we stopping?"

"They found us," Jan said.

Five men had sifted out of the trees to stand still as fence posts across the path before them. Not a one of them even brushed at the mosquitoes sputtering about. A tall man with a shaved head led the group. He was dressed in a shiny green suit coat; alligator skin came to mind after listening to Haywood's stories, but the material wasn't shiny or scaly. Ten feet in front of them, he stopped, handsome as the chief of some tribe of movie stars. Jan supposed that made him Z.Z. Rip. The men fanning out on either side of him weren't anywhere near as pretty. At least two of the others stood poised with hands tucked inside the warming pockets of hooded sweatshirts that should have been in mothballs for at least another three months.

"It don't look like you came alone," Z.Z. Rip said. "You needed help, should have asked."

"I told you what I need help with—findin' my brother. You bring him along?"

"You gets right to the point, don't you?" Z.Z. Rip said. "You got any peepers 'hind them glasses?"

" 'Bout as much as I got leg in these pants."

"You are a package. I like your manners, though. Real shitty, the way they should be. Like your style too. Who else got a motor white as yours?" Z.Z. lowered his voice and purred to Jan, "What your name, honey?"

"Far as you concerned," Haywood said, "her name my name. "Now what 'bout my brother?"

A man next to Z.Z. leaned closer to say something behind a cupped hand. There was barely enough light for Jan to recognize him as the man the FBI had taken into custody. The one they called Po'.

"I'm being told," Z.Z. said, "that your woman there's some kind of heat."

"Not any kind will burn you."

"I work with his brother at the hospital," Jan said.

"That so?" Z.Z. Rip said. "You know this mess-up standing beside me?"

"No," Jan told him, unable to think of anything fancier.

"That the right lie to tell," Z.Z. said with a slow nod.

"So where you got my brother?" said Haywood.

"Ain't got him nowhere."

"You told me . . ."

"Told you I knew where you could get your hands on him. Didn't say any Sevens has him. We ain't got no reason to have him. Rainy's somethin' for a lawyer, not for grabbin' bodies. That kind of empty thinkin' don' go with the color green. You just lucky your TV special got people talkin', that all. It turn out that one of your bro's guards gots a way with women. Too many women. Turn out that one of them women got tired of his spreadin' hisself all over town. She cried to her brother, who like his lucky number Seven. That how we know all this."

"And you goin' to tell me?"

"For fifty thousand dollars? I'll do you one better. I'm goin' to give you an expert." He gestured at Po'. "Someone to help get your brother free."

"What kind of expert?" Haywood said, suspicious.

"An expert at rescuin' people. He been pullin' hisself from fires hot as this all his life. You get close 'nough to him, he even smell smoky."

"Why don't you send a crew down there and get my brother? Now, that be earnin' fifty thousand dollars."

" 'Cause this situation call for delicacy. You go rammin' down there with an army and your brother goin' to get broke. The people holdin' him is Golds, and they don't like leavin' nothin' behind in workin' order. But you go down there nice and easy with our expert, you just might get your brother out of there 'fore anyone know what happened. See?"

"You 'fraid to start some war?" said Haywood. "That it?"

Z.Z. laughed softly, saying, "There somethin' you better learn here. I ain't 'fraid of nothin' on two legs, 'less it be me. I scare myself considerable from time to time."

"I ain't on two legs," Haywood said, which increased the volume on Z.Z. Rip's laugh and made everyone uneasy.

"How are we supposed to get there?" Jan said to break the tension. "There's a curfew on."

"Your ride's waitin' back at the lot," Z.Z. said, stopping in midlaugh. "And if you has to shoot anybody, feel free to plug your expert here. He in need of an extra lesson or two."

"Why you really doin' this?" Haywood said.

"Why?" Z.Z. said, as if the answer was obvious. "To right a wrong."

The head of the Sevens laughed about that all the way to the line of trees he disappeared in. Meanwhile, Po' had already slipped around Jan and Haywood, heading toward the parking lot. He stayed ten yards in front all the way to the hill above the lot. When Jan caught up to him there she saw why he'd stopped. Parked next to the van was a squad car.

"Our ride," Po' said.

"A cop?" Jan said.

"That the first thing what does make sense," said Haywood. "At least we won't be picked up for curfew."

"He'll drop us off where we need to be," Po' said.

"Then what?"

"Shorty here going to call the guard out for dog-earing his sister."

"I ain't got no sister," said Haywood.

"You does now. And when he come out, I'm goin' to lunk him over the head and we move in."

"I get to shoot somebody?" Haywood asked.

"Not unless you brought your own gun," Po' said.

When they climbed into the back of the squad car, the policeman, a young blond with a bull neck, never bothered to look over his shoulder. He just said, "Where to?"

28

By the time they had the new hostage blindfolded and tied to a chair, Lyle felt almost neglected. For one thing, the newcomer got a chair that was two or three feet higher than the chopped-up bucket seat they had slapped Lyle in. The way Lyle's legs were cramping, listening to the new guy talking from that high up felt like listening to a free man. For another thing, the four men who delivered the prisoner came in slapping hands and crowing as if they'd captured a World Cup. There hadn't been any dancing in the streets when they'd hauled Lyle's ass out of that car trunk. Just backbiting and rough handling for him. At least the woman guard on duty was consistent. Her mood remained foul for the new man too.

"What I supposed to do with this one?" she wanted to know.

"Listen," the new hostage said, piping right up as though he'd just had a brilliant idea they wouldn't want to miss out on, "I think it'd save us all time if you just let me talk directly to your head negotiator."

"Head negotiator?" the woman said. "Say, what kind of fool you boys tryin' to dump on me here?"

"Weren't we told to get something white?" a squeaky voice said. "And something doctor too? Can't help it if he talk funny."

"That may be," the woman shot back, "but I ain't takin' care of nothin' that talk this way, not all by myself, I isn't. You tough boys can park it right here and wait like the rest of us."

Groans and complaints about no breakfast all around. Lyle was with them there. The woman guard had been feeling weak and decided to eat his breakfast for him that morning.

"Listen," the doctor said, "this should really be quite simple. My wife's family has money. Give them sufficient time and they'll raise a ransom you can retire on."

"That so?" the woman guard said. "S'pose next you goin' to be tellin' us we can all get on Donahue too?"

"Maybe you don't understand how much—"

"Or maybe Oprah or Sally or that snitty little Regis. Shit, don't you think that I want to hear a word of it."

"Listen, if you could just arrange it so that your head negotiator—"

"Bubbles," the woman called out.

"Name ain't Bubbles," said a sullen voice.

"That all right. Don' care 'bout your name. What I want is one of them pretty socks you wearin'. What you got there? Size thirteen? Come on, now. Don't be shy. We all seen a naked foot."

"What you . . ."

"Come on, come on."

"Listen . . ." the doctor said, starting up again.

"The sock," the woman ordered.

After that the doctor talked with such a thick argyle accent that only another sock could have understood him.

NEAR MIDMORNING THE garage door cranked up and a car pulled in, edging forward until breathing in Lyle's face. Or at least it seemed to be. He could smell radiator coolant. A moment later Lyle heard the head man, the one who got a kick out of dropping blind cats in laps, giving orders. Today the bastard was only interested in the new hostage, which suited Lyle fine. He wasn't sure what might pop out of his mouth if pushed, but at least he still had enough sense to know it would be better if nothing popped out. After the botched swap for Rainy Penshorn, a half-dozen rabbit and kidney punches, delivered at random intervals, had kept him awake until dawn. The night guard somehow blamed Lyle for the trap.

"What's that 'tween your lips?" the head man asked the doctor in a concerned voice, the same solicitous tone that Lyle had heard upon their first meeting.

The doctor answered as best he could, not a word of it understandable.

"Say," the head man said to the room at large, "didn't I order up a doctor?"

"That's right," the squeaky voice said with respect, apprehension too.

"So what kind of doctor talks this way?"

Since no one else was willing to tackle a question that big, the doctor took a crack at it. Same muffled results.

"Say," the head guy said, "they 'pear to be a sock in his mouth. If he ain't got no more sense than to wear a sock over his tongue, I don't see what use . . ."

Someone yanked the sock away and words came tumbling out of the doctor.

"I'm sure we can work out a deal. If only you'll let me talk to your head negotiator, everything can be—"

"You won't get any more head than me," said the man who'd just arrived.

"In that case," the doctor said, "all you need do is contact my family. They'll do whatever you ask of them. Money's no problem."

"Money?" the head man said, surprised. "Who said anythin' 'bout money? We ain't holdin' you for money. We got a bigger picture than that."

"But surely you could use a million dollars."

"Now that makes me mad," the head man said a beat later. "I hate promises that can't be delivered on, and the only kind of people what can lay their hands on that kind of pile is drug dealers. That what you are? I thought I heard someone say you was a doctor."

"My wife's family has money," the doctor assured him. "Real estate money. A fortune. They're very fond of me."

"Open yo' mouth," the head guy said. "Wider . . . Stick out yo' tongue. . . . That look like a liar's tongue."

"I swear to God," the doctor said. "A million dollars."

"That so? Then maybe the big picture can wait a little bit, seeing's how you talkin' such a round, respectful kind of number. You figure you could write a little note for us, tellin' that we want a million dollars and Rainy Penshorn too?"

"I certainly can. Who's Rainy Penshorn?"

"Just a tight-ass punk what's nothin' for you to worry 'bout. You just concentrate on writin' so they can read it, Doc. That's all you need to think on. I seen how you doctors write."

While the doctor practiced his penmanship, the head guy leaned close to Lyle to whisper, "Now don't you wish things work slick as this for you?"

THE FOUR MEN who had delivered the doctor were ordered to stay put until replacements arrived.

"We ain't got some worthless nigger anymore," the head guy told them. "It appear we traded up, so I don' want no jackin' off 'round here. I want a lookout up on the billboard and I want that old truck in back workin' case you needs to de-part in a hurry. You showed you got that real gold color this mornin', so don' go messin' up now."

Once the head man was gone to deliver the doctor's letter, the woman guard started bossing again, ordering everyone to get going on their jobs, and quietly too, seeing as how the early afternoon rerun of *Donahue* was coming up. From then on the only noise, other than the TV, was the rumble of a truck engine somewhere behind Lyle's chair. During a commercial break, the woman went back to cuss them out good for revving the motor when Phil was on a roll. Lyle took the opportunity to check in with the doctor.

"You all right?" Lyle whispered.

"Who's there?"

"Lyle Brown, the hospital security guard they grabbed a few days back. I think we're safe for now."

"Of course we're safe," the doctor answered. "And when I get out, I'll tell them where you are."

"You know where we are?"

"I meant," the doctor said, "that I'll tell the authorities these people have you."

"That's mighty big of you," Lyle said. "But I don't know that I'd care to wait that long. These people ain't exactly perfectly balanced, in case you hadn't noticed. I'd say our ticket out of here is the night guard. He gets hot real easy and we might be able to take advantage of it."

"I want no part of any schemes," the doctor declared. "The safest way out of this predicament is to pay them off, and I don't want you ruining my chances with heroics."

"Didn't you hear—"

"Shut up, you two," said the returning woman guard, "or I'll stuff an oil rag in your mouths. Two in yours," she told the doctor, "big as it is."

Not long after that, relief arrived and the four men who'd swept the doctor off his feet punched out for home. The replacements included the late-night guard even though it was only midafternoon, another woman who couldn't stop singing scat under her breath, and a quiet one who smelled of Bengay and must have been the kid who'd earlier slipped Lyle's blindfold back in place. Right away the gun-loving, late-night guard started in on the doctor.

"I wouldn't even waste a bullet on you," he baited. "When the time comes, I'll just march you to the top of this building and give you a kick over the side."

"You better talk to the man in charge," the doctor advised.

"Right now that's me. And I'm goin' to make you walk every step of the way up there too. Ain't no elevators for you. And don't go thinkin' there but two stories to this place. Forget that shit. This buildin' ten high and squish you up plenty for however long you breathin'."

"Listen," the doctor said, "let's not do anything irrevocable here."

"Think your *irrevocable* mean anythin' to me? Don't even bring it up. When the time comes to shove you off that rooftop, only one thing goin' to hold me up, and that's waitin' 'til a street sweeper comes along. I don't want to be lookin' at your ugly little spot for days. That for sure."

"Listen . . ."

"Havin' to drive 'round your remains, now that would piss me off entirely."

Other than threats like these, each one gorier than the last, the main topic of conversation was what they should order up for lunch, which they'd all missed in their rush to get there. The new woman wanted chopity-chop, Chinese, as she sang it, off-key; the night guard tried to bully them into Mexican; and the Bengay guard voted for hot-and-spicy chicken wings.

"You and them chicken wings," the woman guard from the day shift complained. "Your tongue going to turn into a pepper."

They ended up deferring to Bengay, though, phoned in their order for wings with extra rice, and sent the scat singer out to pick it up. Twenty minutes later—Lyle timed it by counting to sixty over and over—the singer was back and Lyle had his first lock on the garage's location. He was within a ten-minute drive of a chicken-wing joint whose product could blow the roof off your mouth.

The afternoon was quiet except for periodic threats thrown at the doctor. Lyle's sole conversation came with the Bengay guard, who waited until they were alone before approaching him. With the gunslinger up on the roof and the two women supervising the doctor's trip to the bathroom, the guard said softly in Lyle's ear, "You goin' to be all right, man. Don't sweat it."

"Ain't lookin' so cool from here," Lyle whispered back.

"No, man, they promised me. Ain't nothing goin' to happen to you."

"Why would you care what . . ."

But the women returned with the doctor and the young guard shuffled back to his post somewhere near the garage door. For once the doctor had nothing to say, not with the two women discussing his private parts, which were generally a disappointment to them.

The evening-shift guard was late and reeking of perfume. As usual, he got chewed out by the day guard, who wanted to get home in time for *Entertainment Tonight*. The other three guards stayed on, arguing about whether or not the cops were really doing house-to-house searches since a white man got grabbed. They got around to disagreeing about supper too, and this time the woman scat singer won out. The gun lover was up on the roof and Bengay wanted hot-and-spicy chicken wings again, which he wasn't going to get, so he voted with the scat singer for Chinese. Lyle

185

again tried counting how long it took to pick up the food, but he lost count somewhere around thirty counts of sixty, when the blind cat hopped into his lap, breaking his concentration.

Not long after everyone had polished off their shrimp fried rice and snapped open his or her fortune cookie, sharing a hoot over the blank paper inside the doctor's cookie, the gun-loving guard called down from the billboard on a cellular phone, ordering battle stations.

"Some funky on the street," said the scat singer, who had taken the call.

A light went out to Lyle's left, darkening the garage by half. Somebody's foot stubbed what sounded like a toolbox. A stifled curse. The blind cat tripped somebody and hissed. The TV went mute, which made it possible to hear the guard's quickened whispers.

All voices stopped with a pounding on the garage door, followed by a ranting voice. Lyle tried to tell himself that the foaming mouth he was now listening to didn't sound familiar.

"Honeyman," the voice called out, "I know your worthless ass in there, and I'm goin' to tear it right off you, if you ever go close as a block to my sister again. Hear?"

It didn't sound like the voice of a man who had a sister. It sounded like the voice of a man who had a brother. It sounded like Haywood.

"Someone seem to know you here," the woman guard told the lady's man.

"What we goin' to do?" asked Bengay.

"Wait 'em out," said Honeyman, sounding practiced at it.

"That real smart," said the woman. "All that shoutin' he's doin' probably scare the police away. That what you thinkin'?"

"What, then?"

"Maybe bring him in and let him have yo' ass."

"Not my ass."

"Name us some other options, then. We *all* ears."

"Plunk him."

"Who goin' to do the plunkin'?"

From outside, Lyle's brother shouted, "I'll set fire to the whole damn block if I has to."

"I don' even know what sister he's talkin' 'bout."

"Take your pick," said the woman. "Maybe we should just shove your ass out there, see if you can talk your way out of this one."

"I think we better do something," Bengay said.

There was more pounding on the garage door, which boomed and rattled like corrugated metal. The lookout from the billboard joined them in the middle of a peal.

"Three of them," the gun lover said, having to stop for a breath. "Dude in a wheelchair's doin' all the yakkin'. Some white bitch pushin' him. And some flabby muscle hidin' right beside the door. What the hell he hollerin' 'bout?"

"One of Honeyman's women."

"Damn, we got to shut him up. Honeyman, get over there and start talkin'. The rest of you help me move these two motherfuckers into the shithouse where they be out o' sight."

"Then what?" asked the woman.

"We teach these suckers that this the big time."

Lyle heard a click from what sounded like the safety on a gun. Within seconds the guard known as the Honeyman was at the garage door, jawing with Haywood, who was threatening terrible things, forecasting doom as he had a talent for doing. The woman pushing Haywood's chair was an unknown, and with Wonder Woman being a long shot, Lyle began to rub the tape binding his wrists against a bolt on the back of his bucket seat. Whatever muscle Haywood had drummed up would most likely be steady as his last stiff shot of bourbon. His brother's bitterness about life had stripped him of his ability to judge character beyond a man's taste in blended whisky.

As Lyle was working his wrists, one of the guards jerked him up by the shoulders. The bolt on the back of the chair dug into his wrists, but he didn't cry out, for it also ripped the tape. His hands were almost free.

The woman guard prodded him forward toward the john. Behind him, the doctor was promising his complete and neverending cooperation. And then, judging from the barnyard smell of things, Lyle and the doctor were shoved into the cramped bathroom. When he bounced against Lyle's back, the doctor gasped, "Not me."

"Settle down," Lyle said.

"Just give me some room," the doctor said, regaining his self-control.

"Don't I wish I could," Lyle said, straining against the tape without luck, "but my hands are almost free. All you got to do is bite through some tape and I'll have my hands."

"For what?"

"Maybe I can get us a gun."

"Listen," the doctor said, pushing Lyle away, "the safest thing for us to do is sit tight. I'll pay for you too, when the time comes."

Two gunshots silenced them.

"What was that?" the doctor said.

Imagining his brother slumped in his wheelchair, Lyle couldn't make his tongue answer. A minute or two later there was another gunshot. The doctor started backpedaling and fell on top of the toilet.

"Close that!" someone shouted out in the garage.

"It's closed," Bengay answered.

A spray of bullets got through anyway, nicking the Wedgewood, splintering the Chippendale, raising hell with the frilly curtains. Whatever rummy Haywood had scrounged up must have packed a Gatling gun. The amount of flying lead would level them all, a thought that revived Lyle's tongue.

"Let me turn around," Lyle said, "so you can reach my hands." Contorting, he turned his back to the doctor.

"He's trying to get away!" the doctor shouted. "He's trying to—"

Lyle sat on him to shut him up, but it didn't matter. The bathroom door jerked open and a light came on. The woman guard disgustedly said, "You boys is all alike." A hand with sharp fingernails jerked Lyle upright.

29

Their cop chauffeur dropped Jan, Haywood, and their escape expert on Vanderbilt Avenue, an old cement-slab street that ran beneath a freeway viaduct. After a brief and conflicted conference with himself, their expert pointed north and said, "That way." As they advanced, they met no cars at all on Vanderbilt and seemed to be bucking the flow of what little traffic passed above them on the freeway. Curfew had taken hold. The only light was from the cumulative glow of the city itself, enough to see shapes but no details. Eyes looked recessed, teeth unnaturally white. During the "Crisis," as the media had now taken to calling the riots, anyone who owned a light left it on; apparently no one owned lights in the buildings they now passed.

Po' matched Jan stride for stride, his head constantly swiveling to all points of the compass. One out of four or five times, he glanced upward as if expecting a car on the freeway to fall through a crack. He repeatedly poked a finger in one ear or the other, as if mining for wax, and once said, "You hear that?"

"Hear what?" asked Haywood.

"That music, man. Some kind of country western shit."

Jan stopped pushing Haywood's chair to listen but heard only a truck on the above highway. Maybe it was Nashville bound.

"Don't hear nothin'," said Haywood.

"That 'cause the cops ain't put a radio inside yo' head."

"Why help us now?" Jan asked. "Why not by the lake?"

"The price right," Haywood answered for him.

"Always somebody thinkin' for me," said Po'.

"I'm serious," Jan said. "Why not just run again?"

"Where to?" Po' asked, stopping to stare at the highway above them.

"That way, way over her head," Haywood commented when Jan said nothing.

Sensing there was no convincing them otherwise, Jan dropped the matter, moving on in the semidarkness. They continued beneath the freeway for three blocks, the occasional rumble of a car overhead making her feel as though she were far underground. The air seemed to gain weight with each step as a new heat wave slowly got its mouth around the city. Gastric smells crept out of crevices and grates. Po' marched them to a spot in front of a two-story building with a Camel cigarette billboard up top, on the level of the freeway. There might have been some movement in the shadows beneath the billboard's catwalk, but it ducked so quickly it could have been her overactive imagination.

"There." Po' pointed.

"Use more words," Haywood said.

Jan obliged when Po' wouldn't. She described the white garage door they were facing, the billboard two stories above it, and a bluish light visible through a grimy window off to the right.

"Make it good," Po' said, leading the way across the narrow side street. "Won't be much time."

Jan fell in behind Po', asking what he meant by that but not getting an answer. Once out from beneath the viaduct, Po' stopped, cocked his head, and stared up at the sky as if hearing something fall, an angel, maybe, or a meteorite. He tapped the side of his head and covered the remaining short distance double-time. His sneakers never made a sound. Flattening himself against the building, he pulled out a handgun and waved them forward.

Jan positioned Haywood directly in front of the garage door, but sideways so that his shoulder touched it. Once she pressed his hand against the door, he went to work with his mouth.

At first no one answered Haywood's taunts. Then a man demanded to know who Haywood thought he was, interrupting his studies this way. Haywood filled the man in on exactly who he thought he was.

Somewhere amongst all the insults, Po' started mumbling to himself loudly enough to distract Jan. At first it sounded as though he was refusing orders, although Jan couldn't hear anyone giving orders but Haywood. Then his mutterings grew sterner, and it sounded as though he was *giving* orders. Jan looked around but couldn't see anyone taking orders, either.

"That's enough," Po' suddenly shouted. Pushing himself away from the building, he pulled off two shots at something above them, maybe the Milky Way.

"Who's blastin'?" demanded Haywood.

"The antenna's up there," Po' answered, still aiming upwards. "And it workin' again."

Before Jan could gather her wits enough to ask what antenna, the squeal of car tires made any answer meaningless. From opposite ends of the block tore two cars, white sedans without headlights on, both bearing down on them. They accelerated until the last instant, when they nailed their brakes and fishtailed in near unison, almost kissing as they formed a *V* pointed at the building. At first Jan assumed they'd been ordered up from inside the garage, but when the first wave of passengers, six all total, piled out on the far side and crouched behind the cars, they took aim at the building as if intending to lay siege to it.

"What's this shit?" Haywood wanted to know.

Jan was about to fill him in when the rear door of the closest car opened and out stepped the well-dressed Z.Z. Rip. He scanned the building in a leisurely fashion, as if daring it to hurt him, then looked back at his troops hiding behind the cars and snorted at their cowardice. Turning back to Po', he wagged a finger at him and said, "I don't see no open doors."

It was almost the last thing Z.Z. Rip ever said, and Po' wasn't even listening. He was too busy searching the building's upper story for an antenna that was bombarding him with honky-tonk. Or at least his hands — one still holding a gun — were covering his ears like a man hoping to silence demons wearing hand-tooled shit-kickers and playing steel guitars. The tail end of Z.Z.'s words must have caught Po's attention, though, for swirling about, he leaped for the car door like a man seeking asylum. The fact that the gang leader was unable to clear out didn't matter. Po' tackled him, carrying them both into the car.

At the same instant Jan flinched, hearing another shot. This one came from above them and was aimed at Z.Z. Thanks to Po's dive for safety, it missed, hitting only glass.

There was a moment of confusion, during which Jan dumped Haywood forward, out of his chair, and threw herself down on the cracked cement beside him just as the air above them started whistling.

"Lyle!" Haywood shouted once the gunfire stilled.

The only answer he got was another, shorter round of lead aimed at the garage door, which boomed as though being pounded by baseballs. More than one person shouted from inside the building; more than one set of footsteps could be heard running. Jan didn't bother pointing out to Z.Z. that he'd been misinformed about the number of guards. At least there was no further return of gunfire. An engine started up somewhere behind the door as Jan, wanting to get out of the line of fire, pushed on Haywood's shoulder.

"Roll," she said with a grunt.

They cleared the front of the door in time to be missed by a surplus army transport that burst forth, nicking a corner of Haywood's chair and pitching it aside as it wrenched the garage door from its mounts. The truck shoved the door forward like a floppy shield until ramming the cars blocking its exit, a collision that shed the door and gave the driver enough vision to crank his wheels onto the street running beneath the viaduct. A car fender got dragged, sparking for twenty yards before falling off and being run over by the truck's rear wheels. The driver just kept crashing through gears and gaining speed and disappearing into the semidarkness. The truck was nearly a block away before a single shot was fired at it. The gunmen had been too busy diving for cover to be pulling triggers.

In the aftermath, one car's front end was so crumpled it wouldn't start, and no one was eager to get in the other to give chase. They could hear Z.Z. Rip laughing in that car. The sound had them glancing sideways at one another. When the laughter stopped, they grew even more uneasy and edged away from the car. From inside the car, Z.Z. Rip said, "You mothers couldn't protect nothing." Emerging from the backseat, he had an arm affectionately around Po'. When he tried to look each of his men square in the eye, they kept their faces averted. So he spoke up for the benefit of everyone present.

"Don't matter how many ways you fucked up before, Po'. Your fortune's made. You just saved my ass."

Po' looked willing to be convinced this was the case.

"What the hell's goin' down?" Haywood said.

"Take a look inside for your brother," Z.Z. said. "But somethin' tells me he just got moved."

"Was he in there?"

"Word had it that way."

"Then what all this shootin' 'bout?"

"Takin' care of old scores."

"You can kiss that reward good-bye," Haywood warned.

"Hear that, boys?" Z.Z. said, voice raised and amused, as if fifty thousand was petty cash. "We out of the runnin', so let's load her up. Po', you drivin'."

"What about us?" asked Jan.

"Don't pick up no strangers. That my advice to you."

Po' slid in on the driver's side, looking as though he'd been there since he was tall enough to see over a steering wheel. He ordered everyone else to pile in and drove off, leaving Jan and Haywood to search the warehouse. The first thing Haywood said was, "Don't go savin' my ass ever again."

30

The garage had been emptied of Lyle, but Jan did pocket a hospital name tag that read *Dr. G. Knox*. While she rubbed her thumb over that, Haywood lifted his chin in the general direction of a faded ottoman that had tangled bed sheets and an embroidered pillow on it.

"They had him right over there."

"How can you tell?"

"Blind man's vision."

Jan didn't comment but, seeing a phone, picked it up and started dialing.

"Who you callin'?"

"FBI. They might learn something from this place that we can't."

"Shit," Haywood said, but nothing more, not even anything with teeth when Jan got a pager and had to leave Agent Ford a message.

They waited fifteen minutes without a callback and, despite all the gunfire, without any sirens coming to the rescue either.

"Seems we all alone," Haywood said with satisfaction.

"For now," Jan answered, hating the way she felt obliged to defend Special Agent Ford.

"I can be all alone at home."

"And I want you to be," Jan said.

After being clipped by the truck, Haywood's wheelchair scraped all the way back to City Park. The only event on the long walk was a nonevent: Haywood fell completely silent, wouldn't even answer questions. Jan fell under the same spell, feeling spent and worse than useless. They got in Haywood's van, drove back to his place, and parted without saying a word to each other.

IT WASN'T UNTIL she got home after dodging three curfew checkpoints that she was forced to return to the land of the talking. As soon as she pulled into the drive, she knew something was wrong. Every light in the house was blazing and she found her youngest, Tess, at the picnic table in the backyard. Wearing the pajamas with the carrot design and her bunny slippers, Tess sat gazing skyward, counting stars with her index finger.

"What's going on?" Jan asked, remaining on her feet.

"Dad was over."

"Why?" Jan said, glancing toward the house despite herself.

"Said he wanted to make sure we were OK."

"What happened?" Jan asked, slowly lowering herself beside Tess.

"Grandma wouldn't let him in."

"Then?"

"Amy said she'd invited him over and he could come in if she wanted him to."

"And?"

"Everyone chose sides and your friend came upstairs in the middle of it. She didn't stay up long."

"She's still here, isn't she?"

"Oh yeah, back in the basement, waiting for you to give her a ride home. Dad wanted to know what in the blank-blank she was doing there. And Grandma told him it was none of his blank-blank business. And Felicia said some blank-blank too—I don't remember what—but it made Dad get all red, that way he does. And Amy got into it too. Leah thinks Amy owes your friend some kind of apology for calling her a jigaboo. I forgot to put that part in. Amy started calling her that and that's when Felicia said what I don't remember."

"I think it's bedtime," Jan said, forcing herself to stand.

"It's too crazy to sleep."

"Not for long," Jan promised, taking Tess by the hand. "Come on."

Just as Jan was about to open the back door, Tess said, "Jigawho?"

"What?"

"That's what Felicia said," Tess said, opening the door for her mother. "And some other blank-blank things too, and she was crying too until Grams took her downstairs. Amy talked with Dad. Leah got on the phone with that creep she hangs out with, and I don't know, I guess Katie and me were angels. You might have to split Leah and Amy up, you know."

"We tried that once," Jan said. "Remember?"

"I'll say," Tess said with a yawn.

Inside, the television was going, turned on by Katie to drown out her older sisters, who, though in their bedroom, could be heard all over the house. On the way back there, Jan turned off the TV, warning Katie that late-night television would make her teeth crooked. The usual protests were lodged and duly noted. The door to Jan's bedroom was closed, signaling Claire's withdrawal from the field of battle. The door to Leah and Amy's room was closed too, no doubt by Claire, for Jan's two oldest loved an audience for their operas. Once Katie and Tess were pointed to their room, Jan held up in the hall a moment, curious. Her two oldest daughters—half sisters, actually—had gotten along about as well as *Ms.* magazine and *Good Housekeeping* from the start.

"You wouldn't even know what to do with plastic gloves." A volley from Amy.

"That was always your specialty," said Leah.

No telling what that was about. Current arguments were always laced with retorts from old battles. Jan entered without knocking and found the two girls in their usual sparring positions: on their separate beds, curled on their sides, backs to one another. She ordered Leah to move into Jan's bedroom for the night and to do it quietly in case Claire was sleeping.

"Ha," Claire called across the hall.

The girls broke cleanly, though, and with the house quiet, Jan took a minute to compose herself before heading downstairs to mend fences with Felicia. A minute was too long, and she didn't make it all the way downstairs. Felicia met her on the steps, purse in hand.

"There any word?" was Felicia's first anxious question. Followed by, "You shouldn't have let me sleep."

"Nothing definite," Jan said, unwilling to go into the near miss at the garage just yet. "What happened here?"

"I met your ex. Appears he doesn't like black folks."

"God, I'm so sorry, Felicia."

"No reason to be. My ex isn't any better."

"But you didn't need to hear that kind of stuff."

"I didn't hear it," Felicia said. "Told him right off, which was maybe the healthiest thing for me. I feel much better and probably should be getting on home, in case there's anything to hear about Lyle."

"You can hear that from here."

"I think everyone might be more comfortable if I was at home."

"Not true," Jan said. "Everyone wants you here."

"Jan, I appreciate what you're doing, really I do, but maybe I'd be more comfortable at home. It's not exactly *everyone* who wants me here."

"At least wait until morning," Jan said. "The curfew's still on."

"I won't sleep again," Felicia warned.

"You can stay awake here just as well as at home."

They stared at each other until Felicia smiled tiredly and said, "First thing in the morning?"

"Guaranteed."

"Before breakfast?"

"Right out the back door."

"Done."

"Good," Jan said. "Now there's something else I should fill you in on."

They sat down on the basement steps and Jan filled her in on how close she and Haywood had possibly come to springing Lyle. At the end of it, Felicia took one of Jan's hands in both of hers and said, "Thank you, Jan. If I hadn't been acting up you wouldn't have needed to do any of that."

"At least it seems he's still alive," Jan said.

"That's about all we do know," Felicia said. Making a fist, she hit her thigh in frustration.

Jan said something comforting that neither of them listened to. It was past three before she dragged herself to bed, surprised that her legs were long enough to manage the stairs, seeing as how she felt about three inches tall for still not being totally up front with Felicia.

31

In the morning Jan had more opportunities than she could stand to make a clean breast of everything. The girls were sleeping when she and Felicia left, so there weren't any distractions from that quarter, but the shameful memory of Amy's outburst dampened her impulse to do right. During the drive across town, Felicia was striving to be upbeat. Jan didn't have the heart to kill that. And although Haywood was nowhere in sight when they arrived, the thought of his hearing about her sins of omission sealed Jan's lips, sending her scurrying to the General rather than accept the offered cup of coffee.

Once at her desk, she stared at the telephone all morning. Felicia could be reached on that thing. Instead, she paged Agent Ford again, without luck, and tried Lieutenant Crenshaw, who called her excursion with Haywood grandstanding but had to admit what she'd learned might save two lives. At least now they could start bird-dogging the right gang, if they could free anyone to do it. The mayor was calling for a new peace initiative, to be headed by the police. Then Jan was back facing the phone. In the end what silenced her better instincts was the early-afternoon arrival of Agent Ford, who looked as though he'd been to the edge of the world and was back to report it was a long drop off. He spoke in a soft, respectful voice that made Jan want to look away. She didn't risk it, though.

"Crenshaw tells me you had some excitement," he said.

"If you'd answer your beeper, you could have heard sooner."

"Sorry, I had to take a flight to Washington for a meeting. Tell me about it now."

She did, but he kept checking over the top of her cubicle's partitions the whole time, as if expecting a messenger with winged feet. When Jan leaned back in her chair for a peek at how Miss Pepperidge was taking their conference, the agent turned with her, his gaze flushing the secretary toward her boss's office. Jan chose that moment to play her trump.

"The Sevens aren't the ones holding Lyle or the doctor."

"Doesn't matter," the agent said, waving it off. "Not at the moment, anyway. Maybe later, but right now that means next to nothing." He scanned over the top of the cubicle to make sure they were alone and said, "We're taking your advice, Jan. Penshorn gets traded for the hostages."

"What in the world . . ." She stalled there, finding herself staring at the phone again as she tried to piece everything together. When her mind flashed forward to the answer, she felt a sudden prickle in her cheeks. "It's the doctor, isn't it?"

"The fact that they've kidnapped two people," he said reasonably, "that's bound to change our thinking. We're not inhuman."

"One issue at a time," Jan commented. When she looked up, the agent avoided eye contact and started twisting his gold bracelet. "Why do I get the feeling there's more?"

"Sad but true," the agent said, taking an interest in her phone himself. "The people who have Lyle Brown and Dr. Knox have contacted us. They'll only do business with Brown's brother, the one they saw on TV." His voice became robotic for what he had to say next, as if repeating something word for word. "And if that's the way they want it, then that's the way it's going to be."

"Is that what they told you in Washington?"

"Among other things."

"And Penshorn's going along with this? Knowing it's not Sevens you're handing him over to?"

"We can't be sure who we're handing him over to," Ford said, turning heavy-handed. "You've only some gang banger's word on it."

"So you haven't told him?" Jan said, wanting to hear him say it.

"He wants to go," Ford said, becoming defensive.

"I see," Jan said. "And what do you want from me?"

"Me personally? Nothing. But this Haywood says you're the only honky he'll let go to the exchange, and we have to have someone there we can trust, don't we?"

"Why's that make me feel like a rat?"

"You've done great so far, Jan. Don't give up on us now. We've nearly got your man."

"Nearly," Jan echoed. "Where will you be when all this is going on?"

"Close as possible."

"When's the historic moment?"

"Tomorrow morning, after the doctor's family gets the ransom pulled together. By the way, they're paying for your man's release too."

"Am I supposed to be grateful?"

"I'd say so."

"I'll try to work it in," Jan said.

THEN CAME A full day of nothing. She had twenty cups of coffee and nearly as many conversations with Felicia, each of them assuring the other that everything would be all right. There were plenty of openings for Jan to reveal what she had known from the beginning, but what purpose did it serve—other than hushing Jan's conscience—to dredge it up now that they actually were going to trade for Lyle? During all the conversations there was never any question but that Felicia would be coming with them too.

At the end of her shift, Jan had to drive home for supper as if it was any normal workday. All her daughters were contrite but Amy, who stormed off to her room when Jan informed her she owed Felicia an apology.

"I knew you'd take her side," Amy shouted before slamming her bedroom door.

After supper, TV. Despite all the coffee, Jan was asleep by ten.

She dreamed about the *Mary Tyler Moore Show*. In the episode she watched, Mary was trying to convince Mr. Grant that she hadn't really meant to do what she hadn't meant to do. Mr. Grant got it, sort of.

THE NEXT MORNING Agent Ford ordered a tracking device taped to her ankle and swore it would allow them to follow her from a distance of up to ten miles, although they planned to stay much closer. The Little Admiral had donated his office for the cause, having gone on an inspection tour of the hospital's perimeter rather than watch Jan roll up her pant leg.

"So where's the exchange going to be?" Jan asked, feeling spacy and unable to concentrate on details, which she supposed was a blessing. At least it left her feeling as though her worries weren't real.

"They'll call in directions," Ford said, handing her a cellular phone. He also handed her a small key, adding, "For Penshorn's cuffs. Just follow their instructions and don't worry. Once you've got the hostages, we'll move in and make sure nothing happens to Penshorn. He's still going to trial."

"So you're not planning on making the trade this time either?"

"Not true," Ford said. "Penshorn's a free man. For about five minutes."

"This time," Jan said, "you *are* going to let us pick Lyle up?"

"And the doctor," Ford confirmed.

"What about the ransom?"

"The brother has to carry it," Ford said, patting a briefcase at his side.

"Real money in there?"

"And lots of it," Ford said without offering a look.

"Tell Penshorn anything?"

"To be a good boy."

"Are we done here?" Jan asked as the agent who'd been taping the tracking device to her ankle stepped away.

"I'd say so," Ford answered, leading the way out of Hodges's office.

They drove to Haywood's in five cars ranging from a Volkswagen Golf to a Mustang with a sunroof. There were at least two agents to a car and when they pulled up in front of Haywood's bungalow around midmorning, five men and two women accompanied Jan and Agent Ford into the yard. They were dressed in such crisp casual clothes—creased blue jeans and billed hats without stains—that there couldn't have been much doubt who employed them, and if there was, the aviator sunglasses took care of that. Jan went in the middle of the pack, following Rainy Penshorn around the side of Haywood's house. The prisoner still wore handcuffs, and his head remained bandaged, his arm in a sling. All the way around the house he made glad talk, offering to kiss their pimply asses one last time if anyone wanted to drop his or her drawers. No takers, not even when he said, "Ladies first."

Haywood accepted the ransom briefcase, setting it on his lap and asking Ford if they couldn't put something big in Penshorn's mouth, a lug wrench or something. When Haywood tried unlatching the briefcase, he found it locked and warned them there better not be paper dolls in there. Felicia had no idea what he was talking about and reacted as though she'd spent the night cutting the aforementioned dolls out of the newspaper. Taking Jan's hand, she asked her to do the driving. Jan agreed, thinking the activity might turn out to be a godsend.

Penshorn talked all the way to Haywood's van and didn't stop once they were inside it. Most of what he said didn't register with Jan, although every once in a while a word, usually a simple word, got through and she repeated it to herself a half-dozen times or more before remembering its meaning. The FBI drove off before Jan even started the van. That was for the benefit of any neighbors who might be watching on behalf of the kidnappers, and for Haywood too, who swore he wasn't going anywhere if they tried to follow them. Jan kept quiet about the tracking device around her ankle.

Then came a full morning of aimless driving, as per their initial instructions. *Drive until contacted.* They had to stop to fill up the gas tank, and not until lunchtime did the cellular phone finally chirp. When it did, Jan hit the brakes and almost got them rear-ended.

"Let's hear it," Haywood said into the receiver. He listened a half minute before saying, "I got you." A few seconds later he hung up and said, "Lexington and Ingersol."

The only other person to comment was Rainy Penshorn, who said, "Home, James."

Haywood told him to shut up, which he did, after a good, long laugh.

THE INTERSECTION OF Lexington and Ingersol was at the top of Knob Hill in a quiet residential neighborhood with tidy lawns, long driveways, and two-car garages. There was no sign of any hostages, unless a squirrel or two was holding them. The eastern half of the city spread out before them, which must have been why they'd been ordered there. Someone with a spotting scope could observe them from almost anywhere down below. Jan pulled over and there they sat for five minutes, until the phone rang again. Haywood fumbled it this time, dropping it to the floor.

"I'm in good hands," Penshorn commented as Jan retrieved the phone.

Felicia shut him up with an elbow, an action that so surprised Jan she turned around as if she hadn't glimpsed it out of the corner of her eye.

"Let him step outside," Haywood said, repeating what he'd heard over the phone.

Felicia slid open the side door and pushed Penshorn out. He stood next to the van for a half minute, waving down at the city, until Haywood received more instructions and told him to get back inside.

"Downtown," Haywood said, hanging up. "The Danford Building, underground parking."

The Danford Building meant nothing special to anyone but Penshorn, who boasted, "Fifty stories up and connected to everywhere by tunnels. We in for a ride."

Two or three blocks before their destination the phone rang a third time. This time Haywood reported they were supposed to park, take the garage elevator to the fourteenth floor, and look for an open door.

"We take Chuckles too," Haywood said, jerking a thumb toward Penshorn.

"Shouldn't we be calling somebody?" Felicia asked.

"You go callin' anybody," Penshorn said, "and I'll be shoutin' my brothers off."

That was as close as Jan came to telling him they weren't necessarily going to be his brothers.

"We're fine," Haywood said, quieting Jan's impulse.

It took them five minutes to cover the last three blocks to the Danford Building and another five minutes to get into the underground parking, which was full. Traffic was heavy and drivers aggressive, as the business day was shortened due to the riots. During all that time Jan didn't spot any of the FBI agents who had driven to Haywood's house.

They descended to the fourth level before finding an open parking spot. The only conversation on the way to the elevator came from Penshorn, who had begun narrating the trip like a sports announcer hyped up for Super Bowl Sunday. Haywood told him to shut up or he'd run over him with his wheelchair, a threat that Penshorn wove right into his coverage.

There was barely enough room on the only elevator that seemed to be working, and breathing was tight, given the amount of air that Penshorn's mouth was consuming. The elevator car stopped on the third level for a businessman, who took one look at Penshorn's handcuffs and stepped back, refusing to get on. Penshorn kept right on broadcasting. The elevator stopped again on the second level, and Jan readied herself for another backpedaling business suit. Instead, she found herself face-to-face with four men. Three of them were masked by silk stockings and wearing green running suits. The fourth was not. The fourth was Lyle.

Two of the men had to hold Lyle up by his armpits. His head was slumped down, chin resting on his chest.

"This what you want?" the man not supporting Lyle asked. He held a large-bore pistol on them and blocked open the elevator with his foot. Jan couldn't be sure but thought he was the man she'd talked to at the first aborted exchange.

"Lyle?" Felicia gasped, moving forward, only to be shoved back by the tip of the gun barrel.

"Biz first," the gunman said. "You got cash?"

"Here," Haywood said, holding up the briefcase.

The gunman leaned into the elevator to relieve him of it.

"That good," the gunman said. "Now our man."

With a wide grin, Penshorn stepped in front of Jan and held his handcuffs up as high as he could, waiting for the key.

"Where's the doctor?" Jan asked.

"Around the corner. You push ol' Rainy out here, and you get this one." He nodded at Lyle. "Then you push that wheelchair out here, and you get the other one."

"That wasn't—"

"You heard me. We gonna teach this wheelchair there a price for knockin' on our door."

Before Jan could argue, Haywood started to wheel himself out.

"Not so fast," the gunman said, stopping Haywood's chair with the bottom of his foot. "Rainy first."

"Now you talkin'," said Rainy.

After Jan undid Penshorn's cuffs, he put a hand out for the talking man's gun, as if he had some immediate use for it, but the gunman waved him off, and nodded for his two helpers to give up Lyle. They did so by shoving him into Jan's and Felicia's arms.

What happened next came fast. Jan and Felicia staggered under Lyle's weight. Felicia cried out. Jan heard a stairway door to the left of the elevator open.

"Hold it right there," a man shouted. It sounded as though he'd shouted that line before, maybe for the FBI.

The gunman in front of them acted as though he'd heard that line before. Without holding anything, he shot from his hip. End of that conversation. There was no return fire from the FBI.

"Running time," the gunman shouted.

The elevator doors began to shut and the last thing Jan saw on Rainy Penshorn's face was a look of childlike astonishment. The gunman had raised his barrel to Penshorn's nose. As the elevator started up, Jan heard another gunshot that she knew she'd carry all the way to her grave and beyond.

32

Jan and Felicia yoked themselves to Lyle's arms and dragged him off the elevator. Haywood brought up the rear, rolling himself forward and barking for directions. The procession made it as far as a bank of telephones in the Danford Building's main lobby. Jan was punching up 911 when FBI agents with drawn guns began pouring out stairway doors in their field jackets. Their faces were flushed from sprinting up and down fourteen flights to the floor Haywood had been ordered to. The growing crowd of spectators knew right away what to do and flattened to the marble floor. Everywhere Jan looked she saw black briefcases identical to the one Haywood had just been relieved of; they were all being clutched against someone's chest.

"Where?" Agent Ford shouted across the lobby.

"Lower level two," Jan answered just as the emergency operator came on the phone line. Ford waved his team toward the elevators and stairways. Jan ordered up an ambulance.

The Danford was slightly over a mile from Jackson General, and two ambulances arrived within minutes. As the paramedics were transferring Lyle outside, Ford returned to say they only needed one stretcher down below, for the downed agent. Rainy Penshorn had caught one between the eyes. They were trailing the paramedics when Ford delivered that news. He managed to sound blameless. Jan was pushing Haywood, and Felicia was hovering near Lyle's stretcher. Holding Jan back by the upper arm, Ford motioned for one of his men to take over pushing Haywood's wheelchair.

"There may still be time to catch them," Ford said. "What did you see?"

"Three men," Jan told him, staring at the hand on her arm. "Black. They wore nylon stockings as masks."

"How dressed?"

"Green running outfits, kind of shiny."

"What else?"

"Red high-tops."

Releasing Jan, Ford broadcast the description over a two-way. The details were accurate enough for the agents to tag a pile of running outfits ditched in a stairwell. Jan didn't find out about that until later, though. As soon as Ford started talking into his radio, she cut for an exit to catch the ambulance. She didn't get far.

"Jan," Ford sang out, "they've already called again. They want another million."

"Another?"

"The first was for Lyle. They want another for the doctor. If you can find out anything from your man, it could save a life."

The delay was enough that she missed the first ambulance, the one taking Lyle, and had to flag a taxi whose driver kept his English in a pocket dictionary above the sun visor.

SHE REACHED THE General in time to find Haywood in the middle of a scene with Frank Huey, the guard in charge of controlling access into the emergency room. Since the riot, Security had initiated a locked-door policy. One visitor per patient, and that visitor cleared through a checkpoint.

"My brother's in there," Haywood was insisting.

"The woman went in with him," Frank Huey said.

"Can somebody tell me," Haywood said, raising his voice to the room at large, "is this a *man* sittin' in front of me?"

"Keep it up," Frank Huey said, "and I'll have you escorted outside."

"Escorted!" Haywood cried.

"Voice down," Frank Huey said.

People were beginning to gather in the ER entry area to listen. Frank Huey, the only guard in sight, sat behind a portable counter blocking access to the ER. There was a line of people waiting to plead their case with him, but he wasn't paying any attention to the audience. A warm glow to his face, he was concentrating on Haywood. To reach the front of the line, Jan had to step between two wide bodies with dreadlocks and around an East Indian mother dressed in a sari and holding an infant on each hip. Other people were drifting down from the TV lounge, drawn by Haywood's lung power.

"How about God?" Haywood was saying. "Would you let God in there?"

"This *is* Lyle Brown's brother," Jan said, adding her voice to Haywood's. "Let him in."

Frank Huey crossed his arms and leaned back in his chair, looking as though Jan's arrival made everything perfect. He didn't bother saying no.

"I mean it," Jan told him.

"No doubt," Frank Huey said.

Stepping back, Jan told Haywood to hold his horses and crossed to the triage desk to use the phone. She called the Little Admiral's office, getting Miss Pepperidge on the line. Before the secretary could put her on hold, Jan informed her that riot number two was brewing in the ER and she'd better put her boss on the horn. The Little Admiral came on just as Haywood was bellowing in the background, "I suppose you think I couldn't be God."

"What's that?" Hodges demanded.

"Frank Huey being sensitive."

"I'll have his goddamn ass," Hodges said.

Jan told him where he could find it.

Within two minutes footsteps were galloping down the hall. Three security guards arrived, including the day-shift supervisor, Robert Yost, just as Frank Huey wrestled Haywood's chair out of Jan's grasp and was shoving it toward the pneumatic doors as if to dump its contents outside. The East Indian woman had skittered to the side, but the two men with dreadlocks weren't giving an inch. More people were arriving. Haywood was blindly groping behind himself, trying to get a handful of Frank Huey.

And then things got worse. Haywood quit grabbing for Frank Huey, clutched his chest, went rigid.

"Nurse!" Jan yelled to the triage desk.

"Out of the way," the day-shift supervisor called out, forcing his way through the crowd.

"He's faking it," Frank Huey said. Stepping around the wheelchair and leaning over Haywood's face, he said, "Come on, you."

Feeling a breath on his cheek, Haywood quit playing possum and punched Frank Huey square on the chin, rocking him back on his heels, crumpling him to the floor.

And then the unexplainable.

The impact of Haywood's fist on Frank Huey's chin drained all the tension from the room. No one else threw a punch. Everyone opened their fists. The two men in dreadlocks returned to their place in line, stepping over Huey without saying a word. The East Indian woman followed suit. Several people turned back toward the TV lounge.

"Who's next?" Haywood shouted, fists raised.

Shortly thereafter, once Jan had explained everything to the day-shift supervisor, she and Haywood made it through the locked double doors to the ER. They went in right behind a woozy Frank Huey, who was being held up by another guard. Jan pushed Haywood to the back cubicles, where they found two nursing assistants cutting off Lyle's uniform, a nurse conferring with the paramedics who had rolled him in, and Felicia holding on to Lyle's hand as if it was a lifeline. Haywood put it all into perspective.

"Is he breathing?"

He was.

THE MEDICAL STAFF working on Lyle catalogued a concussion, a hematoma that closed one eye, cracked ribs, lacerated heel, heavy bruising on his flanks, possible kidney damage, a broken nose, badly sprained ankles, three broken toes, a fractured tibia, and severe dehydration. He also appeared to have bitten his tongue. As Jan learned later, he had his own brother to thank for much of the list. The truck ride out of the garage where they'd been holding him was a rough one. But that news came later. While in the emergency room Lyle never came far enough around for the staff to judge his mental status.

They hustled him through X ray and CAT scan, and admitted him to a medical intensive care unit with a diagnosis of multiple trauma, which the young doctor in charge assured Felicia only meant they wanted to keep a close eye on him. Everything should be all right. Haywood put that into perspective too.

"That's what they told me when I lost these." He was pointing at where his legs used to be. "What I want to know is how the FBI got there lickety-split? Without 'em, everything would have been cool."

But Felicia shushed him and said the worst was over. She said it often enough for Jan to think the worst might just be returning. Out of guilt, she slipped off to a restroom, undid the FBI's tracking device, and stuffed it deep into a wastebasket. But her twinges of conscience didn't clear up until Lyle came around enough for his one unswollen eye to flutter open, barely. Taking in Felicia, he said, "That's nice." Before anyone could second the motion, he faded. But afterwards, Felicia gained strength and, although spending half a day sitting in various waiting rooms, required no hand-holding.

By early evening they'd all arrived at the intensive-care family lounge, Felicia dozing in a chair, Haywood arguing over the phone, Jan figuring there wouldn't be a better time to slip home for some rest.

Before she'd gone twenty steps in that direction, she heard her name called and turned to see Agent Ford rising from a nurse's desk, where he'd appropriated a telephone. He dropped the phone and approached quickly, speaking in a church whisper and keeping away from the hall windows of the family waiting room.

"What's he saying?"

"He's not. Probably won't be for a while."

"I'll talk to his doctor," Ford said, as if that would speed things up. "Listen, the other hostage's family wants to meet you. They know you were at the exchange."

"I didn't see their doctor."

"The lady's lost her husband, Jan. The old man, a million. I'd say they're entitled to hear something."

"I don't remember you saying that about Felicia."

211

"Something, Jan." The agent signaled for a time-out. "I didn't say we would tell them everything."

"What aren't *we* telling *these* people?"

"To get ready for the worst."

THE MISSING DOCTOR'S wife and father-in-law had been ushered into the executive administrator's office, hallowed ground whose carpet Jan had been called on before. It was also a room that Felicia had never seen during her ordeal. The exec himself was nowhere in sight, but the ceiling was high as ever. There was shelving lined with old books, a simple wooden desk with two facing chairs, and a view of the courtyard where Felicia and Jan had first become friends. It was empty out there now. A cart with a coffee service had been rolled into the room. The coffee in the engraved cups was untouched and looked as though it had gone cold.

There was a fierce odor of hair oil loose in the room, and since Agent Ford went for the blow-dried look, the only other candidate was a hunched old man encamped behind the executive administrator's desk. He wore a blue blazer with a crest on its pocket, a white button-down shirt, and a natty tie that must have been silk. If he was aiming for preppydom, what hair he had left wouldn't need an oil change before he got there.

"Well?" the old man demanded.

"Nothing," Ford said.

The old man brought his cane down so hard on the desk that Jan flinched, though nothing broke.

"That's not what I'm paying you for."

"You're not paying me for anything, Mr. Waltzer."

Agent Ford looked more satisfied than he should have while delivering the rebuff, but Jan didn't care about that. At the moment she was more interested in the woman sitting in front of the desk. In her thirties, she held herself stiff as porcelain, was attractive but pale, and looked wound up tight as a nun with deep doubts about the pope. While one hand bunched up the material of her charcoal-gray dress, the other held a tan cardigan together at her throat. The sweater draped over her shoulders probably belonged to the exec, who went in for things like leather elbow patches. Sleep had evaded the woman for days. Dark ovals extended below her eyes, which concentrated so intently on the lips of whoever was speaking that Jan at first imagined she was deaf.

"Father," she said, voice almost hoarse, "they're trying to help."

One look at his daughter stifled the old man's impulse to thump the desk a second time.

"Do you have anything more to tell us?" the wife asked.

"That I'm afraid it's a waiting game," Ford said.

The wife nodded, as if she'd suspected as much, and moved her vision to Jan. Being studied by those wired blue eyes took Jan back to the morning she'd had to tell Felicia why Lyle hadn't come home. It was as though a demon had fled from one woman to the other.

"This is the security officer I told you about," Ford said. "The one who was at the exchange."

"Did you see him?" the wife asked, letting go of the cardigan and leaning forward. "My husband, I mean."

"I'm sorry," Jan mumbled, "but no."

"We would have found him if he'd been there," Agent Ford assured them.

"Meaning they intended all along to ask for more," said the old man. To Jan, he said, "What happened to the first briefcase?"

She answered but directed her words to the daughter.

"Sounds as though the same thing will happen to a second briefcase," the old man told his daughter.

To which the daughter said nothing. To which the old man said nothing.

"You have some time to think about it," Ford told them. "And in the meantime we'll continue tracking down every lead. We've a full technical team going over the crime scene."

"Is it hopeless?" the wife asked.

"I think," Ford said, fingering his gold bracelet, "that your father may be right. Paying a second million may not bring your husband back either."

"Are you saying we shouldn't pay it?"

"Not at all. Paying may be all that keeps him alive long enough to save him."

"Paying and paying and paying," added the old man.

"It may come down to that, yes, sir."

"My husband's a good man," the wife insisted.

Rather than argue the point, the old man told Jan and Agent Ford to get out. Before they reached the door, the wife made one last request.

"If there's any way to help . . ." she said, but was unable to finish the thought.

Turning, Jan found the woman gazing at her.

OUT IN THE hall, Jan asked, "So what do you want me to do?"

"Just what I said," Ford answered. "Find out whatever you can."

"And then?"

"Let me do my job."

BY THE TIME she got back to the family lounge it was empty. She panicked and dashed down the hall to the intensive care unit, but everything was all right. Lyle had regained consciousness. As soon as Jan saw his one unswollen eye weakly open, she knew she wasn't up to telling anyone where she'd just been. Felicia was spooning ice chips into his mouth. Haywood had rolled along the other side of the bed and was pitching a five-part miniseries based on Lyle's ordeal and injustice in America.

"Our big problem," Haywood predicted, "will be getting a sponsor. I've been thinkin' on Hallmark."

Lyle's one good eye studied his brother as if he'd been hearing similar schemes for years.

"Who's going to play me?" Jan asked, making her entrance after a deep breath.

"Maybe Whoopi," Haywood said.

"I'll take that as a compliment."

"You better."

Then came another, slower voice, one that sounded as though it was talking around something stuck in its mouth.

"I hear," Lyle said, "I owe you a big thank-you."

Jan didn't correct him, and Felicia seconded what he'd said with a firm nod. Haywood even made a point of keeping his mouth shut, which was probably as much agreement as anyone could expect from him.

"I'm just glad you're safe," Jan said, pulling a chair beside Felicia. "Do you feel up to answering some questions? They're still holding another man."

"That doctor?" Lyle asked, his one good eye blinking.

"Hold on now," Haywood interrupted. "These mothers never once budged a finger to bust you loose, so what business is it of yours to be helpin' now? Answer me that."

"What about *my* itty-bitty fingers?" Jan protested, too loudly, she supposed, but she couldn't forget the way the doctor's wife had looked at her. "I suppose they don't count."

"Your fingers? They some kind of aberration."

"Felicia?" Jan said, as if appealing to a higher court.

"She's been there for us," Felicia said.

"Yeah?" Haywood said. "So see if you can answer me this. How come nobody coughed up Rainy Penshorn until there was a white ass on the line? Fill me in on that, if you can."

"I can only tell you what they told me," Jan crossly said, fighting to keep her voice level. "But I don't imagine it'd do much good."

"Might give us a laugh," Haywood said.

"No laughs," said Lyle.

With that, Jan and Haywood quit crisscrossing the bed with looks and found a corner to stare off into. Felicia patted Lyle's hand, indicating he should go on.

"This guy they got," Lyle slowly said, "I don't know if he's worth rescuing, but if you've got your heart set on it, Gallagher, then I got about one thing that might help you."

Lyle caught his breath there. Jan bit her lip.

"Spicy hot chicken wings," said Lyle. "That's about all I can tell you."

33

There were eleven chicken-wing joints listed in the yellow pages, and Agent Ford's frown deepened as each name on the roll call was read. Not until Jan said it was as hot a lead as they were likely to get did Ford dispatch agents for eleven orders of extra spicy. He also informed her that he wanted a word with Lyle Brown himself, with some help from her, of course. They were seated in the Little Admiral's office, Ford behind the desk. The green-glass desk lamp was on, but the Little Admiral wasn't in port.

"Don't expect the welcome wagon," Jan said.

Smiling as if back on familiar ground, Agent Ford picked up the phone and two calls later had arranged for the medical staff to shoo all relatives out of Lyle's unit. To let the patients rest, he suggested. Setting the receiver down, he tightened the knot of his necktie, and said, "That ought to even the odds a little. Shall we?"

Ten minutes later, Ford let Jan lead the way to Lyle's bedside. The patient was resting, but didn't appear to be sleeping. Although his eyes were closed, the TV in front of his bed was on and his fingers were tapping to the tune of a commercial.

"Lyle," Jan quietly said, "do you feel up to talking?"

His one good eye opened to take in Jan and the agent behind her.

"He's from the FBI," Jan said.

"Why'd he bring you?" Lyle asked, seeing through the game they were playing. Before Jan could answer, he said, "Don't matter. He's going to ask his questions anyway."

"But will you answer?" Ford asked, stepping around Jan.

"Why wouldn't I?" Lyle asked, the mockery in his tone making it sound as though Haywood had bent his ear good.

"No reason that I know of," Ford said, pretending everything was sweetness and light. "So tell me about these chicken wings."

Lyle closed his good eye before starting. He didn't open it again while Jan and Ford were there.

"Took them ten minutes to get them when they had me in that first place," Lyle said. "I counted it out. Eight minutes when I was cooking on that rooftop they moved me to."

"Same food both times?"

"Same wings. There's no mistaking that taste."

"Good," Ford said. "And it was always the same woman who made the runs for food?"

"Same."

"And she was always singing?"

"Never stopped," Lyle said. "Never got any better, either. Nonsense stuff, she sang. Scat."

"Was she young or old?"

"Young and old. But she didn't sound like much more than a kid, if that's what you mean."

"OK. So tell me about this second place they moved you to."

"A blacktopped roof. Hot. They just let me blister in the sun. Right on the international's flight path, too. Had to shout half the time. Smelled ripe, like maybe near the lake."

"The doctor they kidnapped was there too?"

"Telling them how to run things."

"How did they get you down off that roof?"

Lyle gave that some thought, as though its possible importance hadn't occurred to him before. Jan edged closer despite herself.

"Marched me down," he said. "Three or four of them. Had to guess, I'd say we went down five floors, but no more than seven, no less than four."

Ford rubbed his chin before saying, "Why are you so sure they'll go for chicken wings again?"

"One of the guards was always wanting them. And the other guards went along with what he wanted."

"He the boss?"

"Nothing like that," Lyle said. "He had something else over them. What, I can't say. But they kind of catered to him, like they owed him something. And I can tell you this much about him. That boy saved my ass one time while they had me. My blindfold had slipped down, and he pulled it back up without saying a word."

"You saw him?" Ford asked.

"Did I say that?" Lyle asked. "If I saw a one of them, they'd have dragged me ten miles down the freeway before they cut the rope. But I'll tell you this—I'd like to repay that boy's favor, and that's for sure."

"Have anything in mind?"

"Let him go."

"I can't make a promise like that."

"Then I probably can't identify any chicken wings," Lyle said, settling on his pillow.

"All right," Ford said, caving in without missing a breath. "Say I look the other way. How do I know which one to look the other way for? Or did you want me to ask them which one pulled your blindfold back up?"

"Look for whichever one smells like Bengay," Lyle said. "He may have a limp, too."

"You want it in writing?"

"Just want to hear you say it in front of Gallagher here."

Jan closed her eyes at that. When she opened them, she found Agent Ford smiling as if everything was falling into place.

"I'll do it," Ford said.

So the boxes of extra-spicy chicken wings came rolling in, and on the eighth one, Lyle gestured madly for a glass of water, which he chugged down. Once the flames were quenched, he said, "That one." He didn't want to taste the rest, but Agent Ford sent word that in the name of thoroughness he should.

"No contest," Lyle said, after pushing the last carry-out box away.

SURVEILLANCE WENT UP that night on a place called Jack Green's Chicken Machine. After hours an agent slipped the lock and planted a bug right under the counter in front of the cash register.

The Chicken Machine did its deep frying in an old storefront that had once belonged to the Reverend James Hapgood, whose sign still hung above the current one, which showed a volcano spewing out smoke and chicken wings in equal parts. Most of the storefronts on that block were boarded up and the boards covered with graffiti, although there was a fortune-teller above the Chicken Machine, a Madame Paridiso, direct from New Orleans, who did enough business to afford a neon light in her window, and at the far end of the block was a Sicilian tailor whose customers all arrived with bodyguards. Except for some hourly-wage earners in needle heels and shrink-wrapped dresses, foot traffic was nil. Customers for the chicken wings came by car, and over the lunch or supper hours they were double-parked out front.

Jan learned all this when she requested frontline duty and was told to report to the surveillance site the next day. Even though the kidnappers Jan had seen all wore masks, no one else had seen even that much, so they were glad to have her. By ten in the morning she was following Ford's directions to the back of a two-story cinder-block building with no roof. A tornado had hit the neighborhood a few years before, and several structures had never fully recovered. She knew it was the right roofless building because of the two identical Chevies, both black, parked behind it. One car held an agent waiting to tail any suspicious take-out orders.

Up on the second floor of the building, the first thing the two agents in business suits said, after introductions, was, "You know anything about watermelon diets?"

That was Agent Garcia, who might have had an ounce or two to shed around his Adam's apple but otherwise looked as though raising his fist and saying a magic word would bring on a superhero's outfit. His partner, Agent Manning, was more of the same rock pile, though black-skinned, not brown. The two of them were standing in a room with no roof on it as if it were nothing out of the ordinary. Maybe they'd torn the roof off to get in. The room had two windows that overlooked the Chicken Machine and were eye level with Madame Paridiso's parlor. Plywood covered both windows, but holes had been cut out of the plywood and then covered with tinted plastic. In front of one portal stood a camera on a tripod. A jet landing at the international airport drowned out Jan's answer to the watermelon question. By the time the plane had passed, Agent Garcia was talking again.

"My wife thinks I need to lose a few pounds."

"A few?" said his partner.

"That's what she says," Garcia explained to Jan. "She thinks it might bring the romance back. What do you think?"

"Are we still talking about diets?" Jan asked.

"Why not?" Garcia said. "I've never been on a bigger goose chase."

"Chicken chase," Agent Manning corrected.

"You had lunch yet?" Garcia asked. "We've been thinking about trying some of Jack Green's volcano specials."

He showed her a take-out menu he'd lifted while planting the bug.

Over the lunch hour rush, three of the customers came into Jack Green's singing. Two of them were young rappers with a message about the AIDS conspiracy. The third was a saggy streetwalker stuck on some snatches of Smoky Robinson.

After the lunch hour Manning drove in a roundabout way to a parking space in front of Jack Green's. Once inside the takeout place his voice came over the radio loud and clear and a little too theatrical.

"Say," Manning asked the man behind the counter, "this the place that gets some crazy girl customer who won't stop singing scat?"

The electronics didn't pick up the answer from behind the counter.

" 'Cause if this is that place," Manning explained, "a friend told me you got the best spices north of Memphis. He couldn't remember your name, just that girl singing. Said she was a regular, sounded bad as a washboard."

The counterman answered.

"That so? Well, why don't you get me three orders from the same volcano, extra rice, and maybe I get out of here before she makes it. There a charge for that extra rice?"

A muffled answer.

At the same time, Garcia was saying, "Listen to that cheap bastard."

By the time Manning got back to them he'd polished off one dinner and was eyeing another. Having no appetite, Jan let him chow down on hers. By midafternoon the agents had run out of insults to trade and were talking about supper. The woman scat singer, whom Jack Green swore was a regular, never made it that day.

IT WASN'T UNTIL lunch of the second day that a white van, with red doors transplanted from another, less rusty, vehicle, pulled up in front of the Chicken Machine. A young woman got out on the passenger side. As soon as she opened Jack Green's door, Jan could hear her singing over the radio.

"Be-bap, be-bap, be-bapity-bap. You got that order ready, Jack-ity-Jack?"

The woman was dressed in oversized bib overalls hemmed at the knee and a puffy blouse the color of a canary. She wasn't any songbird, though. Her voice was flat and nearly as husky as the rest of her. Garcia was already on the radio, telling the agent down in the car to get ready for liftoff. Manning was at the camera, clicking.

"And don't forget that extra hot sauce," the woman was telling Jack Green. "You always shortin' us on that."

There was an answer from behind the counter.

"What you mean someone askin' 'bout me?"

More from behind the counter.

"Shit," was all the answer she had time for.

A moment later she came busting out the doors with two grocery bags full of chicken wings. From over the radio came the owner shouting, "What about that extra sauce?" The woman wasn't waiting for it. Just as she hit the street, the FBI's unmarked Chevy stuck its nose out the alley across the way. It was enough to spook her.

She jumped in the van, screaming at the driver, who hit a U-turn in front of an oncoming school bus. Before the woman could close her door, one sack of chicken wings flew out on the sidewalk. Braking, the school bus skidded sideways, blocking the unmarked car. With the bus stalled across the street, the FBI agent had to pull onto the sidewalk to give chase. Too late.

Twelve blocks later, though, at the Oak Hills projects, the pursuing agent had some luck and radioed to Jan and agents Garcia and Manning, who were arguing over whose fault this was, that he'd found the van, empty and parked behind a utility shed. One sack of chicken wings was still inside. By the time Jan, Garcia, and Manning arrived, the agent was interviewing nine youngsters who appeared to have been jumping rope nearby. They were all lined up, tallest to runt, and silently shaking their heads no. When Agent Garcia opened his door, every kid except the smallest scattered through holes in the fence easy as smoke would have. Too scared to make a break for it, the smallest child was left holding the jump rope. Her eyes were shiny wet and her jaw so quavery that Manning kneeled down, rested her on his knee, and dried her eyes with a paper napkin from Jack Green's Chicken Machine. After she'd blown her nose, he asked for her name. When she couldn't remember it, he told her she'd have to come with them.

BY SUPPER JAN was back in front of Agent Ford. This time the Little Admiral himself was present, dry-docked in a corner with a faraway look in his eye, as if he could hear a dinner bell toll, but it did not toll for him.

"We need something fast," Agent Ford was telling Jan. "The second million goes out tomorrow. I don't think they'll be waiting around for a third, and all we've got is a four-year-old kid in custody who can't remember her name."

"She must be terrified," Jan said.

"The agent did the right thing, though, Jan. That little girl may be our only link to who piled out of that van. Some of the older kids who were there must know who it was, and the one kid we've got will know who they are. The only problem is, we can't get her to talk."

"You want me to try? Is that it?"

"I was thinking," Ford said, "that Lyle Brown's girlfriend might be a better bet."

"Felicia?" Jan's stomach turned.

"She's a social worker, isn't she? She might have some contacts in those projects, and it's the same old story, Jan. We need to have some trust."

"I don't know if I can ask her," Jan said. "She's been through so much already."

"There's a man's life on the line, Jan, so you'll have to ask her. We can't afford to mess up on this. And while you're at it, you might as well ask her to help interview the woman who owns the van they were driving. We tracked her plates and tried talking to her but got nowhere. Claims her van was stolen. She's fifty-four years old, so it's doubtful she's involved, but closemouthed as she was, she might have some ideas. Here's her unit number. Her name is Elvera Malbarth."

Jan had started reaching for the paper but stopped.

"Something wrong?"

"No," Jan said, recovering by accepting the folded slip. "I was only wondering if we'll find this doctor in time."

"Did you want me to say something positive?" Ford asked, studying her closely.

"Sincere would do," Jan said, knowing that the chances of her meeting two Elvera Malbarths weren't worth calculating. When Ford rose to accompany her, she waved him off, saying, "I'll get more cooperation without you."

"True," Ford answered, easing himself back down. "Don't forget to remind your friend that her guy was in the same fix not too long ago. And report back as soon as you find out if she's willing to help. I'll be over at the Fifth Precinct, with the little girl."

"What do you want me to do?" the Little Admiral asked from the corner.

"Stay right where you are," Ford told him.

It was the best exit line Jan had ever heard in that office.

SHE FOUND FELICIA reading "Dear Abby" to Lyle. A woman's fiancé was paying more attention to his collie than to her, signed *Lassie in Seattle*. At least Haywood wasn't present to comment on the columnist's pedigree. Lyle was on his back with the bed controls resting on his chest. His eyes, good and bad, were closed and there was an idyllic smile parting his lips, as if the hospital room were a spring meadow, Felicia held a bunch of grapes, and his aches and pains were nothing more than violin music.

"I think I know who helped you," Jan said, not daring to sit.

Without lifting his head, Lyle opened his good eye and squinted at her as if he couldn't remember anyone helping him, ever.

"The guard with the limp and Bengay," Jan reminded him. "I think it's Isiah Lawrence."

"Oh, Lord," Felicia said, the newspaper slipping from her grasp.

"Old boyfriend?" said Lyle, making a feeble joke.

"The boy I told you about," Felicia answered, hands positioned as if still holding the newspaper. "The one we pulled out of that basement."

"That'd explain some things," Lyle allowed. "If he'd been in my shoes."

"He drove your scat singer to the chicken-wing place," Jan said. "Went in his mother's van."

"Elvera's?" Felicia asked.

"I'm afraid so."

"You tell them about the boy?" Lyle asked, not having to clarify who *them* was.

"Not yet. I wanted to see what you thought."

"See," Felicia said to Lyle, nudging Lyle's shoulder as if he'd been voicing doubts about Jan.

"Maybe Felicia and I should talk to him," Jan said, the words coming fast so that she wouldn't have to think about them.

"You do that," Lyle said after a moment of consideration. "Tell him what's what and that we'll keep him out of this mess if we can."

"What if he won't tell us anything?" Felicia asked.

"Tell him I never saw him if that doctor's let go."

"And if that doesn't work?" Jan asked.

"Tell him he's busted," Lyle said, closing his good eye as if hoping he wouldn't have to witness it.

34

"There's something else," Jan said, the words labored. Her hands were clinging to each other on her lap. She was riding in Felicia's car to the Fifth Precinct for a word with the child left holding the jump rope. Having talked it over, they didn't expect to learn anything more than the girl's name, if that, but went to cover up knowing Elvera Malbarth.

"It doesn't sound like something I'll want to hear," Felicia said, signaling a turn.

"Not something I want to tell," Jan admitted. "But I guess I have to live with myself, same as everyone else."

"That the end of the good news?"

"Mostly. Here comes the rest." Deep breath, eyes forward. "I knew from the first that the FBI wasn't going to trade for Lyle. No deals, they said. It took that doctor to start them dealing."

"They told you?" Felicia pulled over to the curb for a reconnaissance of Jan's eyes.

"And I never told you," Jan answered with a solemn nod. "I didn't want you holding back anything that might help them. I figured they had the best chance of getting Lyle out in one piece."

For a moment both Felicia's hands gripped the steering wheel as if there was a current running through it. Her eyes rounded and she made a low, penned-up sound in her throat.

"You thought you knew best," Felicia said through her teeth. "Is that what you're saying?"

"I can't lie about it anymore," Jan said, "and now that Lyle's safe, I thought you should know."

Felicia raised a hand as if to slap Jan. She held it in the air for maybe five seconds before dropping it back on the steering wheel and saying, "That makes things hard."

Before Jan could agree, Felicia pulled back into traffic, cutting off a taxi and attempting several other ill-advised shortcuts through traffic. No time for speaking. Squealing into the Fifth's lot, she slammed next to a squad car and didn't have to cut the motor. It died all on its own, flooded. She stared at the barred windows before them long enough for another squad car to gun in beside her. By then Jan had turned sideways on her seat to face Felicia. The only sound was the ticking of the cooling motor. Felicia didn't notice Jan or the new cop car until the officer got out of his car and walked in front of them, left to right. Her eyes tracked the cop until he was even with Jan and then her stare skipped to Jan.

"How am I supposed to know when to trust you, and when not to?" Felicia asked at last.

"How about from now on?" Jan asked, stealing a line from one of her daughters.

"That might be easier than you think."

"Why's that?"

"We might be done being friends."

"I didn't want you helping with this doctor unless you knew," Jan said. "I thought one of the reasons you might lend a hand would be me."

"You'd have been right," Felicia said, nodding mechanically. "What if I don't help?"

"I'll try talking to Isiah Lawrence myself."

"Why not give his name to that FBI agent?"

"I figure I owe you something."

"Fair's fair," Felicia said, opening her door. "I suppose I owe you something, too."

THE DESK SERGEANT wrinkled his nose when they asked for Agent Ford and jerked a thumb toward the back of the first floor. Passing a line of frosted-glass doors whose offices were dark, they finally heard Ford holding court. He'd gotten the last office, which had no important-sounding title stenciled on its glass and held nothing but two folding chairs, a card table, and a black rotary phone sitting atop a city directory covered with scribbled numbers. Ford sat on the windowsill, crooning over the phone. The room's two folding chairs were occupied, one by the little girl, who still held her jump rope, the other by a police matron who appeared to be made from last year's wax.

Seeing Jan enter the room, Ford got off the phone by saying he was being paged and promising he would be in touch the instant there was any breaking news. There was a moment between pulling the receiver away from his ear and setting it down when he looked as though he knew his destiny included an office exactly like the one now surrounding him, with maybe a desk and filing cabinet thrown in for years of service. Tearing himself away from the crystal ball, he returned to duty.

"The doctor's wife," he explained. "Her father has arranged for a community organization to offer a hundred-thousand-dollar reward for help in finding his son-in-law."

"Does that mean we can go home?" Jan asked.

"Maybe not yet," Ford said, watching Felicia, who ignored him in favor of the little girl. "We should probably keep going through the motions."

The first motion Felicia went through was to ask Ford to leave her alone with the girl. Once the agent and the policewoman had stepped outside, Felicia kneeled down to eye level with the child and asked, "You hungry?"

A small nod.

"Come on, then," Felicia said, taking the girl's hand. Opening the door, she asked the woman cop waiting in the hall, "Vending machines?"

The cop pointed. A Snickers and Coke later they'd learned that the child's name was Starla Langston and that her mother would be spoiling about her staying out so long with strangers. Felicia promised to help smooth everything out. The girl wasn't so little that she was reassured.

★ ★ ★

FOLLOWING THREE FBI cars, they reached the Oak Hills projects shortly after dark. Agent Ford had offered them a ride, but Felicia flatly refused. She did begrudgingly agree to an escort as far as the entrance of the projects, but no further. She didn't want anyone seeing the company they kept. All the way there Jan wanted to say something conciliatory but never found an opening. Felicia made a point of chatting with the little girl as if there wasn't another adult in the car.

Per their agreement, the FBI cruised past the projects, allowing Felicia to peel off the tail end of the convoy and glide into the parking lot alone. The agents sped ahead to the next National Guard roadblock to await their report. Jan and Felicia's only concession to teamwork was to carry a two-way radio in case of emergency. They stuffed it in a purse. Felicia went along with that for the simple reason that, as she put it, the only fools her mama raised were somebody else's kids.

The parking lot was well lit and, except for a small National Guard detachment gathered around a Jeep, empty of people. Although Felicia parked as far away from the Jeep as possible, four weekend soldiers in camouflage fatigues and oversized helmets intercepted them before they reached the sidewalk. Three of the soldiers carried rifles. The fourth, who led the way, had a pistol on her hip.

"It's after curfew, ladies," said the woman officer.

"We're taking this little girl home," Jan said.

"That makes you Gallagher, I guess. We were radioed that you'd be showing up. Would you like us to accompany you? It's been pretty quiet tonight, but you never know."

Jan was about to pass, reluctantly, when Felicia spoke up.

"Have you been walking other people home?"

"Yes, ma'am. If they want it."

"And do they?"

"It runs about fifty-fifty."

"Well, we're with the fifty that would appreciate your company," Felicia said. To Jan, she coolly added, "Any sensible person would."

With the little girl holding their hands, Felicia and Jan led the way. The four soldiers fanned out behind them, not crouching as though they expected sniper fire, but sticking to the shadows nevertheless. Starla lived four identical buildings—thirty-two dead bolts—removed from Isiah Lawrence's mother. When they knocked at the child's home, voices quieted and Starla's mother came to the door. With a cry of relief, she jerked her daughter inside as if pulling her away from a fire. Once the mother got beyond hugs and kisses, Felicia explained where Starla had been and what she had witnessed.

"She don't know nothing about that bunch she was playing with," the mother informed them and eased the door shut in their faces. The living room behind her was full of kids straining to see what was going on.

"I don't blame her," Felicia told Jan.

"No one's asking you to," Jan said, leading the way down the steps. The National Guard officer radioed in their coordinates and they moved on to Elvera Malbarth's.

"What do we say?" Jan asked, keeping her voice low because of the soldiers.

"Just what Lyle said, I guess."

"Think it will be enough?"

"Maybe not. But I can't think of what else would be. Can you?"

"Not yet," Jan admitted. "Who'll do the talking?"

"It better be me. Lord knows what you might say."

To which Jan said nothing.

"Or not say," Felicia added a few steps later.

To which Jan still said nothing.

The light pole nearest Elvera Malbarth's unit tilted sideways, away from her front steps, casting long shadows across her door. Its light coated everything from the taped picture window to the shake siding with a waxy yellow glow. From inside the unit came gospel music, but not loud enough to rattle glass. When Felicia knocked, a black cat flushed from beside the steps, jolting her backwards and making her titter. Jan put a hand on her back to steady her.

Isiah himself answered the door, and did it so quickly that Jan got the impression he was expecting someone. The volume of the gospel music doubled with the door open, and Jan, but one step lower than Felicia, had to strain to hear what got said.

"We need a word with you," Felicia told him.

"Nothing to say," Isiah answered, gazing past them at their armed escort, who remained ten yards back but cast shadows almost to the steps.

"There's still a man needs your help."

"Ain't got none of that to give," he said. He tried to close the door but wasn't fast enough. His mother appeared at his side, putting a hand out to stop him.

"Again?" Elvera Malbarth said. It sounded like a question her son had heard before. Opening the door wider, she impatiently waved Felicia and Jan ahead. To the National Guard, she nodded and politely said, "Evening," before shutting them out. Setting Jan and Felicia in the living room on a flowery love seat, she prodded her son toward a facing couch, then disappeared toward the back bedroom and the gospel music. Isiah limped to a place across from them, assuming a totally elsewhere expression on the way. To reach his seat, he had to detour around two coffee tables and squeeze between a pair of unmatched wing chairs. It didn't appear that anything was ever thrown out in that house. The walls were crammed with enough family photos to say it was a tradition stretching back at least to the Emancipation Proclamation. The music slackened and children's voices could be heard in the kitchen.

"You know why we're here," Felicia said.

No answer. Isiah's elsewhere only got farther away, somewhere that didn't understand English.

"My mother can't hear so well," Elvera Malbarth explained upon her return. She settled herself down in an armchair halfway between the facing sofas. "At least this time you had sense enough not to bring that wheelchair. *Now* what do you want from my boy?"

"To find out where a man is," Felicia answered.

"What man?"

"A doctor. He was grabbed down at the hospital."

"That so?" Elvera Malbarth asked her son.

He continued being elsewhere.

"Don't be messing with me," she warned him.

"It's on all the news," Isiah said.

"Yes," Elvera said, losing her patience, "but do *you* know his whereabouts?"

"Not likely."

"Plenty of not likely things happen 'round here," his mother observed.

"Lyle Brown said to thank you," Felicia said to Isiah, who looked, then looked away.

"For what?" Elvera Malbarth asked.

"For helping him while he was being held."

"That so?" the mother asked her son.

"Not likely."

"Don't be giving me that tune," Elvera Malbarth said, leveling a finger at her son. "I know that tune. What I don't know is why I'm getting visits from the Federal Bureau of Investigations about my van. And why you disappearing at all kinds of odd hours."

" 'Cause I'm no good."

"You'd like to think so," his mother said.

"Lyle Brown sent me to tell you something else too," Felicia said when the mother and son didn't break cleanly. "He can't get out of his hospital bed or he'd have come himself."

A shrug from Isiah, who finally glanced away from his mother.

"He said," Felicia told him, "you help this doctor and he never saw you at that place. You don't, you're busted."

It was Elvera Malbarth who answered. "That's some thank-you."

"There's a man's life at stake."

"They ain't got nothing on me," Isiah promised his mother.

"If you know where this doctor is," his mother told him, hands now folded on her lap as if awaiting a judgment, "they don't need to have nothing on you. You got it all on yourself, and you won't ever outrun it."

231

The rest of what got said was hardly worth listening to, except for one tiny contribution that Jan made when the same toddler as on their last visit came gurgling out of the kitchen with a wooden spoon in her hands. Cookie dough covered most of the child's chubby face and some of the spoon, which she carried to Isiah.

"The doctor has children," Jan said. "About that age."

Isiah flashed her a look that could have set a spider's web afire. It lasted but a second before it was gone and the elsewhere look returned. He ignored the spoon the toddler was waving, ignored his mother's order to pick up the child, ignored Felicia and Jan when shortly thereafter they got up to leave. On the way to the door, Jan asked for pen and paper to write down her home phone number.

"In case you change your mind," she said when nobody offered her one.

The only answer she got was a click of Elvera Malbarth's tongue. Isiah had already left the living room with his daughter. Felicia didn't waste any time leaving either, but on the way out Jan spotted a red crayon abandoned against a baseboard and scooped it up. Stopping at a small table near the front door, she printed her phone number on a piece of junk mail addressed to Resident, an invitation to the grand opening of a furniture store. Easy credit was promised. The only acknowledgment Jan's effort got was a small nod from Elvera, too small to promise anything.

Outside, Felicia waited for her near the tilted light pole, standing apart from the National Guard soldiers. She fixed Jan with a cold stare and asked before Jan even reached her, "That doctor really have children?"

"I don't know."

"Then I doubt," Felicia said, turning on her heel and leaving, "that it's time for me to be believing everything you say."

Jan had to hurry to catch up and when she did, couldn't think of a thing to say.

"What are you going to tell this agent?" Felicia asked without looking at her.

"To get the second million ready."

"Don't be trying to tell me that's all you'll tell him."

"I'm willing to give Isiah until morning," Jan said, grabbing

Felicia's arm, which brought them both to a stop. "If his conscience hasn't caught up with him by then, it's probably out of the race."

"We're agreed on that much."

"Felicia," Jan said, "I'm sorry."

"Me too," Felicia said. "Me too."

They parted for the night without saying anything friendlier.

35

Jan got the phone call shortly after the stroke of midnight, the timing adding a dash of unreality. Amy had moved to the basement, so Jan was back in her own bed with the lights out, wishing she could stop thinking about Agent Ford and how she hadn't told him everything either. The ease with which she was spreading half-truths frightened her.

When she and Felicia had met up with the agent at the next National Guard checkpoint, his reaction to her report had been out of character. He mumbled some Joe College inanity about everyone having given it their best shot, then sent them home for some well-earned rest. Instructions on where to deliver the second ransom were due in the morning, he said, and their help might be essential. "Absolutely essential" had been his exact wording. Before they left, however, he did manage to pull Jan aside and urge her to call if she remembered something. "Anything at all," he'd said, as if they still shared a secret. Felicia had seen their little sidebar but never asked about it, acting instead as if she knew exactly what they were up to.

And now the phone was ringing. Picking it up, she expected to hear Ford's voice.

"I'm only going to tell you this shit once."

It took her a moment to realize it wasn't Agent Ford but Isiah Lawrence.

"Let me get a pen," Jan said, knocking the bed lamp off its stand and having to scramble to flick on the ceiling light. The commotion woke Claire, who pulled a pillow over her face. All that Jan could find to write on was the inside cover of a paperback romance her mother had been reading. The only thing to write with was a stub pencil dulled by countless crossword puzzles.

"Ready," she said into the phone.

"I doubt it," he told her. "First, you call that friend of yours and that stump too. You'll need 'em both."

"Felicia and Haywood?"

"You know their names. I don't. You and that woman go to three-eighty-one Marsh Street, down by the lake. Take two cars. You park up front. Her in back. Get there around four. This morning. Can you handle that?"

"Yes."

"Look like cops on a stakeout. Smoke cig, pick nose, scratch butt. I don't care. But sit there 'til five sharp. At five you have that stump call the heat down on that building. He tells 'em there's been a cop blown away."

"That's not going to make you any friends."

"Don't want friends. Want cops. Plenty of cops. Want 'em fast. Loud, too."

"Wait, wait," Jan said, scribbling. "What's this about?"

"Getting your doctor out of there. Ain't that what you wanted?"

"It is."

"All right, then. Soon as you hear a single siren, you go up to the front door of that warehouse, the one right under the stone block that says Kelly Paper. You can read, can't you?"

"I can."

"You get to that door, then. You shoot the lock on that door. Blast it two or three times. Get it good."

"What if it won't open?"

"It already open. You shootin' to let us know you right on our ass."

"Us?"

"I ain't going to be in there alone, lady."

"Oh. Then what?"

"You'll probably hear some shoutin'. That'll be me tryin' to sell the other guards that we ain't got time to be draggin' no doctor along with us. The heat has arrived. Now. Any luck, they'll be buyin' and we'll be flyin', 'cause by then those sirens your stump ordered up should be shit close."

"What about Felicia?"

"She just sits out back, make us feel surrounded, so there ain't nowhere to drag that doctor to."

"And where will the doctor be?"

"Top floor. Little room at the back. Just follow the blubbering sounds. You got all that?"

"I think so."

"Ain't no room for *thinkin'* so, 'cause I'm going down there right now."

"I got it."

"You bring the heat on early, that doctor all done blubberin'. I'll see to it personal."

"I understand."

"What questions you got?"

"Should I thank you?"

"Don't you be thankin' me for nothin'."

He slammed his receiver down so hard it must have broken. The line squeaked before the dial tone returned.

SHE RANG FELICIA before Claire could lift the pillow off her face. Twenty rings later Felicia answered, roused from her first secure slumber since Lyle had been grabbed. And now, when she should have been able to sleep at last, without fear of causing Lyle's death, Jan was waking her with this business.

"He called," she told Felicia. She had to repeat herself before Felicia came around enough to ask who had called. "Isiah Lawrence," Jan said. "With an address."

"What address?"

"For the doctor. I'm going to need help, and he says it has to be you. We'll need Haywood too."

There was a pause before Felicia said in a fated voice, "That's the way, then."

"Do you still have that gun?"

"They haven't given it back, but Haywood has plenty."

"One's enough," Jan said. "I'll lay it all out when I get there. Give me an hour."

When Claire wanted to know what the gun was for, Jan told her they needed to shoot a lock open.

"Isn't that what locksmiths are for?"

"There won't be time," Jan said.

Out in the hall she had to order every daughter but Amy back to bed. Before she left, she called to Amy down in the basement. "I'll get to you later."

SHE ONLY NEEDED half an hour to reach Felicia's. The freeway was empty except for squad cars running with their flashers on—no sirens. They were all moving too fast to bother pulling her over for curfew violation. After the first three or four units whizzed by, she caught their slipstream and drove eighty all the way across town, passing a National Guard convoy on the way. There were smoke and rosy lights to the southeast, and she saw so many police pointed that way that she found herself praying there would be enough cops left over for Isiah Lawrence's needs. At Felicia's she found Haywood sitting outside his half of the bungalow, waiting for her.

"What'd you do to 'licia?" he asked before Jan could close the gate. "She's actin' like there some kind of fire been lit 'neath her."

In the dark, Jan couldn't see Haywood's expression, but he sounded as if he approved of Felicia's newfound grit.

"Told her the truth."

"Which truth that?" Haywood asked, his head back, strong teeth showing.

"The one about how I knew up front that the FBI wouldn't trade for your brother."

"And that surprised her?" Haywood said. "That's some joke."

"Nobody's laughing," Jan said. "At the moment all I'm asking you to do is make a phone call in a little while."

"I suppose you think that's all I'm worth?"

"That's all Isiah Lawrence needs," Jan said. "Felicia and I are supposed to handle the rest."

"Who he got me calling?"

"The police."

"No way." Haywood shook his head slowly.

"To tell them a lie."

"Have to be a whopper."

"There might be a reward too," Jan said. "If we help get the doctor back, that is."

"Think I care 'bout rewards?" He said it as if she was pitiful. "I'll do it 'cause of Lyle. That's all. Just lay out what I'm s'posed to tell these jackals."

"To get somewhere fast and loud."

" 'Licia said something 'bout a gun. What you need that for?"

"To add to the loud."

"I got just the piece. I generally like my artillery louder than accurate. What am I lyin' to these mothers about?"

"Getting there fast enough. They won't be able to, at least not to catch anyone."

"All right, then," Haywood said, satisfied, maybe even pleased. "Feed me the rest of it."

FELICIA WASN'T ANYWHERE near as easy. Not that she had to be talked into anything. She was ready to go when Jan knocked. What was hard about Felicia was the way she stepped outside without a word of greeting. Her stare made Jan feel like something washed up on a beach a week ago.

"It was probably your little lie that got him," Felicia said.

"Lie?"

"About the doctor having a family. You going to let this boy go home too when everything's said and done?"

"I'll do my best."

"That a lie too?"

"Not that I know of."

Felicia nodded grimly, as if that sounded about right. "What are we doing?"

"Creating a diversion. I've apologized once, Felicia. Would you like me to do it again?"

"Once was enough," Felicia said, softening, her voice now sad. "I only wish there hadn't been a reason for you to do it then."

★ ★ ★

THE OLD WAREHOUSE district they drove to had been built over a swamp eighty years before. The foundations had been sinking ever since. Marsh Street was four blocks long and ended at the Cawsy River, which flushed into the lake two blocks away. One of the warehouses at the front of the street was a produce distributor, and a couple of refrigerated trucks were being unloaded of citrus and potatoes. The abandoned Kelly Paper building bubbled away at the other end of the street, on the banks of the mighty Cawsy, about twenty years mighty at that point and possessed of a faint green glow and curling sewer fumes. Jan made a pass of the building at ten to four to make sure they had the right place, then doubled back to tell Felicia this was it.

"We'd better get in place," Jan said. They were sitting in their separate cars, pointed in opposite directions, windows rolled down.

"You're going to play this out right to the end, aren't you?"

"Play what out?"

"You do that perfect."

"Good luck," Jan said, wishing she had no idea what they were talking about.

"Good-bye," Felicia answered, sounding certain enough about it to give Jan a chill.

ROLLING DOWN MARSH Street, Jan turned off her headlights and edged around the produce trucks. A bald-headed man on the loading dock watched her roll past, a sight that made her go faster. In her rearview there was a flash of light as Felicia made a U-turn and went to her appointed place. Jan found herself holding her breath and gazing at the now dark mirror. The bricks of the street brought her back to the here and now, making such a racket through the floorboards that she lifted her foot off the gas pedal, tried to calm herself with a cliché or two, and let the slight downward slope of the street pull her forward. There was one weak streetlight near the Cawsy River—across it, actually—barely enough to show that the six-story Kelly building was abandoned.

She tried rolling down her window. There were mosquitoes. She turned the radio on to the all-night talk shows. Law and order was frequently mentioned. She reached under the seat to make sure Haywood's pistol was still aboard. The only movement at her end of the street was a rat on top of a sewer grate, an orange peel in its paws. The dash clock in Jan's Pontiac had died long before she ever owned the car, so at intervals she had to strike a cigarette lighter to check her wristwatch. At least she didn't have to worry about giving away her position.

Even though she'd spent fifteen years and two marriages lighting up every chance she got, at the moment she didn't feel the slightest temptation to sneak a drag on one of the cigarettes she'd pilfered from her eldest daughter's stash. For appearances, she lit one and let it burn in the ashtray. When the first butt was almost out, she chain-lit another off it, rolled down her window, and flicked the first onto the street. She refused to do any picking or scratching. Whether her antics were being observed, she couldn't tell.

Parked there in the slightly luminous dark, the whole proposition seemed ridiculous. She found it hard not to believe she was parked in front of a totally empty building. Isiah Lawrence was probably having a high old time telling his associates how gullible she was. The only thing she was glad of was that she wasn't camped with Felicia, wondering what to say.

At 4:36, she heard a siren and panicked, thinking that the battery in her wristwatch had died, putting her timing off. She had a hand on the door, but by then the siren was close enough to identify as an ambulance whistle headed away from her.

At 4:45, with the sky turning a milky gray and without a single strand of mist lifting off the Cawsy River, which remained in the shadows, she became incredibly drowsy, could barely keep her chin up. The weariness came on so fast that it had to be her mind trying to shut down any way it could. She still had time, she realized, to pull around back, collect Felicia, and head somewhere serving warm pie and strong coffee. She didn't budge, though. The thought of facing Felicia left her sluggish.

Cracking a window, she inhaled some fresh air, or at least air fresher than in the car. It didn't help. She nodded off only to come to with a start. A minute had passed. Knowing that timing was everything and that she had to wait another quarter hour, she took a long drag on a cigarette just to keep herself pumped. The tobacco triggered a coughing fit that ended in a gasp. A face was staring at her through the passenger-side window, the pretty face of Special Agent Kyle Ford.

She didn't rub her eyes. It wouldn't have mattered if she had. The agent stayed put, neither smiling nor blinking, only making a circular motion with a hand, indicating she should roll the window down. Leaning across the front seat, she did so and asked the inevitable question.

"What are you doing here?"

Her jaw was in need of oil.

"Your friend just went in the backside of the building," the agent said. "Maybe you're the one who should answer that question."

Her head whipped toward the Kelly building.

"Who's inside, Jan?"

"Your doctor," Jan said, a burn in her gut.

"Who else?"

"Apparently Felicia. You've been following us?"

"It all comes down to trust, Jan."

"Strange," Jan said, holding her stomach. "That's just what I was thinking."

"Who else is in there?"

"I don't know."

"What's your friend talking to them about?"

"You, I imagine."

"Jan," the agent said, swinging into full-scale confidential, "we can still get her out, but we need to know who's with her. We don't and somebody gets hurt—bad."

She checked her wristwatch, tilting it toward the lone streetlight. Ten before five.

"You're in over your head, Jan."

Looking back on it, as she would so often try not to do, she was never quite sure what made her talk. Worse, she was never sure if *not* talking would have made a difference. In the end, what made her talk might have been something as simple as being weary of not talking. But maybe it was something more complex, something like the fatherly tone of the agent's voice, the way it promised to take care of everything.

"At least two guards," she told him. "Top floor, somewhere near the back. We're supposed to wait down here until five. One of the guards is going to release the doctor."

"Good girl," Ford said, already moving away from the car and talking into his two-way.

Her reaction to those words was something she often played back, too.

Before the agent was halfway across the street, Jan reached under the seat and pulled out the pistol. Stepping out of the car, she fired three times into the air.

Ford crouched and spun toward her, gun drawn, but never fired, never said a word to her, only to his radio. Then he was sprinting toward the building, a half-dozen other agents joining him from the shadows. Without checking the front door's lock, the agents blew it in with a shotgun and disappeared inside.

Jan took a running step toward the door herself. What stopped her cold was a muffled gunshot from deeper inside the building. Everything in her veins turned to sludge with that retort. She never doubted for an instant whom the shot was aimed at, just as she never had any choice but to stop. Her body wasn't hers anymore. It belonged to a madwoman who was shouting at the building. She never was able to remember what that woman was shouting.

Then came a silence so deep that Jan felt as though she were losing her balance listening to it. She tried to fight it by imagining that the building across the way was nothing more than a warehouse. That fantasy was bumped by a firefight somewhere on the top floors. She watched in a stupor, expecting muzzle flashes, shattered glass, falling bodies. There was none of that. Only the irregular pounding of gunshots that sounded so much like a string of explosions deep inside the earth that she found herself expecting the entire building to implode and collapse. To steady herself, she put a hand on her open car door.

Without warning the gunshots moved outside the building, drawing her vision upward. The silhouettes of three men could be seen on the warehouse roof. Several times one of them stopped running to fire behind him and pin down any pursuers. At last they scrambled onto the lip of the roof where it overlooked the Cawsy River. They were perfect targets against the lightening sky, but now there was a pause in the shooting. Apparently no one was close enough behind to fire on them. They argued until one of them, she thought maybe Isiah Lawrence, grabbed the others' hands and leaped.

For the short while she could see them, their legs cycling as though trying to run on air. A second later came a splash. Her back now against her car, Jan slid down to the brick pavement. Twice she tried shake the gun out of her hand. She couldn't get rid of it.

FOR A TIME there was no time. She was split between several places at once, all of them points in her life when something had changed her forever. The death of her first dog and of her grandmother, which were strangely equal in her mind. The departure of hubby one, the arrival of hubby two. The divorce of her parents. The voice of Eldon Hodges telling her there would be no promotion. And now this. None were as clear as this. None as bad.

WHAT BROUGHT HER out of it was the FBI agents shouting from the roof of the building. Within a minute agents were piling out the street-level door, headed for the river. After that, there was no more shooting and only occasional shouts. Frustrated ballyhoo from up and down the banks of the river.

SEVERAL MINUTES PASSED. An ambulance arrived. From up on the roof an agent directed the paramedics inside the warehouse. Jan stayed seated. She could feel mosquitoes landing on her face and arms. The buzz of mosquitoes—one more thing to remind her of this scene forever.

Eventually, agents started filing out of the building. More came out than Jan remembered going in. The paramedics came out, their stretcher empty. The doctor who'd been kidnapped came out, or at least Jan assumed that's who it was. A sandy-haired man, he was rubbing his wrists and ordering anyone who would listen to take him directly to the hospital. The instant Jan saw him, she thought of his wife, the way her eyes had something trapped behind them. She knew her eyes looked that way now. She could feel something lurking inside her, looking out, using her eyes to see the world.

Ford helped the doctor into the back of the ambulance and closed the doors without getting in himself. As the rig pulled away, the agent crossed the street to Jan.

"They got away," he said. "But you know their names, right?"

Jan shook her head no and stared at the ambulance, now a block away.

"We'll need their names."

"Who's still in there?" Jan asked.

"Your friend was down when we got there," Ford said.

"Down where?" Jan asked, thinking the words sounded foreign.

"We did what we could," Ford said.

"Did you tell her I was waiting for her?"

"It was too late," Ford said. "She did have some last words."

Jan thought about covering her ears, couldn't.

"She said she knew we'd be coming," Ford said. "How did she know that, Jan?"

"She thought I'd called you in."

"She didn't know you very well, then, did she?"

"Better than most."

"Those names, Jan. We need those names."

Looking into his blue eyes, she said, "I've forgotten."

"They killed your friend, Jan."

"No they didn't."

Whatever he said after that she didn't hear.

36

Jan avoided Felicia's funeral. For weeks she could do nothing but sleep. She slept while talking, while in the shower, while at her desk; she slept behind the wheel of her car and at the dinner table. She slept through all her daughters' questions and slept through her daughter Amy's refusal to apologize. There wasn't anyone to apologize to. Gradually her family lost interest in the riots as the evening news hurtled onward. One day she found herself passing a Catholic church. Pulling over, she sent her youngest daughter inside to light a candle. Jan stayed in the car, still sleeping.

She slept through August and September and a good chunk of October. One day she was standing in her backyard, sleeping under a brilliant autumnal sky, when she got a phone call from a producer at Tele-Star Enterprises. He wanted to know if she would consider talking to an actress about an upcoming role she was playing. They were making a TV movie about Felicia and Lyle's ordeal, and the lead actress needed background. She needed authenticity. She was having trouble understanding where the Felicia character was coming from, and they'd been told that Jan might be able to help.

"Who told you that?" Jan asked.
"The husband."
"Lyle?"
"That's right. His name was Lyle."
"They were never married."

"What we're hearing," the producer said, "is that they got hitched in the hospital, shortly after Lyle was rescued."

Needing to know whether that was true, or just some scriptwriter's improvement, Jan agreed to meet the actress. A day later she was sleeping in one of the city's finest restaurants, or at least its highest, gazing out on the lake to the east and the business district below them. The actress sitting across from her was ten years younger than Felicia, prettier, and talked four times faster. But there was something thoughtful about the movement of her eyes that reminded Jan of Felicia. The other thing in her favor was how seriously she took her job.

"Can you tell me what happened that last night, Jan? That's what no one's been able to do."

Not until then did Jan feel something wake inside herself. Suddenly, she needed fresh air. *Now.* It was that or be sick. She made it as far as the restaurant entrance before hugging a vase of cut gladioluses. The elevator ride to the lobby had its moments too. She staggered out of the building, gasping for breath, and never went back. Never heard from the actress or producer again.

The nausea and flush that had overcome her left, but she called in sick to work every day for a week. Being awake was thousands of times worse than sleeping through everything. She didn't eat much and mostly sat in front of the television in her bathrobe. When her sick time was spent and she had to have a paycheck, she went back to her job without saying a word to anyone at work about what ailed her. That wasn't so hard. Nobody asked. She went out of her way to avoid the Social Services area.

Winter came on hard and early that year. She was awake through all its endless cold and dark. Now she couldn't sleep and paced the house, usually ending up in the dark basement, staring at the flickering light of the furnace. Once she found herself reaching out to touch the flame.

The miniseries finally aired in March. Although she'd vowed not to watch it, she found herself drawn to the living room at the appointed hour. There were the expected discrepancies: Lyle was portrayed as too sensitive; Haywood was given back his legs but not his vision; Jackson General was fifty years younger than Jan had ever seen it. But from the opening scene, what seized Jan was the actress who played Felicia. She took Jan's breath away, so accurate was her portrayal. Somehow, she'd stepped inside Felicia's skin. She had the walk, the talk, the desperation. Jan had to sit, then couldn't stay seated. Twice she had to get up and leave the room. Both times she crept back.

So totally did Jan relive what had happened that it wasn't until the end of the opening episode that she realized she'd been written out of the script. Amy wanted to know if she would show up in Part II and suddenly, with relief, Jan knew that she wouldn't. She'd been bracing herself to face herself, but she wouldn't have to. Her presence had been entirely erased from the story. Her gratitude lasted until she saw her own relief mirrored in her daughter Amy's face. That was when she knew she'd have to tell them what really happened. Getting up, she crossed to the TV and hit the mute button. With the credits still scrolling across the screen, she turned to face her daughters and say, "There's something I better tell you."